The Life and Opinions of Amy Finawitz

The Life and Opinions of Amy Finawitz

By Laura Toffler-Corrie

Roaring Brook Press | New York

Text copyright © 2010 by Laura Toffler-Corrie
Published by Roaring Brook Press
Roaring Brook Press is a division of Holtzbrinck Publishing Holdings Limited Partnership
175 Fifth Avenue, New York, New York 10010
www.roaringbrookpress.com

Distributed in Canada by H. B. Fenn and Company Ltd.

Cataloging-in-Publication Data is on file at the Library of Congress
ISBN: 978-1-59643-580-3

Roaring Brook Press books are available for special promotions and premiums.
For details contact: Director of Special Markets, Holtzbrinck Publishers.

First Edition August 2010
Book design by Stephanie Bart-Horvath
Printed in June 2010 in the United States of America by RR Donnelley & Sons Company,
Harrisonburg, Virginia

10 9 8 7 6 5 4 3 2

To Tom, Hannah, and Rachel,
for roots and wings.

The Life and Opinions of
Amy Finawitz

*D*ear Callie,

According to the latest fortune cookie fortune:

WHEN YOU MAKE CHANGE, COME BACK A DOLLAR.

Very inscrutable, these fortune cookies. Although I think it's safe to assume that the message is not about money, but about life. So, you get it? (Change and become more, etc., etc.) These fortune cookie people sure know how to squeeze profound ideas onto a tiny slip of paper. And then, of course, they add a cookie for free. It just doesn't get any better than that.

And speaking of change (your big change, not money), I'm glad you're adjusting to farm life. You're a braver girl than me. Even the mention of the word "udders" would send me packing. So I'm beside myself with admiration for you actually having the nerve to touch them, much less pull on them. Are they slimy? I know, fresh milk is "just like cream." But they actually sell cream at the corner deli. It comes in a carton!

Now, I know it's not as much fun to reach into the dairy section and grab a carton as opposed to, you know, reaching under a cow and grabbing its udder, but what can I say? Life is dull here in New York City.

1

I'm also glad to hear that the school in Kansas doesn't bite. I was afraid it was gonna be very *Little House on the Prairie*, like, you'd keep getting your braids dunked in the inkwell by the boy who sits behind you, some big, blond hulk who's really twenty-four but is still in high school.

On the home front, my life remains unchanged, and the screaming continues. Kevin and my parents are fighting all the time now. They think he's a bum for dropping out of Tufts to move back home and become an actor, and I agree. He's dramatic all right, and every day he stars in the same little play, which I've affectionately titled:

THIS IS HOW YOU REPAY US, BY BECOMING A BUM?!

(A play in one scene, by Amy Finawitz)

CHARACTERS: MARV, LILLIAN, and KEVIN FINAWITZ. Special cameo performance by AMY FINAWITZ, who plays herself.

THE SCENE: The FINAWITZ living room. The FINAWITZES are shouting so loudly, that LOU, the doorman, calls from downstairs to tell them that the chandelier in the lobby is starting to vibrate.

LILLIAN
(to KEVIN)
Why have you dropped out of school?!
What's the matter with you?!

KEVIN

There's nothing the matter with me.
I'm following my inner chi.

MARV

Can't you do that at college?
(to LILLIAN)
What's an inner chi?

KEVIN

I don't need college to become an actor.

LILLIAN

Couldn't you have figured that out four tuition pay-
ments ago?

MARV

Do you know how hard it is to make it as an actor?
You and your chi will end up a bum!

KEVIN

You're just urban pseudo-intellectuals with no feeling
for the aesthetics.

MARV

I don't even know what that means! See how smart
you are?!
You should finish college!

LILLIAN

Didn't one of the Jonas Brothers go to college?

KEVIN

What on earth does that have to do with anything?!

At this point, AMY passes through on her way to the kitchen.

                    AMY
        Hi, 'scuse me. I'm running away to Italy to press
        grapes with my feet.

She is unceremoniously ignored. The fighting continues, until
LOU the doorman calls and threatens to have them evicted.

                  THE END

According to some doctor guest on *Oprah*, it's often the
unstable, emotionally needy child, a.k.a. pain in the butt,
who demands all the attention in a family. Very insightful,
these doctor guests, don't you think?

    And by the way, do you like the picture I sent you? I'm
finally wearing those contacts. They kind of show off my
eyes, if I do say so myself. And how about the hair? Can
you see how that lemon juice worked its magic?

    I am a little concerned, however, that my boobs are
getting too big for my torso. I told my mother that I
wanted to get them reduced. She said I was crazy and that
I should exercise. Exercise? I was like, "Mom, they're boobs.
You can't exercise them away."

    And speaking of boobs, please don't suggest that I hang
out with Judy and Claire while you're away. I know that
Judy is angling to be my replacement friend, but those girls
are bigger dorks than we are and so BORING. The point

                    4

is, there is no point now that you've left. You know I'm not going to find a replacement friend to suit my discriminating taste.

I
remain
forsakenly
yours,
Amy

*D*ear Callie,

Well, it seems that God, in his infinite humor, has decided to intervene in my life by sending me an actual replacement friend after all. Unfortunately, she is older than He is.

Who, you might ask? Why, none other than little old Miss Sophia who lives up the hall in 4B. Remember I told you about her? She used to baby-sit for Kevin and me sometimes when we were little, and she'd tell us these super long stories about "when she was young during the depression," blah, blah, blah, and how her "bubbe" made borscht and how she put sour cream on it and it was better than any expensive, fancy restaurant because it was made by her bubbe's loving hands, blah, blah, blah.

She was always so happy talking about Bubbe's beet soup of love that Kevin and I didn't have the heart to tell her that all we wanted to do was watch cartoons. One time she even made us a couple of bowls which we tried to ditch (cat bowl, down the sink, etc.) when she wasn't looking, but that stuff is like some kind of red globby glue that stains everything in sight. We were finally forced to choke it down, and our teeth were red for two days.

My mother still invites Miss Sophia over every once in a while for one of her, thankfully infrequent, experimental vegetarian Friday night Shabbat dinners (tofu brisket anyone?), and Miss Sophia always insists on bringing another one of Bubbe's made-from-love recipes, many of which smell disturbingly like gym socks.

You know how my mom is. The week after some Jewish holiday, she gets into the Jewish version of the Christmas spirit and it's always the same thing: out comes the good china and the candles and a challah that she bought from the Italian deli (because it's crusty). And then she's like, "Isn't this nice? Taking a break from our whirlwind week. Surrounded by family and friends. Taking time to be grateful to God for what we have."

And then she gets all pious, throws a doily over her head, lights candles and reads the Shabbat prayer phonetically from *Judaism for Dummies*. She rambles on about the luminous glow from the candles, then immediately blows them out so she doesn't set her sleeve on fire like she did that one time.

Of course, by the next Friday, we're back to our "whirlwind lives" (a.k.a. ordering Chinese food) until the God mood strikes Mom next.

Remember when your family came over for Shabbat a few months ago and how, after dinner, we were gonna be religious and finish that Hebrew school project about Moses and the ten plagues (lice, frogs, etc.) but instead watched *Night of the Living Dead* on cable? And your dad had his ear up against the den door and was like, "What's all that weird groaning?" Which of course were the zombies eating people, but we said, "Oh, we're praying and really feeling it."

And he was, like, "Uh . . . okay."

And we almost died laughing.

Sigh. Good times.

Now I'm feeling depressed. I'm going to channel surf for stupid, non-slasher horror movies.

But before I do that, I must finish my story about Miss Sophia.

So, you know how every morning I pass by Miss Sophia's apartment on the way to the elevator, and how I hear her cats yowling and get that slightly disturbing whiff of cat pee mixed with air freshener which wafts out from under her door, and how I have to wait while she hobbles down the hallway in her cute Lord & Taylor ensemble, pulling her little metal shopping cart with the wheels?

Yes, I know I'm being mean. She's always liked me. I'm just so popular with the geriatric set.

Well, anyway, on Tuesday morning, I am rushing to the elevator because I'm late, as usual, but I still tiptoe past Miss Sophia's door in the wild hope that she won't hear me.

At the elevator, I peck vigorously at the open door button. Then I scoot in and peck vigorously at the close door button, but am stopped by a familiar cry.

"Yoo-hoo, Amy, dear. Hold the elevator!"

Groan.

But, of course I do. She bolts her thousand locks and bumps her metal wagon across the rug, ducks into the elevator and is about to ask me when my little friend is coming home (that's you) which it seems like she does every morning, but I beat her to the punch.

"She's gone for the year, Miss Sophia," I sigh, with all the politeness I can muster.

"I see," she nods. "And my, you've gotten bigger since I last saw you!"

(Another one of her favorite remarks, which I don't appreciate even though I'm assuming she means height.)

"Thanks, Miss Sophia," I sigh.

At this point, the elevator opens and there's Mr. Klein from 8B who wants to get in, but he extends his hand to help Miss Sophia out first.

He spots me and says, "Good morning," in that tense, nasal voice of his, when I know he really wants to say, "Why do they let children live here?"

So there you have it. My two new best friends in the building, since your departure.

I am so never forgiving you for this.

Amy

PS: Mr. Lee, down at Lee's Chinese says, "Hi." He wants to know when you're coming back for our after-school egg rolls. I told him that might be a little hard since you're living in the heartland while your parents travel Europe.

9

9/14, 10:50 p.m.

What do you mean they're not lice; they're locusts? What the hell are you talking about?

9/14, 10:55 p.m.

Don't have a cow! How should I know you're still thinking about the ten plagues. Mrs. Goldstein would be so proud! That is, of course, only when she's doing her side gig at Temple Beth Shalom. When she's teaching history at PS 126, I don't think she thinks about Moses at all. Except maybe when the cafeteria is serving Middle Eastern–inspired falafel.

9/14, 11:10 p.m.

You're so right! Lice are grosser than locusts. At least locusts don't lay eggs in your hair. Besides, don't locusts make that crickety noise by rubbing their little sticky legs together? What was that supposed to do? Annoy the Egyptians to death? Was the Pharaoh like, "Nefertiti, for Golden Idol's sake, close that damn window. Those crickets are driving me crazy. I can't think straight. My hieroglyphics are turning into a jumble."

And then was Nefertiti like, "Then free the slaves already so we can get some peace. And forget about those hieroglyphics. No one can make heads or tails of them anyway. And BTW, they're not crickets; they're locusts." Get it straight.

9/14, 11:15 p.m.

What about this? What if, maybe, the frogs and the locusts were, like, fake-out plagues. Maybe God was like, okay, now you've got your guard down and you think I'm just some bogus idol . . . when Bam! Here come the boils! . . . Who's sorry now?

9/14, 11:20 p.m.

Yes, I am totally losing it. Thank you for pointing that out. Going to sleep now. First though: have to perform our ritual check the closet for zombies. Hope you're doing it too. I hear they've got some nasty zombies out there in the heartland, where the undead are, like, super bored.

*D*ear Callie,

Okay, latest, latest fortune cookie fortune:

JUST WHEN YOU THINK LIFE IS WEIRD, IT GETS WEIRDER.

Actually, it didn't say that. It really said something about how confronting personal challenges builds character and that my lucky number is seven. But if fortune cookies could really predict the future (remember how we always thought they could?), that's what it would say.

Allow me to illustrate. My school day was boring as usual. Judy, dense backup friend extraordinaire, has taken up crocheting. (Yes, even Judy wants to distinguish herself as a unique and purposeful individual.) Unfortunately, her plan only distinguishes her as a weirdo. For example, she sits in the cafeteria and knits these little circles. She says she's gonna sew them together to make an afghan. An afghan! What is she trying to accomplish with this? I mean, seriously, why she wants to be perceived as Grandma Girl is beyond me.

For lack of a better plan, during lunch, I learn how to crochet a circle, but tell her that I absolutely refuse to make an afghan. So, instead, she talks me into making a circle sweater; that being, of course, a sweater made up of dozens

12

of circles. She shows me a picture in her new magazine, *Crochet, Circle, Go!* and I tell her it looks like a giant doily. I also tell her that if she takes up mah-jongg and starts shoving tissues up her sleeve, I'm leaving. But then Judy looks hurt. So for about five minutes I watch her sulk and push her potato logs around her plate while I try to make guilty small talk about crocheting.

"Remember in *A Tale of Two Cities*," I remark with false cheeriness, "when Madame Defarge practically spearheads the French uprising by knitting secret messages into a blanket? That was something, huh? Talk about crocheting, circle, go."

"I never know what you're talking about, Amy," Judy gently rolls her eyes. "By the way, knitting is not the same thing as crocheting."

And I'm like, whatever. See what I mean about dense backup friends?

"Why do you have to be so weird?" she says.

I'm weird!

Then she leans in up close to my face and squints into my eyes, jumps up, grabs onto my arm, and pulls me out of my seat.

And before I can say, "Excuse me, but what are you doing?" she yanks a little cloth ruler from her backpack, turns me around, and instructs me to hold both my arms out straight, which, of course, I refuse to do. She exclaims that she's suddenly become inspired to crochet me a vest to match the tiny green flecks in my eyes.

Then she pulls out this big knitted patchwork of multi-colored circles, as a color guide, and tucks it into the top of my shirt. Of course, by this point, I'm totally mortified and I'm trying to get away from her, when she wraps her arms around my middle and starts measuring my waist. I grab for her little ruler and yank, but just at that moment she lets go, and I stumble back right into you're not gonna believe who! John Leibler, Mr. Hunkaliscious himself, that's who! Carrying a tray full of food!

Fortunately, John is a sports god with Olympic-like athletic reflexes. With one hand he swings his tray away from my stumbling body, just in time to save his food, and with his other hand he stabilizes me by grabbing on to my arm.

But not before Judy's knitted patchwork sample jolts loose from the top of my shirt and plops directly into his tomato vegetable soup and quickly sinks to the bottom of the bowl.

So me and Judy just stare, totally mortified for what seems like an hour, until John gingerly pinches the drippy, pukey-looking, knitted patchwork out of his soup, which is, grossly enough, tangled up with tiny pieces of potatoes, carrots, and bits of string beans.

"Er . . . sorry, John," I manage to croak.

Then, unbelievably, he flashes me his 100-watt smile and, referring to the puke patchwork, says,

"Did you knit this?"

I swear to God.

So Judy's jaw drops open like eighty feet, but nothing comes out except little clicking noises because her tongue is bumping up against the back of her throat.

"I . . . um . . . am making a sweater," I say, for some unknown reason.

And for a split second, I have this fantasy about him standing around with his homies wearing some big awesome-looking sweater that totally matches the blue flecks in his eyes, saying something like, "Oh, you all like my sweater? Yes, the color does match my eyes. My girl-friend made it out of little circles. Isn't it off the hook?" Then beaming with pride, John throws his arm over my shoulder, and gives me a squeeze.

But back at reality central, he just gently places the gross thing onto my lunch tray and slides his wet fingers over his napkin.

"Em . . . since we kind of destroyed your lunch, would you like my sandwich?" I offer.

"Nah, I'm good," he says. "Don't worry about it."

Hot and a good sport! Who knew?

And then, as he's walking away, he glances over his shoulder and says,

"By the way, my mother knits stuff too."

Can you believe it?!

I hear it's not good when you remind a man of his mother, but I feel flattered nonetheless.

Yeah, I'm pathetic.

Amy

9/15, 10:15 p.m.

Yeah, I am.

9/15, 10:20 p.m.

Yeah, I so totally am. And what do you mean, "Try not to be pathetic"? How can you try not to be pathetic? You either are or you aren't.

Dear Callie,

Mrs. Goldstein took us today to the Metropolitan Museum to see the "Immigrants of New York" photo exhibit in the New American wing since we're studying immigration right now in social studies. Yes, I have good old Mrs. Goldstein this year. She's okay, but, like, I don't see enough of her in confirmation class at Temple Beth Shalom?

Anyway, all I kept thinking about was the time we wanted to be like Claudia and Jamie from the book *From the Mixed-up Files of Mrs. Basil E. Frankweiler* and hide out there for a week.

Remember the mystery about the little angel statue and how Claudia just couldn't go home until she discovered it was made by Michelangelo? Remember how we mapped out an awesome plan to run away, even though it meant cruelly deceiving everyone we knew and loved?

Sigh. More good times.

Well, I'm sorry to report that there were no mysteries on this trip. John Leibler hung tight with Horrible Susan and her friends. Judy glommed onto me and became delirious with joy when she discovered ye olde American tapestry and quilt exhibit. She dragged me all around the place and kept calling the colonial women "the mothers of the modern fiber arts revolution."

Fiber arts had a revolution?

Overall, I was bored, bored, bored.

Now, why can't I uncover a mysterious Michelangelo statue or something, and why do cool things only happen in books?

Amy

9/16, 5:01 p.m.
What do you mean, "Don't feel alone" with a little smiley face. You know how I feel about those little smiley faces.

9/16, 5:04 p.m.
Yes, I know I'm cranky and I would rather be here than there. I just wish you were here too. Sue me.

*D*ear *Callie,*

So today I'm daydreaming my way through English class and Mrs. Milnak is talking about *A Tale of Two Cities* and telling us that important historical events happen around us all the time, we should read the newspaper, history is a living entity, yak, yak, yak.

But here's the part where you'll be proud of me. Because of the social opportunity that recently presented itself (vis-à-vis John Leibler talking to me in the cafeteria about knitting), after class I screwed up my courage, went up to him and said, "Hi."

Then he looked up at me, like he seriously remembered who I was, and said, "Hey!"

But it wasn't a generic "Hey." It was more like a "Hey, I know you," or "Hey, glad to see you," or "Hey, I love you." (Well, maybe not that one . . .)

But, anyway, it was still pretty darn awesome.

Now, that's history in the making!

Amy

9/17, 8:03 p.m.

I do see your point about the "Hi." "Hi" doesn't leave much room for conversation, other than a return "Hi." But your "ask him a question" idea is stretching it. What the hell kind of a question am I supposed to ask him? "Hey, John, I was wondering why God gave you all the good genes and left none for the rest of us?"

9/17, 8:08 p.m.

Yes, excuse me, but there is a reason to be sarcastic. Make a suggestion I can live with. You have to have some common ground with someone to ask a question, and we all know that I have no common ground with the cool kids! What am I supposed to ask, "Could you direct me to the main office?" Duh!

9/17, 8:14 p.m.

All right, all right. I know you were just trying to help and, yes, I guess I'm still cranky.

Bah humbug.

But enough of that. Instead of being obnoxious, I'll be intriguing and tell you about the latest fortune cookie fortune which says: SOMETHING UNEXPECTED WILL FILL YOUR PLATE.

Now that's something to think about!

PS: Unless of course the fortune is in reference to the actual Chinese food, in which case that could be incredibly gross and disturbing.

*D*ear Callie,

So I'm in Mrs. Goldstein's confirmation class at Temple Beth Shalom and this is our unit on morality tales, which I actually find kind of interesting, although I could live without all those Yiddish, throat straining guttural ch's and all that accidental spraying of other people with saliva.

And you know how Mrs. Goldstein is. If she senses in the slightest that you're not paying attention or sees you doodling, she calls on you to "get those creative juices flowing!"

Remember that time she got mad because she saw me doodling in *Moses: The Man Behind the Legend* (even though, excuse me, it was my, paid for, textbook). I mean what was the big deal? I can totally doodle a do-rag on Pharaoh and pay attention at the same time.

So anyway, she's blah, blahing about how these stories use animals as metaphors to make a thematic point about the role God plays in our lives, or something to that effect, and she catches me taking one of those "Which Celebrity is Half Jewish?" quizzes in *Hip and Hebrew: The Magazine for Jewish Youth* that I'm hiding under my *Yiddish Morality Tales* book.

And she's like, "Amy, what is your favorite Yiddish morality tale?"

So I panic, because I never actually read the book, wrote a report, or made a project (which was the homework).

"Well," I say, thinking fast. "I saw this documentary on PBS the other night. It was about emus that are sort of like these birds who don't fly and they live in Australia. Their story kind of reminded me of a Yiddish morality tale."

"Oh," says Mrs. Goldstein, presumably suddenly super excited that I'm making a connection between life and Yiddish morality. "Why don't you tell us all what the documentary was about?"

"Well," I begin, "there was this herd of emus grazing around and then these dingoes attacked and the herd took off, totally leaving behind this one, poor little emu, who got ripped to shreds by the dingoes and then they ate him.

"Hmm," says Mrs. Goldstein, looking sorry she asked me.

And then, believe it or not, I actually do feel my creative juices flowing and start to improvise.

"But see the interesting thing is that the filmmaker didn't shoot off his gun to scare away the predators to save the emu. He just reported the incident in this detached way, and started lecturing about survival of the fittest and the food chain, while the emu was writhing and his flesh was being torn away from his body."

I stop, and there's this dead silence.

The rest of the kids stop their doodling, turn, and smirk at me, like, what the hell are you talking about? And, you are so busted.

Then poor Mrs. Goldstein, who has this confused look on her face like she's trying to understand what the hell I'm talking about, but is sincerely trusting that I actually have a point, says,

"And, this reminds you of a Yiddish morality tale because . . ." she coaxes hopefully.

"Well," I say, "let's say the emu is very discriminating, so she doesn't really hang out with the other emus. But then something happens, like her friend, another emu, leaves the herd to visit relatives in another herd, so she's distracted when the dingoes come, and nobody cares. And then, the narrator, who let's say represents . . . God, sees the emu is in trouble and alone, but he doesn't care either because she's just not that important to him. And so she's tragically ripped to bits and dies, a slow, sadistic, tortuous death . . ."

More silence. Mrs. Goldstein looks perplexed and blinks.

"And no one cares," I say again, just to sum things up.

And then the clock strikes eleven and we're all out of there.

Later that morning, I'm congratulating myself on my fast thinking, saved from one of those makeup homework assignments that Mrs. Goldstein is so famous for, when she stops me in the hall and gives me this little disappointed half smile, the one we used to think meant she had gas and says,

"Amy, your emu story. It was . . . a little . . . troubling," she says.

Uh-oh.

"I was wondering if you could come to my office for a minute."

I'm thinking, well, this can't be good.

But I say, "As tempting as that sounds, Mrs. Goldstein, I'm kinda late for Comparative Culture in the Kitchen." Mrs. Greenberg is making sushi-inspired falafel. How about later?"

"I'll tell you what," she says. "Tomorrow at school, after social studies, come to my office. We'll talk then!"

Then she waddles away.

Groan. Double groan and sigh.

Why does Mrs. Goldstein need to talk to me? As a matter of fact, why does she have to be one of those teachers who really care about their students? Moreover, why does she feel the need to teach all the time? Can't she just teach at public school during the week and be done with it? Isn't there some support group out there for people who can't stop teaching, like Teacher's Anonymous or something?

I'd love to see her in some church basement, surrounded by a circle of other teaching addicts all sitting around in bridge chairs.

She'd be like, "Hi, I'm Hannah Goldstein, and I just can't stop teaching."

And all the other preppy nerd teaching addicts would respond in unison, "Hi Hannah."

And another thing, why do I have to live out my mother's dream of understanding Judaism? Doesn't she realize that no one understands Judaism? That that's the whole point: to study the Torah and just keep asking questions until you drop dead or someone else kills you. I already studied and asked a million questions and had my bat mitzvah for God's sake, which BTW, FYI, I never did get any straight answers from.

Amy

Dear Callie,

What do you mean, I'm getting so preoccupied with my own feelings of perceived abandonment and lack of inspiration that I'm being insensitive to you? Of course I know that this has been hard for you too, going to a strange place, not knowing anyone, having to go to a new school in the heartland, where the wind comes sweeping down the plain and the corn grows as high as an elephant's eye, or, ya know, whatever. So how are you? What are the kids like out there? Any cute guys? What's school like? Do you feel like you're adjusting at all?

Just remember, a year is not such a long time. People in prison sit in tiny cells for years at a time, and they don't even have any bathroom privacy. Plus, they're probably kind of unbalanced, which must make it harder for them to cope. So if prisoners can hold on over time, I'm sure you can too!

And speaking of holding on, you won't believe what happened to me today.

So I'm in science class and you know the seating plan: brainiacs way up front, cool kids (i.e., Horrible Susan, hunkaliscious John Leibler and co.), in the middle Judy

26

and a few other nondescript people around the back middle, and juvies (you know, those most likely to end up in juvenile hall) all the way in the back.

While we're waiting for Mr. Spinelli to show up to his own class (still always late), I'm thinking about all the work I have to do this semester, especially to keep that obnoxious honor roll thing up that my parents are so crazy about, when Judy starts yakking about her exciting (her words not mine) after-school knitting class and how cool it is to work with such sumptuous (another one of her words) yarns and wools. So, I'm nodding politely and feigning interest, which she misinterprets as genuine interest, when she opens her backpack, and pulls out some kind of knitted tube (sleeve?) made of spiky multicolored fuzzy wool and is like, "This is soooo soft. You need to touch it, touch it . . . Go ahead. Touch it," she says, rubbing the tube sleeve against her cheek, her expression getting all relaxed and dreamy.

And now I'm totally mortified and Horrible Susan and co. turn around, roll their eyes, and give her a "You are such a geek" look. And the juvies in the back start snickering because crooning "touch it, touch it," over and over sounds totally obscene. And Judy, of course, mistaking the snickers for interest, extends the tube sleeve toward the juvies and says, "Go ahead. You can touch it, too."

This sends everyone into gales of laughter. And Judy, so naïve, is completely perplexed. I'm inching my chair away from her when (get this!) John Leibler turns around, sees what's going on, gets this exasperated expression like the whole class is totally immature, reaches out, and actually touches Judy's tube sleeve!

"It feels nice, Joanie," he says with a supportive smile, melting my heart like butter on a warm countertop. Then he turns back around and continues to chat with "Horrible."

Isn't that awesome?! That John Leibler! I mean, even though he's been through, like, ten grades with Judy and thinks her name is Joanie, he's such a nice guy!

9/20, 7:42 p.m.

*D*ear Callie,

Just finished homework and dinner, which was some kind of vegetarian pork (?) in case you're wondering, and I wanted to fill you in on the rest of my day.

So I'm in Mrs. Goldstein's class thinking about how she's really piling up the work this semester and she's like, "I have something very interesting to discuss with you. I think it will really get those creative juices flowing!"

Some people sigh and shift in their seats and I'm thinking, Oh no! Don't say assignment. Please don't say another assignment!

"I'd like to give you all another . . ."

No, no, no!

"Assignment," she says with a satisfied look.

I groan. Everyone groans.

"Now everyone," she says, holding up her hand in a gentle warning. "This is an experimental assignment that the district has developed, and I think you're going to find it very enlightening.

"Each one of you is going to receive pages from a diary

29

by an immigrant who lived around the turn of the century. This immigrant diary program was developed by a New York philanthropist who, working with museum curators and ancestry documentation professionals, obtained about fifty diaries to copy and circulate among city students."

Mrs. Goldstein then hands each one of us a little packet of papers with our names on them. "I'll be handing out installments of your assigned journal each week. I want you to really try and relate to what your immigrant is writing, to put yourselves in his or her shoes, feel what it must have been like for him to learn a new language and customs, to practice his religion. Try and imagine how it must have felt adjusting to a whole new life."

I look at my journal packet. The name across the front says Anna Slonovich.

"Are we working in groups?" "Horrible" asks, so totally hoping to hook up with John, I'm sure.

"No, you'll be working independently, but you can share ideas and insights with one another. Oh, and no Internet."

No Internet.

Now the groans are so loud that it's sounding like the flesh-eating scene in *Night of the Living Dead*.

"However, I'm encouraging you to do old-fashioned research. I want you to obtain information from a variety of living sources, get family involved, grandparents, seniors you know, etc. Extra credit for those of you who do," she chirps.

"Now this is not a desk assignment. I want you to travel! I want you to use the whole city, go where your immigrant would have gone, see the city through his or her eyes! I want you to—"

"Get those creative juices flowing," the class mumbles unenthusiastically.

"That's right!" Mrs. Goldstein claps her hands together. "Use those imaginations! Be inventive, inspired, resourceful!"

"Um . . . so what exactly are we supposed to hand in?" I ask.

"You are to keep your own response journal, detailing your reactions and experiences."

Groan to the tenth power.

Then, thankfully, the bell rings and everyone starts to bolt out of there, grumbling, looking extremely cranky, and thinking all kinds of expletives in their heads, I'm sure.

I, of course, being no different, try to bolt through the bottleneck at the door myself, and I'm almost there when Mrs. Goldstein taps me on the shoulder and gives me this gas smile and is like, "See you in my office? You didn't forget, did you?"

"I'll be there," I give her a gas smile back, feeling like I really did have gas.

Amy

31

Dear Callie,

All right, all right, I'll finish the story. Don't get your knickers in a twist. A girl needs to use the tinkle room once in a while.

So anyway, a few minutes later, I arrive at Mrs. Goldstein's office and she motions for me to sit in the chair across from her and she plops down behind her desk. She leans back and gives me a gas smile while I stare at her organized paper piles, lined up pens, and pictures of her hefty son and husband. After what seems like twenty hours, she says, "You know, Amy. I usually don't cross over my teaching assignments from Temple Beth Shalom here at the public school, but in this case I had an exciting opportunity to do so."

"I'm not following, Mrs. Goldstein," I say.

"Well, I've known you for quite a while now, Amy. You've been my student at Temple Beth Shalom for many years . . ."

"Many years," I sigh.

"And I've come to know you as a very smart, creative student. I know you will do well in school and in life."

"Thanks Mrs. Goldstein. I appreciate your support," I say starting to get up.

"But I was a bit concerned about your interpretation of that emus documentary. And while I was impressed with your ingenuity, I was troubled by how you imagined the emu to be bereft and forsaken."

I sit back down.

"Do you feel like that little abandoned emu, Amy?"

"Um . . . I dunno."

"Do you really believe that God is like an impersonal narrator in our lives? That he stands by while unpleasant things happen, or that life is just a series of random events?"

"Well, mine seems to be," I say.

Then she leans forward and locks her eyeballs onto mine, "I know you're very discombobulated about Callie Gold leaving for Kansas this year. I know the two of you were very close. I have the impression that you're feeling a little lost without her. Perhaps you need some purpose this year. Some goals."

"Well, maybe," I say, sliding my eyeballs from her gaze.

"Hmmm," she nods, in this all-knowing, motherly way. Then she leans forward in her chair.

"Am I being too personal?" she squints her eyes sincerely.

Yes.

"No, but I am late for AP science. If they start dissecting

those owl vomit pellets without me, I'll be totally lost," I say, starting to get up again.

"Here's the thing," Mrs. Goldstein continues.

And I'm down again.

"I thought this particular journal that I gave you would suit you because your immigrant is a Jewish girl from Russia. I'm sure she had to leave a lot of her friends behind. Maybe reading about Anna will inspire you to discover more about your Jewish heritage."

Why oh why did I ever have to tell Mrs. Goldstein about that emu documentary? Why couldn't I have just made some simple Moses diorama like that suck-up Ellie Bleckman?

Mrs. Goldstein is all pleased with herself and is waiting for some excited response.

"Oh," I say on a high note, trying to sound excited. "So, okay, well, see you later, Mrs. Goldstein," I say, heading out the door.

So it's me and an old diary. Woo-hoo.

Amy

Dear Callie,

I decided to get right on this assignment, so I could hurry on to all the other exciting activities in my life (snort). So tonight over tofu casserole, I was talking about the assignment with my parents and I learned that my glamorous ancestors didn't come from those "so yesterday" places like Paris and Rome. They came from sexy towns in Russia with names like Minsk and Pinsk where they lived in "shtetels", a shtetel being, as far as I can make out, some kind of grouping of straw huts fashioned into a village. And when this dashing lot came to America, they were super excited to live thirty to an apartment on the Lower East Side. They had no education and barely spoke English. Nobody discovered anything, cured anything, or created anything except more ancestors. And the most important thing in their world was to give their children a better life. Snore. I can only conclude that the "boring life" gene runs in my family.

It did, however, make me wonder what would have happened if my present-day family were forced to live under immigrant conditions, which inspired me to write a little play entitled:

PLEASE, GOD, SEND THE FINAWITZ FAMILY BACK TO THE TZAR

(A play in one scene by Amy Finawitz)

THE SCENE: Ten scruffy immigrants wait for the bathroom in a line that snakes down the dark hallway, down the stairs, and into the fetid streets, where the smells of knishes, roast chicken, and urine mingle in the air.

One poor child, who looks remarkably like the Jewish version of Oliver Twist (we'll call him Oli Twistein) raises his skinny pathetic hand and knocks on the bathroom door.

OLI
Please, sir, can I get into the bathroom?

KEVIN FINAWITZ
(his voice ringing out from behind the door)
No, I'm sorry young lad. I need to practice my acting monologues into my hairbrush in front of the mirror.

OLI sighs loudly and heads out the door.

Meanwhile, LILLIAN FINAWITZ is heard screeching in the kitchen. Her dirty black lace-up boots stomp all over the floor as a handful of women chase her around swinging knives and brandishing pots. LILLIAN races from the room, past the bathroom line and out the door.

WOMAN SWINGING KNIFE
And stay out, you bossy, pain in the kishka! We're not going to peel the skin off the chicken, and stop hocking us about low fat!!

36

Oblivious to all the hoopla, MARVIN FINAWITZ hides behind a copy of *The Yiddish Times*, while secretly devouring a delicacy from another ghetto: the Chinese egg roll. In his zeal to conceal his treat, he holds the newspaper upside down.

KNIFE WOMAN turns to her friend, POT WOMAN.

KNIFE WOMAN
Is that whole Finawitz family meshuge?

POT WOMAN
Ech . . . who knows? I hear the daughter is the only normal one.

LIGHTS FADE AS: Life in the ghetto continues as usual.

Amy

Fortune cookie thought for the day:
WHEN ALL YOU HAVE IS A HAMMER, EVERYTHING LOOKS LIKE A NAIL.

*D*ear *Callie,*

So today I'm able to get to the cafeteria a little early as usual.
Mr. Block never seems to know what to say to the menstruation excuse, and I never get tired of seeing him blush, avert
his eyes, wave his hand and mumble, "Grapneekabla . . ."
which in "gym language" means, "Fine, you're excused."

You remember those days, I'm sure. Isn't it amazing that
Mr. Block never got wise to us always both menstruating
at the same time (how do these guys get through college?),
and then we'd slip out and go to the corner deli for some of
those nasty wine and vinegar chips that were so bad, they
were kinda good?

Anyway, I'm sitting there waiting for Judy and Claire
to get their hot lunches, and every now and then I, very
discreetly, peer over to the cool table where Horrible Susan
and co. are picking at leafy salads and flirting with John
Leibler, Mark Wend, and the other hot boys.

Since an invitation to join them is not likely to be forth-
coming anytime soon, I decide to take a look at the first
installment of my photocopied Anna Slonovich journal.
When I open it, a small photocopied picture floats to the
floor.

It's a girl, slim with a pleasant face, wearing some ye old clothing. She's pale, with large, light, buggy-looking eyes framed by dark shoulder length hair, and it's signed underneath in scrawly script: Anna Slonovich, age fifteen.

Despite the ye olde hair and dress, Anna really looks just like any girl you'd see in school today, and it makes me wonder about her. For example, when she came to America, did she have to leave her BFF behind in Pinsk? Was she stuck hanging out with girls from Minsk or even worse, those dorks from Linsk? Did she have a crush on some unattainable boy from the sexy town of Blinsk who didn't even know she was alive?

Idly, I flip through the pages and I see more of Anna's scrawl.

It says "This journal is ideas for my life biography that I will write one day. And, when I am famous mystery writer."

Hmm . . . very kismet that Anna wanted to be a writer because, as you know, I think that I might like to be a writer too someday. What are the odds?

And speaking of odd . . . Why does it take Judy and Claire, like, ten hours to get their lunches when they get the same thing every day?

Judy, who gets the, "Everything looks so yummy!" smorgasbord.

Followed by Claire who gets the, "I'm never eating anything solid again!" assortment of foods made of goo: yogurt, pudding, ice cream in a cup, applesauce, soup of the day, and a smoothie.

And why, you may ask, does Claire's diet now consist of foods most commonly associated with denture wearers and children under two?

Well, ever since that spinach pizza got smooshed in her blue braces fiasco, she's totally paranoid about going through the day with gross food caught in her braces and no one telling her. And before you jump to the wrong conclusion as to why no one (her friends) told her, Judy was absent that day and I didn't tell her because it was probably one of the many days I spent trying to avoid her.

And I can just hear you saying: "Oh, she's not that bad."

And to that, I will respond with a little scene, an example of what I mean: forthwith, the following "conversation":

CLAIRE
(scuttling from the lunch line to the lunch table while slurping her smoothie from a straw)
Ooh sorry, sorry, Amy. I know we took a long time. Did you finish your lunch already?

ME
It's all right, I—

CLAIRE
(interrupting)
So, I ordered my banana smoothie and the lunch lady starts making it and then KAPOW! The machine just grinds to a halt and stops! Can you believe it?

40

                    ME
I can believe anything when—

                    CLAIRE
(interrupting—again)
So I had to stand there and wait for her to un-jam it,
but then Rob Assario starts talking to me, and I don't
care what you say, I don't think he looks homeless. I
think he totally looks like Elvis . . . (does her best pathetic Elvis imitation). "Thank you, thank you very
much" . . .

She breaks into spasms of laughter.

                    ME
(not cute)
Cute.

                    CLAIRE
So the first lunch lady calls over another lunch lady
and they finally fix it, but then she has to mix in that
P.T.A. mandated yeast protein powder, and that takes
a few minutes, but Rob is still talking and, well, I think
he was flirting with me. Isn't that crazy!

                    ME
It certainly seems to be.

                    CLAIRE
(ignoring me)
And he's, like, sooo funny! He says, "Soon they won't
need lunch ladies in the lunchroom, they'll need me-
chanics!" And I thought that was sooo hysterically
funny! And he likes smoothies too, but not banana

                     41

because he hates those little black things, you know, the seeds. But I said, "Rob they're just seeds. You can't taste them," and he's like, "Yeah, but they're gross, and the banana gets caught in my braces." I thought that was sooo funny!

CLAIRE laughs like a hyena, then suddenly stops, looks anxious, leans in toward me, way past the boundaries of my comfort zone, and bares her teeth in my face.

CLAIRE (cont.)
Are there banana seeds in my braces?

Seriously Cal, ever since Claire's father bought her that super duper cappuccino machine for her birthday, she's worse than ever, like a caffeinated Energizer bunny.

And speaking of being energized, is it true that you're making some cool friends? Do you mean cool by Midwest standards (like sun kissed and cheery), or cool by East Coast/West Coast standards (aloof and sexy), or cool meaning indifferent to you generally? Please clarify.

Amy

9/23, 6:31 p.m.
Ah . . . cool as in nice and not totally dorky. Thanks for clarifying. Keep climbing that social ladder!

*D*ear Callie,

So it's Friday night and my Mom has decided it's time for another Friday night Shabbat, this time, with mystery guests (although I'm pretty sure that one of them is Miss Sophia).

So I start going about my usual pre-Shabbat chore, which is to remove all the newspapers, stray homework assignments, and empty cups, etc. from the living room. It is there I find "brother from another planet" meditating, smelling up the place with incense, and chanting off key. When I ask him what he's trying to prove, he says that he is learning to open his inner chi. Remember his chi issue, that being his lame ass reason for dropping out of college?

So I ask him, "What exactly is a chi anyway?"

He says that chi is an energy flow we all have inside and that by meditating on it, it helps us to be more in touch with the needs and feelings of others. Then he tells me to get the hell out of the room.

I'm starting to think that Kevin didn't actually drop out of college of his own free will, but that the other students drove him out with pitchforks and burning torches.

So I finally convince chi boy to practice his new age–inspired religion in his room so I can clean for Judaism, when my dad drops into the living room, looking all comfy in his sweats, and clutters the place up even more by dropping sections of the *New York Times* everywhere.

At the same time, my mom's running around the kitchen with all these pots burbling and timers dinging, and that yummy vegetarian cauliflower-ish smell (my policy on that: Don't ask, don't tell) is wafting all around the place. Every three seconds, she's sticking her head out to nag my father to "get out of his sweatpants already and get dressed."

That's when the doorbell rings.

"Oh no! They're early!" Mom squeaks frantically.

It's Shabbat high alert!

Mom runs into the living room, broom in one hand and a spatula in the other. She sweeps Dad into the bedroom, while kicking newspapers under the couch with her feet. She yells for him to change and "for God's sake comb your hair." She yells at me to finish getting my stuff off the couches.

Dad yells, "Why can't we just relax and have Chinese food?"

And, chi boy, presumably trying to drown out the yelling, turns the new age music up to high.

"Kevin, stop that damn chanting and come out of there!" Mom bangs on his door with a spatula so hard that bits of carrots fly every which way.

And in the midst of all this chaos, I'm like, "Mom, you're getting a little nutso. I think maybe you need to chill . . ."

Shabbat Momzilla turns on me, warning lightning bolts shooting from her squinty eyes.

"Just answer the damn door!" she yells.

Then she stomps back into the kitchen into a cacophony of wild bubbling and pinging timers.

"Ah Shabbat . . ." I sigh to no one in particular. "How peaceful thou art."

As I open the door, I'm accosted by the overpowering aroma of something cabbage.

"Ah, Miss Sophia. Come in. What a surprise."

"Thank you, Amy, dear."

She holds out a big casserole dish.

"I brought stuffed cabbage. It was a recipe from my bubbe."

"No kidding," I smile, reaching out to take it.

"Oh, and I brought something else," she says with a wink and a grin.

Oh God, I'm thinking. Now what? This better not be the ghost of Bubbe.

"I've brought a young man," she winks.

She cranes her head down the hall toward the elevator.

"Now where's he gotten to?" she says.

A young man?!

Panic wells in my breast. My mind races.

Why would Miss Sophia bring a young man? Unless . . . there was more than the smell of cauliflower and cabbage in the air. This was the smell of a setup!

45

Immediately, I had a sudden, frightening recollection of the last person Miss Sophia referred to as a "young man." Do you remember that sixty-year-old pickle guy down at the corner deli? The one with the warty nose, big bulging stomach, and three wispy gray hairs he plastered across the top of his head to give the illusion of hair? Remember, whenever we'd see her in there ordering she'd be like, "I'd like two sours and a dill, young man."

Miss Sophia turns, scurries up the hallway, and disappears around the corner while I set the "cabbage" casserole down on the foyer table. About a minute later she's back at the door.

"He's adjusting his tefillin," she whispers to me and winks. "He doesn't get out much."

Huh?

And then speaking of ghost guests, who approaches the door but one of the palest boys I've ever seen. I peg him to be about our age. But get this, he's totally dressed in Hasidic attire! That's right, a starched white shirt which, trust me, is a poor fashion choice for one so pale, and baggy black pants.

He isn't really bad looking, necessarily, but he seems almost translucent, like a wisp of a person. As if a curl of smoke had come to life.

He looks up shyly and mumbles, "Shabbat Shalom. Good Sabbath."

"Uh . . . yeah . . . shalom," I reply.

Oh. My. God. This? This religious kid is the setup?!

Then we all stand there for about five seconds, until I remember to invite them in.

"Please come in," I say.

He stands frozen to the spot.

"Go ahead, Beryl," Miss Sophia coaxes.

Very tentatively, with eyes averted, Beryl takes about five steps into the living room, careful not to make any physical contact with me even by accident. Then he just stands there.

"All the way in, dear," Miss Sophia says. "Amy, this is my nephew, Beryl Plotsky. Beryl, this is the girl I was telling you about. This is Amy."

Then I'm thinking that I'm not even sure if very religious people even date. It's all arranged by relatives, right? And what if this was a date already?! What if being introduced by a relative was considered going steady?!

At that moment, all the Finawitzes pile out from their respective rooms (kitchen, bedroom, and den) and herd Miss Sophia and Beryl all the way into the living room, with "Shabbat Shaloms" and "How nice to meet yous" and pleasant chatter. The living room is suddenly starting to feel too small and cramped.

"Hello, Beryl," Mom says, "How are you?"

"I'm fine, thank God," he says.

Then she puts out her hand to shake. "Very nice to meet you."

Beryl places his hand over his heart.

"I greet you with my heart," he says.

"Oh . . . that's nice," my mom says, somewhat embarrassed, her limp hand hanging in space until she, self-consciously, lets it drop.

"The religious boys or men don't shake hands with women. Out of respect," says Miss Sophia.

"I see," says Mom, somewhat awkwardly.

And then she adds: "Well, I totally understand, and I brought in special kosher food for you. I hope you like it, Beryl."

"Thank you," Beryl says quietly.

Then Kevin takes one glance around the "room of excitement," and he's like, "I have to . . . ah . . . get some sheet music for my show."

I notice Beryl glance up at him with a mixture of surprise and (maybe?) fear that the only other boy in the room (other than my dad, who doesn't count) is deserting him.

My mom blanches bright red, like the top of the thermometer ready to pop, and my dad shoots her a "leave him alone" look.

"Be back before dinner," Dad gives him the seal of approval.

And bam, Kevin is out the door.

So I, who know a good exit cue when I see one, am like, "Ya know, I'd love to stay and chat before dinner, but I've got reams of homework to do," I say peeking at my wrist under my sleeve, as if I'm wearing a watch, which I'm not.

"Why don't I just pop my head back after candles and right before dinner. As a matter of fact, I might have to take a plate back into my bedroom. Have to keep up that honor roll . . ."

Of course, these remarks are met with angry stares of disapproval, which I try to ignore as I start backing up toward my room.

"Nice to meet you, Beryl," I say. "Shabbat, ya know . . . whatever."

A look of painful embarrassment crosses Beryl's face as he shrinks down into the couch, only to pop back up again because, ironically, he sits down right on my binder with the copy of Jewish immigrant Anna Slonovich's journal inside. He picks it up and turns it over.

"Oh, what a coinky dinky. There's my homework now!" I say taking it from him. "Well, call me when the cabbage, I mean dinner, is ready."

Then my mom shoots me a full-on Momzilla, dagger killer look which brings me quickly slinking back into the room.

"Don't be silly, Amy," Mom says politely through gritted teeth. "Come and sit with us. You can do your homework later. Why don't you sit on the couch next to our guest, Beryl."

So I sit down and then he scoots down the couch away from me, like really obvious.

Then there's this long uncomfortable silence, until Mom spies Anna's journal in my hands, clears her throat, and is like, "Speaking of your homework, I think Miss Sophia and Beryl might be very interested in your latest assignment."

"Oh?" Miss Sophia perks up.

"You mean reverse angle distribution in calculus?" I say.

"No," Mom says icily. "I mean the Jewish immigrant journal. The one you're holding in your hand . . ."

Damn. Caught like a rat in a trap.

"Oh this old thing," I shrug.

"Especially you, Beryl. I'm guessing you're in eighth grade too, right?" asks Mom.

"I'm at Yeshiva," he says, which totally doesn't answer the question.

Then my mother, the reverse ventriloquist act, launches into this whole story about Mrs. Goldstein and how she teaches at PS 126 and Temple Beth Shalom, and Russian Jewish Anna Slonovich's historical journal, plus my assignment to try and relate to Anna's life, while I sit there like Mom's dummy, a frozen smile on my face, my lips clamped shut.

"Did I tell you, Amy, that I ran into Mrs. Goldstein at the market?"

"Er . . . no," I say.

"Well, she said, and I quote," Mom continues, making little quotation marks in the air, " 'This is no desk assignment. Amy is supposed to travel all around New York City to really experience the world through Anna's eyes.' "

Beryl, who looks about as bored as I feel, is coddling a handful of grapes and sort of trying to skin each one before popping it into his mouth.

"Moreover," Mom says, smiling happily, "Mrs. Goldstein specifically stated that Amy was to actively seek out the involvement of family and neighbors."

Oh no!

"Now, I would help her, of course, but I've been so busy, what with my part-time job at the gallery and vegetarian cooking courses at the New School . . . Besides," she chuckles, "what moody teenage girl wants to spend a lot of time with her mother?"

"Or . . ." she pauses for effect, "the other way around."

This "joke at my expense," is received with a knowing chuckling from the adults, but to Beryl's credit, gets the smallest dirty look from both him and me.

"And she's been sooo lonely and testy since her friend, Callie, moved away to Kansas," Mom continues.

"For the year," I interject, starting to get really annoyed. "Moved away for just a year."

"See what I mean," Mom mouths to Miss Sophia, who just nods knowingly.

Hello. Sitting right here in the room. Not five years old.

Thankfully, at that moment, all sorts of whistles and bells start pinging from the kitchen.

"Ooh, have to check on dinner," Mom says, sprinting to the kitchen.

51

At that point, Kevin slips back into the apartment and hugging the wall like an old-fashioned burglar, creeps back into his room unnoticed, except by me, of course.

Then my dad, totally recognizing his good exit cue, is like, "Gotta check on a few work e-mails, folks. Be right back."

I look over at Beryl, who has eaten all the grapes and is now engaged in some kind of microsurgery peeling the bark from the grape stem.

"Did I ever tell you that I was a librarian? For almost thirty years," Miss Sophia nods proudly.

"You don't say," I respond.

"And that was a perfect profession for me," she adds.

"Mmm . . . Beryl, you want some more grapes or something?" I say.

"I'm fine . . . thank God," he says, placing the naked grape tree back on the table, sighing. He turns to stare out the window and starts playing with those string thingies that are hanging out from the bottom of his shirt.

"Do you want to know why that was a perfect profession for me?" Miss Sophia continues.

"Er . . . you like to read?"

"Exactly," she claps her hands together. "And what do you think I like to read?"

"I dunno . . . books?"

Then Miss Sophia leans toward me, all conspiratorially, so close that I can see the super fine light gray fuzz on her cheeks.

"Historical fiction," she whispers.

"And do you know what else I did when I worked at the library?"

"Find books?"

"I helped children with research. Lots of research."

"Sounds . . . interesting," I say, wishing that someone would come back in the room and save me.

And then even Beryl turns around and is staring at her with a quizzical look on his face. Believe it or not, he and I even exchange a look like, whaddaya think, is she getting at something or just nuts? That's when I feel a tiny uncomfortable sensation, like a little feather, tickling at the bottom of my brain. She was getting at something, and it wasn't going to be good.

"Yes, I just loved helping children with research," she sighs.

And, at that moment, I realize what she wants, what she's been hinting at all this time. Miss Sophia wants to be my gal pal and follow me around New York.

Then we're just, like, staring at each other, Miss Sophia, her eyes wide looking all hopeful, her little Lord & Taylor felt headband askew on her head and me looking trapped with a stupid, plastic smile on my face, trying desperately to think of a way to say no without it actually sounding like no. Kevin's Asian music is loudly tinkling again and the kitchen timers keeps pinging and my head starts ponging.

And Beryl is now caught up in the unspoken drama

53

between me and Miss Sophia and is moving his wide eyes back and forth between us.

And that's when I see them: big translucent tears welling up in Miss Sophia's eyes.

"Ever since my Arthur died . . ." she starts.

No, no, no!

"It's been a little lonely for me . . ." she sniffs, takes a cocktail napkin, and dabs at her nose.

No, no, no!

"Although I try to stay busy and cheery . . ."

Help, help, help!

"If only I had something special to keep me busy . . ."

And I'm totally mortified, and Beryl looks like he's going to faint and we're both just sitting there, when my mom sashays back into the room, holding *Judaism for Dummies* under her arm.

"Almost ready to light the candles," she chirps. "I checked the candle lighting time in the *New York Times* and . . . Sophia!"

Mom sits next to Miss Sophia and puts her arm around her.

"What happened? Why are you upset? Are you all right?"

Then she shoots Beryl and me a "what the hell happened look," as we both sink guiltily into the couch.

"I'm sorry, dear, I'm fine," Miss Sophia says patting my mother's knee. "How silly of me to tear up. We were just talking about Amy's project and it reminded me of when I was a librarian and how I was . . . well . . . needed, I suppose."

Mom gives Miss Sophia's shoulder a squeeze.

"Well, now I just had a wonderful idea . . ."

OH NO!

I notice Beryl out of the corner of my eye. He picks up the grape stem again and is examining it, but what he's really doing is biting his lip and trying not to laugh.

"What if you helped Amy with her immigrant journal homework project?!" Mom says happily.

HELP!

All eyes swing over to me.

"I . . . I . . ."

"Oh no, I don't want to burden Amy," Miss Sophia says. Then she leans in toward me.

"Really, dear. I don't."

And she's so sincere that I know she really does mean it, which, of course, makes me feel way worse.

"Nonsense. You're no burden at all," Mom states emphatically. "It's all settled then!"

"It's up to Amy," Miss Sophia looks at me hopefully.

Gah . . . defeat.

"That would be nice, Miss Sophia. I'm sure I could use the help with you being a librarian and all, and you've lived in New York City for, like, . . ."

I was gonna say a hundred years, but I knew that sounded wrong.

"A while."

"Now," Mom beams. "I'm going to get the candles and get the boys and we'll get started. Beryl, maybe you can help Mr. Finawitz with the service."

Beryl nods politely.

Then she happily scurries from the room.

Mom flounces back into the room, holding the candles and calling for "the boys" (Dad and Kevin) to come out and join us.

From that point, the evening was pretty uneventful. Mom did not set herself, or anything else, on fire, but when my dad tried to skip the prayers and segue into his: "Let's eat!" Beryl called him on it and offered some pointers about how the Shabbat service is supposed to go. Fortunately, however, even the very religious get pretty hungry after a few prayers and it wasn't long before we were indulging in a variety of rice, beans, noodles, cabbage, and cauliflower delights. Normally, this would have left me starving, except that later that night, Kevin, my Dad and I made a sneak late night run down to Mr. Lee's Chinese for some real food.

Now it's late. More tomorrow.

Amy

PS: BTW, here is the fortune cookie thought for the day:

BEWARE OF OLD, LONELY NEIGHBORS WHO BRING THEIR SUPER-RELIGIOUS NEPHEWS TO DINNER.

Dear Callie,

Hello, yes I do take offense to your implication that I'm insensitive to Miss Sophia's "so sweet-ness." Oh contraire. I am a sensitive person, very sensitive in fact. Are you forgetting that it was because of my sensitivity to her that I got into this mess in the first place? Perhaps the problem is that I'm mostly sensitive on the inside, as opposed to some show-off people who like to be all gushy and sensitive on the outside.

Anyway, there's another strange and more important matter at hand. You know, I didn't need a fortune cookie to tell me that when you went to Kansas you would change into a dollar just like the fortune cookie predicted. I just didn't think you'd be getting so weird (and expensive) so fast.

I'm referring, of course, to this disturbing story about your hayride with your new cool friends. Exactly how many people were squeezed into this wagon? Where did you meet all these kids? I thought your farm was miles from civilization. We don't have twenty friends here in New York City where our neighbors are practically under our beds.

And you were all, what? Bumping around some pumpkin patch and laughing your heads off? I mean, I'm not trying to spoil your fun or anything. It sort of sounds interesting. But what were you all laughing about?

I've been trying to imagine this, so I've written a little play entitled:

HILARITY IN THE PUMPKIN PATCH

by Amy Finawitz

A wagon, dangerously crammed with kids, bumps through the pumpkin patch on chore night. Bump, bump, bump.

DAISY
Lookey, there, Clem, that pumpkin looks just like you.

CLEM
(incredulous)
Well, duh, Daisy. It is my family's pumpkin patch. A'course there's a family resemblance.

All are brought to tears of laughter by CLEM'S cleverness, although they're not quite sure why.

THE END

And another thing I can't quite digest. Who is this Bucky kid, and in what way exactly is he hunkaliscious? How could you possibly consider, with any seriousness, liking someone named Bucky? Human beings are not named Bucky. Bucky is a pet's name. Bucky is not an acceptable name for someone who is liked by a girl from New York.

I know, I know, it's not his fault that his name is Bucky, but he needs a nickname pronto.

This so reminds me of the time you crushed on that strange kid from Camp Winitucket. You know, the lanky one who could roll one eye at a time? Remember how you made us sign up for all the activities he did? Things we hated, by the way, like any activity that involved changing clothes: i.e., running, jogging, rowing, or sweating in general. I will seriously never forgive you for making me stand in the outfield for ten hours in the sun because you wanted to be on his softball team.

The point here is that he wasn't your type either. Please give this disturbing matter some serious reconsideration.

And on that note, Callie, I'm signing off. But I'll leave you with more earth shattering tidbits: Kevin is in a show. It's called, *Eleanor Roosevelt: Great Woman. Unhappy Smile, A Theatrical Love Letter*, some show that he and a bunch of his misbegotten friends wrote, directed, produced, and are acting in, which is probably the only reason he's in it in the first place.

So the other night at dinner, my poor dad, making this cheery effort to be hip and interested is like, "So Kevin, tell us about this play of yours. What part do you play?"

And then idiot Kevin is like, "Parts in the traditional

sense of the word are not important in modern, avant-garde theater."

"Nobody has parts? Then whaddaya do up on the stage?"

"Our play," Kevin intones, "is an organically evolving performance art interpretation, which explores the inner turmoil of a strong, but tragically unattractive woman who was held in great esteem by the husband who cuckolded her."

There's this big pause, with my dad looking all crest-fallen. "Uh-huh," he sighs deeply.

Woo-hoo! Now this sounds like a play that I'm gonna run out and buy tickets for. I bet the musical numbers will be real foot tappers too!

AND, more exciting news: Judy is having a party in a few weeks. At least somebody invites me somewhere.

Amy

Dear Callie,

Guess what happened today?!

After class, I'm heading down the hall toward English when I see Claire coming toward me, and she's got that manic "OMG, I've totally got something awesome to tell you" look on her face, and her eyes are all caffeinated and beaming, and she's got this crazy manic smile which makes me have to shield my eyes from her blue braces which are catching the light and blinding me with kaleidoscope colors.

So I quickly mouth "I'm late," point in the other direction, and duck around the long way to avoid her. Just as I turn the corner, I see John and Susan by the bulletin board, in this kind of parallel park, romantic huddle position, while the rest of the hall traffic is driving by, and they're both chuckling over something (no surprise here). Then "Horrible Susan" flirtatiously accelerates away from him, heads down the hall, and disappears into a classroom. But here's the weird part. I walk past John and suddenly, he's like:

"Hi Amy."

Can you believe it?!

I stop dead in my track, and I'm like, "Er . . . hi," praying that he did indeed say "Hi Amy" and not, for example, "Hi Andy" to a guy named Andy standing behind me.

Then John pulls out of his parallel park position and cruises beside me, and we're actually walking together up the hall!!

"Going to English?" he says.

"Um . . . yeah."

"What do you think of Goldstein's immigrant journal assignment?" he asks.

"Well," I stall, determined to say the right thing. "What do you think of it?"

"It's kinda cool. I like history," he says.

John Leibler likes history? Who knew.

"Me too," I lie.

At that point, we turn the corner into class. He makes his way to the popular section, winks at me, and says, "See ya."

He winks at me!

And I'm so totally shocked that instead of saying something normal like, "Okay," or something cool like, "You betcha" (well, maybe not "You betcha," but whatever) I mumble something unintelligible. Sounding disturbingly like Mr. Block excusing me from gym for menstruation. Then I scurry to my seat.

So John Leibler was actually talking to and walking with me. What do you make of this?

Amy

You can't be serious. What actual chance is there in this universe that John Leibler likes me? And I cannot believe you are even remotely fantasizing that you, me, Buckyliscious, and John could go on a double date one day. Are you having some kind of Manhattan deprivation induced delusion?

I'm much more inclined to go with your other thought, that John always likes to be seen chatting with someone, and he doesn't hate me.

And, of course, I will keep you up to date. Have we met? All I do is live my (not terribly interesting) life and then come home and keep you up to date.

Alas, pathetic, but true.

*D*ear Callie,

In Mrs. Goldstein's class today she asked us to share basic impressions of our immigrants from their journals. Ironically, some of the kids in class seem to resemble their immigrants, in much the same way that people, over time, start to resemble their dogs.

For example, Judy's immigrant was a sweet wallflower who liked to take her zillions of nieces and nephews to the park so she could sit on the bench and crochet. According to Claire, her immigrant journal is full of long stories and reminiscences that Claire calls "charming."

And John Leibler's immigrant was some hot, vaudeville child star who was fabulous and very popular. Talk about art, or in this case, district mandated homework, imitating life!

My immigrant, however, doesn't seem to resemble me at all. For example, according to the first few pages of her journal, she was quite a "gad about" (her mother's words, not mine), and she had an unsinkable, peppy, "can't hold me down" personality. Plus, she seems to have had "oodles" of friends, loved to give others a "helping hand," and after only a few weeks in New York was running all over the place to "soak up the melting puddle that is the heart of New York."

Oy!

How did I get such a cheery immigrant? Is this a joke? Hello. Morose pessimist here.

Having said that, there are *some* similarities between Anna and me. I like that she's sort of dissatisfied and ambitious for an immigrant, like she wants something more than what other people want for her. It seems that little Anna loves to read mysteries, Sherlock Holmes books, in particular. I also like to read, of course, and I think some Sherlock Holmes books are cool too.

And speaking of mysteries, I just opened up a fortune cookie that I saved from yesterday afternoon's snack of shrimp dim sum (yum!) from Mr. Lee's and it says this:

ATTENTION IS THE MOTHER OF MEMORY.

So here's the question: Do these fortune cookie writers really think they're making sense, or are they just sitting somewhere writing nonsense and laughing their butts off?

Amy

9/28, 10:56 p.m.

BTW, I am so *not* monopolizing our conversations and ignoring your interests! For example, I am very interested to learn that you're taking an organic farming elective. Although I didn't realize that you liked vegetables that much except for maybe the ones in the Chinese food at Mr. Lee's. Do they grow bok choy or water chestnuts in Kansas? What exactly are water chestnuts anyway? Are they like chestnuts soaked in water for, like, two centuries? Have you ever seen the ones that come from the can? They're so gross. They look like the tops of thumbs. Remind me to ask Mr. Lee.

And speaking of Mr. Lee, here's another fortune cookie fortune: IT IS BETTER TO BE LOOKED THAN TO BE OVERLOOKED.

Hmm . . . not quite sure what this one means due to grammatical incorrectness, but it sounds very philosophical.

BTW, how is the half-human/half-pet boy? Has he asked you out yet, or is he still just sniffing your hand?

9/29, 9:24 p.m.

*D*ear *Callie,*

I've been giving it a lot of thought and I have to admit that all this exposure to my cheery, mysterious immigrant has activated the cheery, optimistic side of my nature.

And yes, I do have a cheery optimistic side to my nature, albeit small.

To wit:

I'm walking down the hall with Judy and she's bending my ear saying things like, "Did you know that scientists just discovered that crocheting helps prevent hardening of the arteries?"

Because, of course, that's something that every eighth grader needs to worry about. Then I see her brother Larry in the hall, not looking like his usual Neanderthal self for a change (he usually wears sloppy sweatshirts and shorts so low they expose his butt and so long they cover his knees) but actually dressed nicely. According to Judy, he had to give some class presentation and the teacher threatened to flunk him if he didn't look presentable. He stops to ask Judy something, and it seems like a perfect opportunity to try out my new cheeriness!

"Why, Larry," I say, "don't you look clean and dapper today. And you don't smell like socks."

He looks at me hard then breaks into a slow smile as if he's going to say something civilized like, "Why thank you, Amy. How cheery of you to notice."

But instead he just makes a rude gesture and keeps walking.

Hmph . . . I think I'll go back to being me.

Amy

*D*ear Callie,

Today was the first meeting with my new BFF, Miss Sophia, and I had an idea about where we could go to get a real feel of how Anna lived. We did agree, however, to make the local Starbucks on the corner our meeting place.

So I'm walking up to the glass doors at Starbucks and I catch a glimpse of Miss Sophia from the side, looking swanky in one of her new ensembles: a long black, nubby coat with a brown fur collar, a matching nubby hat with fur trim, and brown leather gloves.

But when I open the door and walk in, WHO do you think is sitting at the table next to her?

BERYL!

Yes, Beryl Plotsky is sitting there, plain as day, dressed in . . . well . . . black (although this outfit seemed a little more pressed).

As if my life isn't geeky enough.

"Beryl," I say, approaching the table. "What an . . . interesting surprise to see you here. How ya doing?"

"I'm fine, thank God," he averts his eyes.

"Amy," Miss Sophia says emphatically. "You know, it was so nice of you to include me in this fascinating Jewish immigrant journal homework assignment, it gave me a fabulous idea . . ."

Beryl blushes slightly and averts his eyes, a shy smile plays across his lips.

Sigh. Here it comes.

"It made me wonder, what if Beryl joined our little team! Then we could explore Anna's immigrant world together, and we'd have oodles of fun!"

Did she say team? Did she say, "oodles of fun" again?

"And besides," Miss Sophia continues, "I told Beryl that I thought it would be good for him. Get some air, see some sights, have some fun. And then he'd be doing us a favor too. It would be like a mitzvah."

She glances at me and mouths, "A good deed."

"Yeah, I got it," I say.

I glance over at Beryl, and much to my utter mortification, he actually straightens up and color blushes into his cheeks.

Miss Sophia leans toward me.

"It will be good for you too, Amy," she winks. "Help to socialize you a little better."

WHAT?!

"And since your friend is away, it will be an opportunity for you to get out . . ."

And thank you Miss Sophia for implying that I'm a social weirdo outcast.

"What do you think?" she asks expectantly.

Beryl looks up hopefully.

"Sure. It'll be great," I lie.

Miss Sophia sits back and sighs happily.

And that's how the "oodles of fun team" deal was officially sealed.

Sigh.

Have to stop.

Time for dinner in the Finawitz house: veggie burgers, carrot juice, and sweet potato fries.

Gag.

More later.

Amy

Dear Callie,

So Miss Sophia orders a round of hot chocolates that I deliver to the table. Then she unlocks her Fort Knox purse and pulls out the pages of Anna's journal I e-mailed her.

"Well," I begin, "since Anna lived in an apartment that she shared with her parents and cousins down on the Lower East Side, I thought maybe we could start there and walk around. Although I'm sure a lot of it's different from when she lived there. Ya know, now there's all these movie theaters, stores, nail salons, massage par . . ."

Beryl shoots me a terrified look.

". . . nail salons . . ."

"That's a wonderful idea, Amy," says Miss Sophia. "But I think I can make our trip downtown even more interesting. When I was a librarian, the teachers and I often took class trips to the Tenement Museum."

"Tenement Museum?" Beryl asks.

"Oh yeah. I remember our class had a trip like that, but I was sick that day."

"Well," she continues, "did you know that they offer tours and little plays depicting the immigrant experience?"

"Sounds cool. Let's call and check their schedule," I say.

Beryl and I sip our hot chocolates while Miss Sophia calls on her cell phone and checks.

"They're open!" she announces.

"Great. Let's go," I say.

So out on the street, Miss Sophia hails a cab and climbs in the backseat. I climb in after her, but Beryl hesitates on the curb.

"Why don't you sit in the front, Beryl," says Miss Sophia, apparently seeing his hesitation.

Beryl doesn't want to (isn't allowed to?) sit next to me presumably because I'm a girl. But he actually looks torn. Now, this is a mystery all its own. Will Beryl take the plunge, I wonder.

"The thing is, you have to actually get in the cab for us to get downtown, Beryl. That's the way it works," I say.

"Yes, of course," he hesitates.

"I don't bite, you know."

"I'm sure you don't," he says.

"But you won't sit next to me?"

He chews his lip.

"No offense, but isn't that kind of old-fashioned and sexist?"

"I don't think so," he says.

"So you'd rather sit next to the cab driver," I lean out of the cab toward Beryl and speak low, "a hairy stranger named . . ."

I peer forward to the driver's ID on the dashboard. It's one of those long names with more consonants than vowels.

"With a name I can't pronounce, just because he's a man?"

I lower my voice even more,

"Who by the way, smells bad?"

Beryl peers into the window. Unpronounceable Name Cabbie grins at him and waves, revealing two gold colored teeth and really wet armpit stains on his shirt. Beryl leans back and crinkles his nose.

"For God's sakes, just sit in the back next to me," I say.

A slow blush crawls up Beryl's neck, burning all the way up to his cheeks. He hesitates and chews his lip some more.

Unpronounceable Name Cabbie lets out a long sigh of impatience. Miss Sophia looks at us expectantly from the backseat.

"Well?" I'm suddenly cross and feeling very feminist. "Beryl, get in!"

"I greet you with my heart," Beryl mumbles quickly and then jumps into the front seat next to the driver, closes the door, crams himself as far into his corner as he can and whirs the window wide open.

"Fine," I say. "Suit yourself."

Needless to say, neither Beryl nor I say much on the way downtown. Miss Sophia, on the other hand, got into a long, somewhat one-sided conversation with Unpronounceable Name Cabbie, mostly because he didn't speak much English. He did grin and laugh amicably, though, at regular intervals while Miss Sophia made pleasant observations about the history of architecture in the city's many and varied brownstone districts.

Finally, we make it downtown and get out in front of the ticket window.

Then we're guided across the street into the museum itself. We're surrounded by a group of about twenty kids, nine years old or so I would guess, presumably on some Sunday School trip. They're looking generally bored and antsy.

"Lower East Side Tenement immigrant show starts in three minutes," announces a lady behind a small reception desk pushed into the corner.

"Is he part of the immigrant show?" a wiry kid demands, pointing at Beryl.

"Todd, sit down!" the teacher barks, clearly reading low on the patience meter.

I look around and wonder exactly where this show is going to take place. There were just a few shabby doors in the lobby, bolted shut, and a crummy stairway heading up, presumably, to apartments upstairs.

Suddenly, a woman, dressed as a poor turn-of-the-century immigrant housewife shuffles down the stairs and stops where we can all see her.

"Velcome, Velcome," she shouts in a heavy, and fake, Yiddish accent. "Come children, visit our poor but filled with love home, for ve are Jewish immigrants from Russia."

So we line up and start to shuffle up the narrow steps.

"My name is Mindele," she continues. "I am a housevife. I have zirteen children, although two died from disease and two have taken a covered vagon out Vest. My husband, Pinsky, vorks night and day selling fruits and bananas from his pushcart."

Then she turns, reaches the landing, and opens the door to a small apartment and gestures for us to cram into the littlest living room ever. It felt as if the whole thing could fit into my living room with space to spare! And you know our apartments are not deluxe by any means.

"Todd!" I hear his teacher scold. "Don't touch anything."

I glance over at Todd, who is caught red-handed fingering an old pipe.

"I was gonna put it back," he insists.

"Zis is our small apartment," Mindele says. "And here are two of my zirteen kindala. Jacob is tvelve and Samuel is eight."

From the other room shuffle two scruffy looking boys, at least in their twenties, trying to look twelve and eight. (Hey, maybe I could get Kevin a job here?)

"We are twelve and eight," they say in unison.

"We share this small space vit my fifteen cousins," says Mindele.

Suddenly, we hear heavy footsteps clumping up the stairs.

"Ah!" Mindele gestures stiffly to the front door. "Here's Tzipora, my youngest cousin, now."

All eyes swing to the door.

"Hello, Mindele. It's me, your youngest cousin, Tzipora. Something great has happened."

"Tell us, Tzipora, vhat great thing has happened?"

"The matchmaker has found me a wonderful boy named Shmuley."

"Vell, Tzipora, that is wonderful news. Since I am a seamstress, I vill make your dress."

At this point, Todd slips into the kitchen and starts making raspberry noises with his armpits, until Mrs. Smith grabs him by the lapel of his jacket and drags him out.

I started thinking that maybe it was comforting, living in close quarters with all your relatives. They looked out for you, and there were no surprises about how your life would go, but I bet it was tough for anyone who was ambitious.

It made me feel a pang of pride for my little immigrant Anna that she had a professional ambition to be a writer. If she was serious about a vocation, though, there were probably some serious fights going on in her house. To her parents, her wanting something other than housewifery was probably like nut job Kevin dropping out of college to be an actor.

So, I've decided that Anna had spunk. Remind me to put that in my response assignment for Mrs. Goldstein.

I take a sidelong glance at Beryl.

"Hey Beryl," I whisper.

"Hmm . . . what?" he says, preoccupied. "Aren't you interested in the show?"

"They kind of lost me after those two college guys said they were twelve and eight."

"Mmm," he says, distractedly.

"Hey, Beryl," I whisper again. "How come guys and girls aren't supposed to shake hands or sit next to each other? I mean what's the point of living in modern-day New York if you hold on to all the rules from the eighteenth-century shtetel?"

He looks at me, amused.

"How do you know what a shtetel is?" he asks.

"I read," I say.

"About shtetels?"

"About anything. That's the point. I can do anything I want to do," I say.

"You can do anything you want to do? I doubt that," he says.

"More than you, no offense, Beryl," I say.

He gazes levelly at me.

"How do you know what I want to do?"

He had me there.

"Well, I know that you couldn't do what you wanted to do, even if you wanted to do it."

"Why do you assume that?" he says.

"Hello. Come on, Beryl. You're kind of a very religious guy. I mean, what if you wanted to . . . start a rock band or take karate lessons? You can't even sit next to a girl."

"Being religious doesn't stop me from doing what I want. It focuses me on what's important," he says.

"Besides, I don't want to start a rock band or take karate lessons . . ."

Then he looks at me, quickly averts his eyes, and that spidery blush starts creeping up into his cheeks and he doesn't address the "sitting next to the girl" part.

Okay, I'm guessing that was an attempt at flirting and I'm, like, this conversation is officially over. Casually, I side-step away from Beryl and toward the window as the show continues.

I look outside the window, past the fire escape, and down onto the street below, and try to envision the streets swarming with immigrants, peddling their wares and foods, horses clomping down the streets dragging buggies and pooping on the cobblestones. I imagine boys playing stick-ball and girls jumping rope in their frocks and black lace-up shoes, their hair ribbons flopping up and down. I imagine teenage Anna, smiling up at me.

"Hey, Amy, it's me, Anna!" she waves. "Can you believe I used to live here?"

She gestures to a steaming pile of horse poop and holds her nose. "Nostalgia is so overrated.

"Oh, wait, look, there goes that cute immigrant John Leiblervitch from Blinsk. I'm gonna go follow him and start a conversation with clever small talk like, 'Hi!' "

Then my fantasy Anna clumsily takes off up the street after some hot-looking boy in knickers.

Just then Mindele turns on a CD player hidden behind an old-fashioned radio.

"Let's do some dancing!" she exclaims.

Beryl's eyes light up, and his shoulders pop up and down to the beat of the music.

Then one of the "twelve and eight" guys grabs some poor kid's hand and starts pulling him into some kind of jig.

"I'm so getting out of here," I say low to Beryl.

"And let's ask all our friends to join us!" Mindele shouts.

"Can't we stay for the rest of the performance?" Beryl asks, disappointed.

"Uh, how about . . . no," I say sidestepping to the beat quickly toward the door.

Then, finally, we're all on the street again. Miss Sophia hails a cab, we all pile in, and head for Beryl's house. By the time we pull up to the brownstone, Miss Sophia is in a soft sleep, her head resting gently on the shoulder of her own fur collar.

"Bye, Beryl," I whisper, as he climbs from the cab. "See you soon."

"See you at Starbucks," he smiles happily.

Then he bounds up his front steps, whistling a little tune.

It's hard not to like a kid like Beryl sometimes. You know what I mean?

Amy

10/3, 7:42 p.m.

Yes, Beryl is nice . . . so?

80

Okay, spill it. What are you implying?

Are too.

Oh come on. I know you too well. You are so totally implying something.

Okay. Fine. Let's drop it.

Sorry, I can't. Why are you so fixated on us having boyfriends all of a sudden? I mean dreaming about the unobtainable dates with John Leibler is one thing. But actually having a committed relationship with a real boy is something entirely different. Is this about half-human, half-pet boy Bucky?

Okay, okay. Fine. Have fun at the movies and the shake shop with your wacky new Kansas friends from time warp, circa 1950s. Don't even worry that I have no plans today . . . whatsoever. On a Saturday. Nothing. Nada. Sitting home alone (hangs lonely head and sighs).

10/3, 8:22 p.m.

Judy just e-mailed me to say she got your e-mail that I was sitting home, bored, so she's on her way over here! She's way super excited and is bringing her "beginners yarn" a.k.a. that gray, cheap stringy crap because she says that now that I know how to make the front of a circle sweater, she wants to teach me to crochet sleeves!!!! Oh totally thanks for that!!!! (NOT).

PS: I hate you.

Dear Callie,

So I'm in social studies and Mrs. Goldstein says, "I'll be handing out the next installments of your immigrant journals today, and thank you for handing in the first of your response assignments. Now before we move on to today's lesson, does anyone want to share anything from their immigrant experience."

Judy raises her hand.

"Yes, Judy?"

"Well, since my immigrant was very interested in the thread arts . . ."

Thread arts?

"I've been visiting a lot of fiber arts studios and boutiques . . ."

A few of the kids snicker and some of the juvies start whispering.

"And I have been talking to some elderly women who crochet."

"Touch it. Ooh, can I touch it? Touch me," the juvies croon softly, cracking each other up.

BTW, remind me never to be associated with Judy in public from now on.

"I've learned that the yarn used at the turn of the century," Judy continues, oblivious to the snickers, "was mostly wool hair that was cheap and very coarse to the touch."

You can imagine the snorts and snickers that broke out at that point.

"Well now," Mrs. Goldstein says, shutting everyone up with a withering glance. "Judy has brought up something that I want to address . . ."

Judy shoots me a proud nod.

". . . because she's touched upon an important point."

"Toouuch meee . . ." someone from the back groans.

Explosive laughter!

"Hmph!" says Judy, turning on them with a "you are sooo immature" look.

So I'm subtly inching my chair away from her again, praying that I don't get associated with this social calamity, and am so totally reminding myself to not even sit in the same row as Judy from now on.

Mrs. Goldstein scowls at us until the muffled snickers die down.

I start doodling (in pencil, because I do not own this book) these little pilgrim immigrants in the borders of *History Comes Alive* and just then Mrs. Goldstein's anti-doodling radar kicks in.

"Amy?" she says. "Would you like to say something?"

"Me? Well . . . I, um . . ." I stutter, still anxious about being associated with this "touch me" fiasco.

And I must sound so caught short that a few kids actually turn in their chairs, hoping for some more comic relief. Even John Leibler has turned full around in his chair and is looking at me with anticipation, which has caused my blank mind to go even blanker.

"I . . . well . . . um . . ." I stammer.

Then John actually nods at me in a supportive way, like, "Go ahead, it's all right." And that in itself is so bizarrely jarring that I go totally brain dead. I mean I can hear that flat line noise somewhere floating nearby.

"Er um . . ." I mumble, my face turning bright red.

And then Mrs. Goldstein gets this expression, like, even she's had it, like holy crap she's so gonna need two Tylenol after this class. Trying to save me, she picks up my homework from her desk and leafs through it.

"Now Amy, I see here that you've already gone to the Tenement Museum and you have some interesting people on your team . . . an elderly neighbor, who was a librarian for many years."

Thirty to be exact.

"And . . . oh?" she reads.

"A boy, who is from a very religious Jewish family. That's very interesting, Amy. Is he giving you any insights into the Jewish immigrant experience?"

Then before I can even give another one of my insightful, brain dead, "duh" remarks, Mindy, one of Horrible's homies crinkles up her nose in this disapproving way and is like, "Is he one of those kids who wears all black? Like one of those guys from that really religious school on 81st?"

Then, thankfully, the bell finally rings and I'm out the door and down the hall even before Matt Saperstein, school team track star and winner of PS 126's fifty-yard dash, can get there first.

Amy

PS: And speaking of immigrant journals, turn-of-the-century life, and knitting, how's that growing vegetables thing going?

10/4, 4:45 p.m.

Whaddaya mean I shouldn't compare you with a dead immigrant and loopy Judy. Baking . . . growing . . . knitting, they're all the same thing to me. Shall we refer to them as the nurturing arts?

10/4, 4:48 p.m.

Touchy again! I'm sure that growing organic vegetables is, as you say, a "modern occupation and an important contribution to the earth's sustainability."

What about calling it the sustainable arts?

Is that permitted?

10/4, 5:10 p.m.

Okay. Ignore me. TTYL.

Dear Callie,
So I'm leafing through the next installment of Anna's diary and she's talking about some chatty, cheery nonsense things: hair ribbons, her cousin Levi's upcoming wedding, etc.

She also talks about how she liked to take walks down to the New York harbor and watch the boats come and go.

This gives me the idea that Miss Sophia, Beryl, and I should go down to the South Street Seaport, which is surely what Anna is talking about, where I can soak up some water/sun rays and have something to write about for Mrs. Goldstein.

So at 12:57 sharp, I walk through the lobby, dressed warmly, in my own properly fitting jacket and an empty bladder. When I reach Starbucks, the dynamic duo, soon to become the terrific triumvirate, are standing by the door; Miss Sophia in a Lord & Taylor ensemble: knee length coat made of some blue nubby material; big, black buttons; and a cute, Peter Pan collar. And, beside her, but not too close, stands Beryl wearing . . . well . . . black. And all I can think of at that moment is, Please, God, don't let anyone from school see me.

So we find a table, Miss Sophia orders some cocoas, and we all sit, with Beryl shyly hanging back, positioning himself so that he's barely at the same table. Miss Sophia takes about three minutes to untwist the silver clickety-clack clasp of her purse and then she takes out the latest pages of the journal I e-mailed her.

"Well, where should we go today, children?" Miss Sophia asks.

But before I can answer, Beryl starts looking all industrious, opens his small black backpack, and rustles through it.

I peer forward discreetly to see exactly what he's carrying around. Inside looks like the school bag equivalent of a hundred clowns in a Volkswagen. There are about ten heavy looking books embossed with gold Hebrew letters, a dozen or so spiral notebooks, a bunch of yarmulkes, a zillion pens and pencils, and at least two boxes of tissues.

Beryl thrusts his whole arm into the bottomless expanding sack and wiggles it around as if he's searching for a particular thing. Victorious, he pulls out one slim old black pen with a slightly chewed top.

He takes a deep breath, adjusts his yarmulke, and leans over the copy of Anna's journal pages, circling words here and there, like he's studying some great Talmudic passage, while chewing on the tip of his pen.

"Hmm . . ." and "Ah," "huh," and "I see," he murmurs.

Finally after what seemed like fifteen minutes, I say,

"Ah, Beryl. It's only, like, a five-page journal entry about Anna visiting the seaport. You want to let us in on what you're thinking?"

"I'm trying to help us better understand the type of person Anna was and her relationship with HaShem," he says.

"God," Miss Sophia translates.

"See here, in the opening phrase, Anna indicates that she loves the harbor. Now, this might indicate a desire for water, which has many symbolic meanings in the Old Testament alone. For example, when Moses parted the Red Sea . . ."

"Beryl," I interrupt. "I think maybe you're getting a little carried away here with symbolism and stuff. I think Anna just liked the water and liked to watch the ships come into the harbor. For example," I say, pretending to circle the journal entry with my Starbucks swizzle stick, "she lived on the Lower East Side, so she could have easily walked to the South Street Seaport."

"And now that I think of it, children, I believe a few of the ships, that were replicated from the originals, are open to the public for boat tours around the harbor."

Miss Sophia, claps her hands together.

"Oh, wouldn't it be delightful to take a boat ride?!"

"A boat ride?" Beryl gulps hard, his eyes widen, the blood in his cheeks fade from his already supernaturally pale face.

"That would be kind of cool," I say. "I could write about that."

Suddenly, Miss Sophia is up and buttoning her coat.

"Well, let's go see if we can catch a tour boat!" she exclaims.

So she shuffles out of Starbucks at a surprising clip with Beryl and me at her heels. And before we can say anything else, she flags down a cab, gestures for me to climb in, and scampers in after me. Beryl climbs into the front seat.

"Where go, kid?" the cabbie says, tapping the meter. "Meter ticks."

A small, strange sound escapes from Beryl, sort of like, "Ach . . . ee . . . ee . . . ach . . . ," as he sits rigidly and stares straight ahead.

"Er, South Street Seaport. Down by Fulton Street," I direct the cabbie.

"You all right, Beryl?" I ask.

Beryl nods his head ever so slightly.

"Iy, iy, ach . . ." Beryl murmurs low.

"Beryl?" I lean forward. "You're not gonna hurl, are you?"

"Hey, no throwy upy in cab!" the cabbie shouts.

"I'm okay," Beryl croaks.

The cab pulls over and we all emerge into the noisy, bustling scene that is the seaport. Because it's a cool, sunny day, there are tourists and New Yorkers, and the awesome smell of cheeseburgers and fries are hitting my nose.

"That smells great, doesn't it, Beryl?"

"Mm . . ." he stares straight ahead, moving like a prisoner on death row on his way to the lethal injection.

We weave past shops and seaport museums to the signs that read: "Public Boat Rides."

"Hey, maybe after our ride we can grab some food," I say, all those awesome smells activating my hunger. "Oh, wait. It has to be kosher, right?

"Hrgrr . . ." Beryl grunts.

"Well, there must be something kosher somewhere around here, right, Beryl?

"Don't be so talkative, Beryl. You're bending my ear," I say sarcastically.

Beryl shoots me his version of a dirty look as we arrive at the docks where a large red tugboat, with the word "Ambrose" written in white along its side, bobs gently on the water.

Miss Sophia scuffles off to the ticket area and comes back beaming, clutching three tickets in her hands.

"We'll just make the 2:00 tour," she says, triumphantly, leading us to the short line that's formed at the bottom of the ramp that leads up to the boat.

Just then, one of those overly enthusiastic tour guides, who's all dressed up like some seafaring Captain Bly, with some weird, faux Scottish brogue, moseys up beside us.

"Mornin', lads and lassies," he announces. "I'm Captain Flanahan. I'd like to be telling ye about the boat yer about to be takin' a ride on. This here is the W. O. Decker, a replica of a ship which sailed in New York Harbor from 1823 until 1967."

"Almost a hundred years ago, Anna could have been

standing right where we are now, watching the *Ambrose* sail into the harbor," I say to Miss Sophia, as we shuffle up the ramp and onto the deck of the boat. "Hmm . . . that's something to think about."

Within a few minutes, we've shuffled up the ramp and are on the boat. Miss Sophia happily scurries over to a free spot by the railing, leans forward, cups her eyes against the sun and takes deep, invigorating breaths.

"Smell that briny sea air, dear," she exhales happily.

I didn't have the heart to remind her that we were still in the New York Harbor and all I could smell were hot dogs, sauerkraut, and fries floating up from the ye old Sabrett stand on the corner and car exhaust from nearby Fulton Street.

"I wonder if the harbor reminded Anna of her ocean journey to America. What do you think, Amy? Why do you think Anna loved to come to the seaport?" Miss Sophia asks.

"I bet Anna must have felt really cramped up in that apartment of hers on the Lower East Side with a million relatives. And what's worse, they were probably people who didn't understand her at all. Who probably thought she should just do her chores and bide her time until she got married. Or just be who they expected her to be, you know what I mean? Beryl, you must totally know what I mean . . ."

I spin around. "Beryl?"

I suddenly realize that Beryl is nowhere to be seen.

"We be sailing off in two minutes!" Captain Bly guy bellows.

"Beryl!" I call out.

Then I spot him, glued to the dock, his face almost as pale as his little white shirt collar, wisps of his orange hair fiery in the sun under his black yarmulke.

"S'cuse me, s'cuse me," I push back through the crowd and make my way down the ramp, back onto the dock.

"Come on, Beryl. What are you doing down here? We're about to sail."

"Amy," he says, his eyes looking wide and wild. "I've never been on a boat before. I can't swim."

"You can't swim? Haven't you ever been in a pool?"

"I've only been in a pool once," he says.

"Just once?"

He nods.

"What do you do in the summer?"

"Sweat."

I sigh long and loud.

"Well, listen, Beryl," I say, motioning him to step onto the ramp and move forward. "These ships are very safe."

Reluctantly, he shuffles along, holding on to the little silver chain railing for dear life.

"You can't swim in the New York Harbor anyway. You'd turn green from radiation and toxic waste."

"Radiation and toxic waste! I hadn't thought of that!" he panics.

"Don't worry about it, Beryl. No one's swimming, okay?"

"I don't know. Maybe I'll stay here," he starts to turn back.

"Come on, it will fun. You'll see," I say, baby-stepping with him toward the boat.

"I don't know."

"Come on, if a turn-of-the-century girl could go on boat rides, a big guy like you can," I coax, figuring that even super religious guys like to be flattered.

"I don't know."

"You can do it," I say kind of herding him, without actually touching him, until he's on the boat.

The ship glides forward from the dock, and Beryl almost loses his balance.

"Is the ship at sea? Is the ship at sea?" he gasps.

"Now, I know you're nervous, Beryl, but just white knuckle it, okay? It's only about a 45-minute ride around the harbor. Hold on to the railing."

I grasp on to the railing to show him.

"See? Breathe. You'll be fine."

So Beryl grabs on and swallows hard. He closes his eyes, and I can hear him praying quietly under his breath. After a few minutes, he opens his eyes and looks around. The cool breeze picks up, the children around us laugh and point at the water, which sloshes rhythmically against the side of the boat. Beryl's face relaxes, and a slow smile spreads across his lips.

"Now, isn't this nice?" I croon.

Beryl sort of nods.

"Hey listen, Beryl, I was just talking to your aunt Sophia about Anna's journal and why she might have liked hanging out here so much. Maybe it gave her the chance to be her own person, ya know, to feel free, to be around different kinds of people, people with interesting lives who were rushing and coming and going," I say, suddenly feeling the wind in my own hair and the urge to sail this mother way out across the sea.

"She could pretend to be anyone here. She could pretend to be sailing to any exotic place in the world."

"Why would she want to do that?" Beryl turns to me perplexed.

"For . . . I don't know . . . adventure."

"Why would she want adventure? She'd just sailed the whole ocean to get here."

"A new adventure," I say.

"She probably had enough adventure running from the Cossacks in Russia. She probably wanted to feel safe."

"Not everyone wants to just be safe, Beryl."

"Why not?"

"Because safe is boring, that's why not."

"Safe is safe," he says. "That's why the Jews came to America, to feel safe."

"And . . . to have a new life . . . and a new life should have some adventure."

"Why?"

95

"Because every soul yearns for adventure," I snap, feeling my blood pressure rising.

"Every soul yearns to know God and do good deeds," he says solemnly.

"Okay, aside from that. I know that you're pretty happy not starting a rock band, but surely you must want to do something . . . I don't know . . . wrong."

"Like what?"

"I don't know, Beryl . . . Start small . . . like wear . . . yellow or something."

"I can wear yellow."

"You can wear yellow?"

"Yes, I can wear a yellow shirt."

"Ah," I say, feeling like I've got him. "But what about yellow pants?! I bet you couldn't wear those."

"Why on earth would I want to wear yellow pants?!"

"Haven't you been listening to a word I said! For adventure! For excitement!"

Pause.

"What's so exciting about yellow pants? Don't you think I'd look, a little . . ." he lowers his voice. "Not like a boy."

"Gah! For God sake, Beryl! You're here, aren't you? That must mean you want a little excitement in your life!"

"I'm here to do a mitzvah. For my aunt Sophia." Then he looks down and blushes, "And for you."

"For me?"

"You need to get out," he says.

"I?!! I? Need to get out?!"

"Yes, that's what Aunt Sophia says."

"Oh, I give up, Beryl. Go look at the waves."

So I put as much distance as I could between myself and Beryl, moving to the other side of the boat. And how did Miss Sophia spend the rest of her seafaring journey?

Well, she ended up having "oodles of fun" chatting with the other passengers, pointing out the sights around the harbor, and just generally enjoying the cool sea air. I found myself actually liking her more in those moments. At least she's more fun than Grandma Nussbaum, who never even visits New York (too dangerous) and thinks a big adventure is finding my grandfather's nose hair clippers.

Eventually, though, Miss Sophia got tuckered out, found a bench, and, with her chin resting on her chest, took a little seafaring nap.

Ironically, it didn't take long for Beryl to get his "sea legs." Maybe it was the free sea air, or maybe he did feel the wind in his yarmulke. He spent the rest of the trip bouncing all around the boat, pestering the crap out of poor Captain Bly with a million questions about ships and history and New York Harbor until I thought the guy was gonna stick his faux sword into his back and force him to walk the plank.

Finally, we disembark and Miss Sophia buys a couple of those awesome smelling (maybe not so awesome tasting) hot dogs, which is I guess why you have to pile them high with smelly sauerkraut. Beryl, who conveniently keeps a list of all the kosher eateries in the city on his cell phone, finds a Ming's Kosher Take-Out nearby and gets his favorite, a small carton of kosher (porkless) moo shu pork.

Then Miss Sophia hails a cab and directs it uptown to Beryl's house. He stares out of the window, absentmindedly twisting the stringy things that droop from the black scarf belt around his waist (what are those called again?).

So we all sit back as the cab weaves through traffic, and I find myself glancing at the back of Beryl's neck, and it hits me that he really isn't that bad looking. Don't get me wrong, he's no John Leibler, but in normal clothes, like jeans and a T-shirt and maybe a little bit of a tan, he could be passable.

Finally, we pull up around to his block, not far from the Chabad Center. I see his family through the kitchen window. A woman, who must be his mother, is busy puttering around, getting dinner ready. Five or six children of various ages crowd around her.

I notice that there's a contented smile on Beryl's face, and he's softly humming a little melody that I can only assume is something religious. Was he happy because he had done a mitzvah for poor "pathetic" me, or did he really feel, deep down, that he had a little adventure of his own? I swear I couldn't tell.

I wondered if, in fact, even for a split second, Beryl ever

really thought about being more of a regular kid; listening to loud, obnoxious music, going to crazy parties; or missing curfew on a date?

Uh . . . wait a second, I don't do any of those things either.

Let's have a moment of silence for my life as a social outcast.

Maybe he was happy because he was getting back to his own immigrant-like life.

Before Beryl springs up the gray stone steps, he turns and pokes his head back into the cab window.

"See you next time, Aunt Sophia," he says. "Bye, Amy. I'm looking forward to our next 'adventure.' Then he blushes slightly, and I swear there's this little twinkle in his eye, and it hits me that it isn't just doing a mitzvah for Miss Sophia that he's looking forward to.

Amy

PS: To make matters worse, Judy's party looms (looms . . . weaving, knitting, get it?). A feisty Saturday night of girls, food, and yarn . . . woo-hoo!

PPS: I really miss you.

10/10, 9:16 p.m.

I've been thinking that my little immigrant dream team and I could maybe start our own immigrant journal research firm. We could take our act global and call it: geeky kid, old lady, and religious kid, or GOR for short.

10/10, 9:32 p.m.
I'm very glad to hear that 'you had a good laugh' picturing me on this boat with Beryl and Miss Sophia. Nothing brightens my day like knowing that my pathetic adventures are bringing sunshine into your life (insert sarcastic tone and eye rolling here).

10/17, 12:05 a.m.

*D*ear *Callie,*

Well, it's now Sunday a little past midnight. I know I haven't written in a couple of days so I'll try and answer your many and varied questions one at a time:

Question: Where are you?

Answer: I'm here.

Question #2 : What's going on?

Answer #2: Nothing.

Question #3: Are you all right?

Answer #3: I've been better.

Etc, etc.

"I've been better" is an understatement. After the embarrassing fiasco in social studies class, I didn't think it could get any worse, but it has.

I've actually written a playlet to memorialize the last few days of my sucky life, aptly entitled:

THE LAST FEW DAYS OF MY SUCKY LIFE: AN OVERVIEW

(A play in a few scenes, by Amy Finawitz)

AMY arrives unfashionably early at 6:00 because she is bored waiting around her apartment for the party to start. JUDY'S

101

brother, LARRY, wearing an undershirt covered in pizza drippings, opens the door. He sprays her with tomato sauce as he talks.

JUDY'S BROTHER LARRY
Whaddaya want?
AMY pushes past him into the room.

JUDY, CLAIRE, and four other unpopular looking girls are sitting in the living room. A few boxes of pizza are stacked on the coffee table in front of them, and a pile of chick flick videos are strewn about around their feet. Stale boy band music plays on the CD player.
CLAIRE waves enthusiastically at AMY.

CLAIRE
Hi, Amy! Have some pizza! Who's your favorite boy band? What movie do you want to watch? How's your cute brother? I saw John Leibler yesterday in study hall. He's so babeliscious! Look, Judy showed me how to crochet a circle. I think, maybe later, she's gonna teach us how to crochet squares, isn't that awesome? Then we're gonna eat pizza and candy, watch a few movies, try and contact Elvis, thank you, thank you very much on the Ouija board, do our nails, and make phony phone calls. I'm so gonna call Rob Assario. It's so awesome that you're here! I never see you. You're always rushing somewhere every time I say hello. Come sit next to me, so we can talk.

At this point, our tragic heroine grabs a poisonous asp from her backpack and slams it against her heart. (No, wait, that's Elizabeth Taylor, playing Cleopatra.)

AMY merely swoons into a dead faint. BROTHER LARRY forgets to call 911, and the girls spend the rest of the evening stepping over her inert body.

THE END

Of course, the fantasy version of the evening would go more like this:

FADE IN: It is Friday night. Our main character, AMY, has been hoodwinked into attending the social extravaganza of the season: a party given by Miss JUDY SWEENEY, daughter of the illustrious HAROLD and SHIRLEY SWEENEY of West 70th Street, Apt 31A. AMY arrives fashionably late at 6:30, the party having been called for the fashionable time of 6:15. She rings the doorbell, which is answered by JUDY'S quick-witted brother, LARRY.

JUDY'S QUICK-WITTED BROTHER, LARRY

Good evening, young lady. Fashionably late, I see.

AMY pushes past him into the room and a fantasy, much like the foggy dream sequence in *Fiddler on the Roof*, unfolds:

A wild party. Cute boys wearing togas made out of sheets and carrying reams of lanyard are climbing up the fire escape and through the windows. Everyone's gyrating to loud music. Couples are getting cozy in corners, knitting doilies and making key chains.

Our hero, JOHN LEIBLER, enters in a swirl of white fairy dust and moves slowly across the room to AMY, who is munching on cheese and salami balls to the beat of the music. AMY spots JOHN moving toward her, quickly spits the remains of a ball into a napkin, and pops a mint into her mouth.

JOHN
Hi. It's Amy, right?

AMY
I love you.

JOHN
Cool . . . wanna dance?

AMY
I'm sorry; I don't dance . . . on principle, you know. But I'd be happy to crochet you a circle sweater and be your girlfriend forever.

JOHN
Sounds like a plan. Oh, and by the way, I love you too.

But, alas, AMY rubs her eyes and the dream sequence turns to dust.

THE END

Amy

10/17, 12:32 a.m,
Forgot to mention that, after the party, I drowned my sorrows at Lee's, and ate, by myself, three shrimp rolls and a small order of broccoli and tofu with sauce on the side. (FYI, I spent half the night belching.) Tonight, I wandered

back into Mr. Lee's for a late-night egg roll. The place was empty and I was feeling philosophical, so I asked him about this "chi" business. He got super excited and launched into this long bit about some dynasty (Ping? Ding? Ling?) and how these very spiritual, ancient people discovered that we all have energy flowing through us. If it's clogged like a drain, then we're selfish, unhappy, and tend to have gastro-intestinal unpleasantness. If it's open, then we are giving, loving, and spiritually advanced.

By the time he was finished talking, I was entering a deep REM state, but I roused myself, thanked him, and went home.

Maybe there's something to this chi business after all. Maybe we should concentrate on becoming better, more spiritual people, enhancing our inner chi and reaching out to others?

Amy

10/17, 12:34 a.m.

Nah. So not us.

10/17, 1:00 a.m.

I'm not sure what to make of your last e-mail. You're to-tally preoccupied with your new friends. And you were out until midnight? At that shake shop again? Drinking shakes and eating gravy fries with Buckyliscious?

Are you joking?

Don't get me wrong. It's not that I'm not happy that you're having fun during your temporary time in Kansas, but could you please try and stay focused on coming home? Like, hello, while you're rockin' 'round the clock with Potsie and Fonzie, I'm back here suffering all kinds of indescribable, despicable social indignities . . . by myself!

Amy

Dear Callie,

I'm very astounded to hear that Bucky boy/Rottweiler asked you to a dance. You did mean a formal dance, right? I mean, he didn't just ask you to do a little boogie woogie with him in the Shop and Save parking lot? I didn't even know you knew how to dance, except for maybe clapping and jumping your way clumsily through the Cha Cha Slide or tripping through the Israeli dances at bar mitzvahs, just like me.

Actually, I can't help feeling a little stung. If I really thought you liked to dance, I wouldn't have suggested we blow off all those tacky school parties. And what about our pact to blow off the dance last year just on principle? Didn't we agree that school sponsored dances violated our civil rights as women and perpetuated antifeminist stereotypes?

Okay, I know you'll say, Amy, you're being ridiculous and maybe I am, but frankly, I'm shocked that you would abandon your principles for the cool smile of a boy named Bucky.

So in honor of your foray into the world of "the others," I've written a play entitled:

GIVING UP ONE'S PRINCIPLES TO DO THE CHA CHA SLIDE WITH A HOT GUY WHO IS NAMED AFTER A PET

(A play in one scene by Amy Finawitz)

WE FADE INTO: A dance at the school gym, decorated with pastel streamers, pastel wall murals, and pastel colored lights.

A long table runs across one wall and is covered with Betty Crocker–inspired snacks, mostly cheese concoctions and little cakes with pastel frosting. There is also the obligatory punch bowl filled with a pink libation and a band who looks as if they've been imported from the Appalachian mountains to play watered down versions of popular country music.

Girls in hoop skirts and high ponytails, looking as if they dropped in from the 1950s (even though this is not a theme dance) sit expectantly in a row of chairs that line the wall. They tap their ballet slipper shoes, and wait to be asked to "cut a rug," while the plain, but superior girls are left behind, publicly humiliated and scarred for life.

CALLIE, our heroine, a formerly principled New Yorker, who has been rendered temporarily insane by her wrenching separation from her beloved Manhattan and her best friend's sensible and compassionate disposition, squirms expectantly in her "girl chair" against the wall. She yearns to be asked to dance by her small town Prince, who may or may not be charming.

Bucky, town hottie, who is wearing a pastel suit and a cool smile, approaches her.

BUCKY

Wanna dance? . . . woof.

CALLIE

Why, Bucky, I'd be delighted, even though by accept-
ing your gracious, although strangely articulated re-
quest, I'm relinquishing everything I hold dear.

BUCKY

Uh . . . is that a yes?

It is a pivotal, dramatic moment for our heroine, who is tragically torn. But alas, she is weak and jumps into Bucky's pastel
arms.

CALLIE

Yes! Yes! I will dance with you, oh Bucky, hayseed of
my dreams. And may God and Mrs. Goldstein from PS
126 and Temple Beth Shalom forgive me!

BUCKY

Woof, woof . . . I mean . . . uh . . . cool.

We fade out as CALLIE and BUCKY turkey trot recklessly into a
wall mural of a pastel colored sunset.

THE END

Well, now that I have expressed myself fairly thoroughly, it's
time for bed. I hear Kevin rehearsing for his play. I think I
mentioned he's in some off, off, off Broadway play (so many
"offs" that I think it's being staged in Outer Mongolia)
about Eleanor Roosevelt.

Kevin is a chorus member/intermission snack manager. Apparently, he has some big number called, "Just because your teeth aren't straight doesn't mean you aren't beautiful" or something like that. Can you believe it?

Amy

PS: Now will you stop playing fetch with Bucky and write me back?!

PPS: I really wish you were here.

*D*ear Callie,

You won't believe this one: So I see Claire in the hall in between math and gym, and I scoot into the girls' room to avoid having her chew my ears right off my head.

But it was really the boys' room. (You know how confusing that first floor is.) So I'm standing there, completely zoned out for a few seconds, wondering who put urinals in the girls' bathroom and who comes out of the stall, pulling up his fly, no less. Yes, you guessed it . . . JOHN LEIBLER!

Can you believe it?!

So I'm, like, completely beet red with embarrassment, fighting the urge to flush myself down the toilet.

"Hey," he says, casually, zipping his fly.

"Uh, hi," I stammer. "I thought this was the girls' room."

"Whatever," he shrugs, washing his hands.

I swear. Like, it's no biggie. I see mortified, stupid looking, beet red girls in the boys' bathroom every day.

And then he's like, "So, do you like your immigrant journal?"

Is he making small talk with me?

"It's okay, I guess. I mean she's okay. She got around,

111

though. Er . . . I mean, not, like, with guys or anything . . . I didn't mean that . . ." I say, followed by dumb chuckling.

"I mean she liked to go places. She liked adventure, I think . . . I don't know too much yet . . ." I say, averting my eyes and letting my voice trail off. All the while the voice in my head is editorializing my remarks with its own remarks like:

What?!? Who?! What are you talking about?! You're not making sense?! He thinks you're an idiot! Shut up, already!

"Oh," John says, looking a little perplexed.

Then there's this big silent pause and he just keeps standing there!

"And you've got some people helping you?" he says, pulling a paper towel from the dispenser.

"My neighbor and her nephew."

"Oh yeah, the religious kid. Does he go to religious school or something?"

"Well, yeah. He goes to a Yeshiva. But he's just doing it, ya know, to please his parents. He's, like, really cool."

Oh my God, and what was I saying? Beryl is cool?

"Huh. Sounds interesting. Did I ever tell you that my cousin is Jewish? He's not that religious, though," he says, rolling up the paper into a little ball.

"Really? That's interesting," I croak nervously.

And we're still standing there . . .

"So, um, what about your journal?" I say. "Is it interesting?"

Even though I totally know from eavesdropping on him.

"I dunno," John shrugs. "My immigrant's kind of boring. His name was Francois and he was some kind of child actor and really thought a lot of himself, like he was all that or something."

John chuckles and then sinks the paper towel ball into the garbage like a basketball.

"But your immigrant sounds pretty okay," he continues. "Did I tell you that I like history?"

I nod.

"Not to brag or anything, but it's my best subject. A lot of people don't know that about me. They think I'm just athletic, but I'm really into the History Channel."

Now John Leibler is confiding his innermost thoughts to me by the urinal?

"I bet you get what I'm saying," he continues. "I usually kind of like English, but it's so boring this year. You seem like you're good in it, though. You're smart. You like to read the books and ask questions and stuff."

"Uh . . . I . . . sure."

But then he still doesn't leave. He just leans up against the sink and is like, "And, um, I wanted to ask you . . ." he turns, smoothing his hair in the mirror and looking back at me from his reflection.

John Leibler wants to ask me something?! Holy crap!

"Did you finish the book in English we're having that test on?"

"*Catcher in the Rye?*" I ask.

"Yeah, *Catcher.* Did you like it?"

"I loved it. Who doesn't?" I say.

"Yeah, well, if you have time to read," he says, turning around, a slight irritation in his voice.

"Well, see ya. But . . . um . . . hopefully not in the boys' bathroom," he moves toward the door and winks.

"Oh yeah . . . no, probably not . . . I mean . . . definitely not."

Then I burst into this lilting phony laughing, like way over the top, with snorting at the end.

Amy

PS: Urinal and slightly funky bathroom smell aside, did I mention that John Leibler is totally hunkaliscious?!

Dear Callie,

Forget the urinal story. What is this about Buckyliscious planting a kiss on you?! You drop this bomb on me and that's it? Please follow this e-mail with more details!

It's kind of ironic that all these years living in the city that never sleeps, you go visit the town that always sleeps and have all these wild experiences.

Yes, yes, I know. You didn't choose to leave the city, and it's not your fault that you're actually liking it . . . but could you like it with a little less enthusiasm? It's not so much fun to be the one left behind.

By the way, New York City does not smell bad. Well, maybe it does sometimes, but only in the summer by the garbage cans. And yes, occasionally some person feels the need to pee on a building, but that's a small price to pay for living in one of the greatest cities in the world.

And what's this bit about loving the fresh air and open spaces? What are you now, a country song? Have you completely forgotten our feeling about the wide open spaces at Camp Winitucket? How we kept talking about what a waste it was, how someone should buy the land and build high-rise apartments on it?

Also, we have Central Park, and don't tell me it's dangerous. You know very well that most of the time, during the day, in most sections it's perfectly safe, especially if you have a big dog and Mace.

Come on, Cal, you used to love the city, and you're a bigger snob than I am.

Of course, there are also giant billboards of guys in underwear, which can be a tad overwhelming if you get my drift, but that just adds to the charm.

Anyway, after this big lecture about how I "heart" New York, in an ironic turn, right now even I wish I lived somewhere else.

Amy

10/20, 4:30 p.m.
Yes, I received the picture of you and Buckyliscious. Okay, I'll admit that he's cute, but he's no John Leibler.

10/20, 4:31 p.m.
What do you mean, even though Buckyliscious may not be John Leibler, at least he's not Beryl. What does Beryl have to do with this? Stop implying that I should hook up with Beryl!

10/20, 4:34 p.m.
What do you mean, "uh-huh," in that sarcastic way. I don't care for your tone.

Yes, I did say that Beryl wouldn't be bad looking if he wore normal clothes and got some sun. And, you're right, there probably is a good chance he likes me. But I AM NOT now, or at any time in the future, hooking up with him!

Don't I have enough problems walking around all day just being me? Wouldn't I be completely making my life worse by being me and having Beryl as a boyfriend?

Besides, you know as well as I do, there's not much dating with the religious. It's probably all, "Hello, how are you." "I'm fine, thank God." "We're engaged."

I have no intention of being an eighth grader with a fiancé, thank you very much.

Dear Callie,

So, the other day, Judy tells me she's dying to see the latest sappy, predictable chick flick and asks me to go with her. I say no at first, because you know how out of control Judy gets at the movies, with her loud outbursts of giggling and shouting out at the screen things like, "Shake that thang, Zac Efron!"

And singing loudly, off-key, along with the soundtrack so that everyone is always "shushing" us and shooting us dirty looks.

And those are the happy movies. Lest we forget those tearjerkers where one of the lovers drowns, gets a disease, or is riddled with WWII shrapnel. Remember when you, me, Judy, and Claire saw *Titanic*, at classic movie night down at the Forum, and Judy kept shouting,

"Find more driftwood, Leo!"

And then she sobbed and wailed so hard that the popcorn guy almost had to call 911?

Anyway, I finally broke down and told her I'd go because (a) she's really okay, (b) she gave me a piece of her mother's awesome cheesecake from her lunch box, and (c) I had nothing else to do. I did try to pitch the idea of

118

seeing the latest bloodthirsty horror, slasher, murder movie instead of a chick flick, but Judy refused.

But, of course, the story doesn't end there.

So, we walk about ten blocks to the theater and the whole way there, she's yakking about the movie plot: something about a shopaholic wedding planner who joins the lacrosse team dressed as a boy; leads a double life as a country singer; discovers she's a princess of a small, obscure country; and then falls in love with the guy she initially hates (I know! What a shocker!) until I'm so desperate I'm ready to jump into oncoming traffic.

Then we finally get to the theater, sit down, and before I can stop her, Judy unzips her backpack and pulls out this huge half-knitted neon-colored chunky granny sweater with these ginormo pink plastic knitting needles that look like they came from the "Land of the Giants" toy store, because that's what gives the sweater its chunky look, don't you know. Then she starts knitting. But not tiny, clickety clack, booty knitting; this knitting is like a whole body aerobic exercise with Judy's arms pumping up and down, stretching and looping the yarn way up over the needles, flapping the knitted part of the sweater back and forth across her lap, gyrating from side to side and grunting.

And I'm, like, totally mortified already and the singing and shouting at the movie hasn't even started yet, so I'm very relieved when the lights finally go down, when who do I see sprinting down the aisle? Horrible Susan and her tribe of homies looking for ten empty seats in a row, which is, of course, the whole row in front of us.

Then Judy suddenly has a sick delusional moment, probably caused by too much yarn fiber inhalation, and decides that these girls are actually our friends. So she reaches forward and starts tapping Horrible on the shoulder with her giant pink knitting needle.

Susan finally turns around, glares at us, and crinkles her nose like we're covered in dog poo. Then she barely mumbles a civil "hi" and turns back to her friends.

But here's where it really gets weird.

So the movie starts. The music swells and Judy gets into position. She shoves her knitting onto the empty seat beside her. She leans forward. Her eyes sparkle. Her shoulders gyrate. Her mouth is open. She's ready to sing. When, suddenly, she is totally eclipsed by the most horrifying yodeling sounds ever!

Horrible and her homies (and every other girl in the theater) beat Judy to the punch! Right before my eyes, the whole place morphs into, like, some weird cult of chick flick zombies, separated at birth, fan girls, all singing off-key to the movie soundtrack!

All through the movie, they're, like, giggling and talking about who's hot and who has cute clothes and who has a tight butt and who's dating who in real life.

And here's where it gets weirder still.

Then Horrible Susan and her homies suddenly start bonding with Judy! They turn around in their seats to chat and dish and guffaw with her (as opposed to at her) while smiling, pointing, and nodding!

But wait, there's more!

So the movie finally ends and I'm packing up my stuff when I spot Judy standing in the aisle, cradling her big chunky sweater in her arms, and she's surrounded by Horrible and co. who are oohing and ahhing over it like it's some big, adorable yarn baby!

By the time we get into the street, it's kisses all around (for Judy, not me) and total ecstatic excitement over Judy's promise to teach them all to knit!!

I've decided that the world, and everyone in it, has gone totally, seriously insane.

Amy

Dear Callie,

What do you mean that I have to understand that most girls want to see happy movies about people falling in love as opposed to seeing gruesome movies about people being eaten by the undead? Have you gone rogue on me now too?

Although I shouldn't be that surprised by that remark since, you're, like, totally obsessing over Bucky lately! So what happened? Pet/Boy wants a longer leash? Needs a bigger pen?

Sorry, I'm not trying to be mean or insensitive. I just think you're overreacting. Just because he hasn't been wagging his tail under your window every day, or continuing to drop little dead bluebirds at your feet in exchange for a biscuit and a scratch (all right, I'll stop with the dog jokes) doesn't mean he doesn't like you anymore and the puppy moon is over (sorry, I can't).

I'm sure he'll trot back home soon enough.

Now while I'm waiting for you to turn your attention to more important matters, like focusing on coming home, I'll fill you in on the more ridiculous aspects of my life, namely my brother Kevin who I am planning to kill. I was wondering if you'd like to be an accomplice. I swear I won't implicate you.

Here's the problem. Well, in addition to the "Eleanor Roosevelt" thing, he's in another play now. This "crowd pleaser" is some idiotic musical about a guy who's dropping dead until he embraces his inner cross-dresser and then he lives. He and his friends pooled their money to buy the rights to it (like anyone else would want it). So now he's referring to himself as an actor/producer and that's how he says it too.

He says, "I'm an actor." Then he makes a slash mark in the air with his fingers, even if he's on the phone, and then says, "Slash, producer."

And he says it, like, all the time . . . I mean all the time. The other morning, my mother asked him if he could stop at the market to pick up some of her organic crap and he's like, "I'd love to, but I can't. I have a rehearsal."

Then my mother squints at the play schedule that Kevin wrote out and taped to the refrigerator, like we all give a crap about his schedule, and she's like, "It says here that you have the afternoon off."

"Well, I'd like to go to the market for you," Kevin says, "but now that I'm an actor slash producer, I have to take meetings."

Then last night, I'm like, "Kevin, could you get your lazy butt out of the bathroom already and stop talking into your hairbrush in the mirror."

He says: "I'm an actor slash producer. I have to rehearse."

And then I say, "Well, I'm a kid slash potential murderer, and I have to pee."

So, if you see any really sharp tools in a barn somewhere, rat poison, or any scarecrows holding sharp-looking hoes, keep me in mind. By the way, can you FedEx sharp, pointy dangerous things with poisonous tips through the mail?

Oh well, I didn't think so.

I should also mention that Kevin's talking about having some play rehearsals in the apartment. Can you imagine how horrendous that would be? Presumably, the actor slash producers are too cheap to rent a theater space, and the homeless squatters won't let them back into their old theater slash bathroom! Two years of college and he's still an idiot.

Judy's oldest brother, Craig, is spending the rest of the year backpacking through Europe. Now, why couldn't I have a brother like that?

Amy

PS: When the hell are you gonna write me back already? Put Bucky in the pen for a couple of hours, will ya! Sheesh!

10/22, 4:01 p.m.

Hello . . . still waiting. Are you there? What's the problem?

YOU'RE WHAT??!! YOU'RE THINKING OF STAY-
ING IN KANSAS FOR ANOTHER WHOLE YEAR,
INCLUDING THE SUMMER??!!

Are you kidding?! Are you nuts?! Have you completely
lost your mind?!

Your parents are going along with this?! They think it's
a great idea?! Have you been abducted by aliens and been
replaced with some automaton replica?!

Is this all about Buckyliscious? Haven't you ever heard
that old adage about if you love something, set it free and
if it was meant to be yours it flies back, or some crap like
that?

And what's this about us being too old to go back to
Camp Winitucket? I thought we were gonna apply to be
CIT's this year, so we didn't have to play sports but could
make the little kids do it. We spent the last nine years as
campers at that dumb ass camp just so we could go back
and be CIT's!

And you're gonna do what? You're gonna stay there and
pluck lettuce at some organic earth friendly farm? The
earth isn't friendly in New York? Excuse me, I think it is.

And what about our plans to go with your family to Rhode Island at the end of August?

And . . . WHAT ABOUT HIGH SCHOOL?!

Don't you "heart" New York anymore?

Don't you "heart" us?

Listen, just promise me this. Don't do anything yet, don't commit to anything, don't sign anything, and for God's sake don't promise anything (other than promising me you won't do anything).

I believe that your complete personality change could only be the result of some serious brainwashing or alien soul sucking.

Amy

10/23, 8:00 p.m.

After your appalling e-mail, I decided to drown my distress in the dinner plate special at Mr. Lee's Chinese. I guess I must have looked upset, because Mr. Lee asked me what was wrong. I confided in him that you'd been brainwashed by a deranged cult of organic lettuce pickers from Kansas. Then he became so upset that he forgot to give his favorite customer extra duck sauce, for which she had to make a second trip. He said he knew of a special anti-brainwashing tea and would order some straight away from his friend who is an acupuncture/herbalist expert.

The latest fortune cookie SHOULD read:

DON'T MAKE RASH DECISIONS YOU WILL REGRET FOREVER.

10/23, 8:54 p.m.

What do you mean your parents and the school want you to make a definite decision after the Christmas vacation? And the sooner the better, like even around Thanksgiving! Thanksgiving is right around the corner! How can you make a decision like this so fast! A decision of this magnitude will, like, affect everything, our lives, ninth grade, high school, and confirmation class at Temple Beth Shalom!

10/23, 9:00 p.m.

Excuse me, I'm not overreacting! I do so care about your feelings! I know you really like Bucky and you really like your new friends and you really like your school and you really like the country . . . so what? I'd really like to run off to the Bahamas with John Leibler. You don't see me actually doing it, do you?

10/23, 9:02 p.m.

Well? . . .

10/23, 9:04 p.m.

Fine. Don't answer me. Good night.

*D*ear Callie,

After agonizing over this latest turn of events, I'm pleased to announce that God has intervened and sent me a message, via Mrs. Goldstein during confirmation class at Temple Beth Shalom.

I was daydreaming through the story of Moses and caught doodling again in the borders of *Hip and Hebrew: A Monthly Magazine for Jewish Youth*, when God spoke to me. He said (in my head of course, don't worry I haven't completely lost my mind yet), "Amy, bubele, why don't you leave?"

And I said (in my head back), "Why, God, whatever do you mean? You know I can't just leave. Mrs. Goldstein would have a fit."

So He said, "No, Amy, that's not what I meant. I didn't mean leave the class. I meant leave the city. Just for a few weeks. Hanukkah and Christmas are coming, and you get two weeks off from school."

"But God," I said. "Where would I go? Grandma Nussbaum sold her condo in Florida, and besides I get splotchy in the sun."

God sighed in exasperation. "Amy, think about it.

Who is the most important person to you in the world? Who do you most need to see?"

"Uh . . . You?" I fished.

"Not me, you idiot." God rolled his eyes. "I'll give you a hint," He continued. "Your best friend . . . faraway . . . in Arkansas . . ."

"Kansas," I corrected.

"Whatever. Come on, concentrate, Amy. School vacation . . . someone who needs your guidance . . . someone whose soul you have to save from soul sucking aliens . . ."

"Oh my God," I exclaimed in my head. "I could visit Callie!"

"There you go," God said, satisfied.

"But wait. I have to get permission from my parents. Do you think they'll let me go?"

"They probably won't even know you're gone, no offense," He said.

"None taken, God, and I'm sure you're right. But here's a problem. Where will I get the money?"

"Not my area," He said.

I paused, and then God said, "Listen, I'm on the clock. There are people with bigger problems than you."

"Oh, okay. Sorry to keep you. But, since I've got your attention, do you think you could get John Leibler to like me?"

"Sorry," God said. "That's too big of a miracle even for me."

So what do you think, Cal? Wouldn't that be sweet?!
Check with the your aunt and uncle and let me know.

Amy

PS: New fortune cookie thought for the day:
7/5TH OF ALL PEOPLE DO NOT UNDERSTAND FRACTIONS.
Ha-ha.

10/24, 7:21 p.m.
So your aunt and uncle said they would be happy to have
me visit?! And they're looking forward to meeting me?
And they said that any friend of yours is welcome? Wow,
they really do talk like the embroidered stuff on samplers.
Anyway, that is so awesome!! I'll talk to my parents and get
back to you right away.

*D*ear Callie,

Just kill me now. Use a sharp object and make it bloody so it stains the carpet and splatters the walls. I want my parents to be pissed off for the rest of their lives.

Why do you hate your family more than usual, you might be asking? Well, I'll tell you. Actually, I'll dramatize it for you in a play that I wrote, entitled:

WHAT DO YOU CARE, MARV AND LILLIAN, IF AMY GOES TO KANSAS TO VISIT HER BEST FRIEND?

(A play in one scene by Amy Finawitz)

AMY, a lovely, charming young girl with big hopeful eyes and little bluebirds twittering around her head, enters the cave of her parents. Therein lives the mean WITCH LILLIAN, dressed in black and OGRE MARV, shoeless, dressed in dirty tatters, hunched, with long arms that scrape the floor when he walks. He's practically toothless and has hair sprouting from his ears.

AMY

Hello, Mother. Hello, Father. Don't you both look lovely this evening.

BLUEBIRDS

Twitter, twitter.

MARV AND LILLIAN

Grunt.

OGRE MARV and WITCH LILLIAN pull chicken bones out of the garbage and begin to crunch them.

MARV

Mm . . . bones crunch good . . .

LILLIAN

Yum . . . Good . . . no carbs.

MARV guffaws and LILLIAN cackles.

AMY

Can I go visit Callie in Kansas over the Christmas break?

BLUEBIRDS

Twitter, twitter, tweet.

MARV AND LILLIAN

(they both howl)
NO! Grunt, grunt, grumble.

LILLIAN

Look! Catch twittering birds. Let's eat! More good low fat.

OGRE MARV and WITCH LILLIAN lunge for the birds who squeal in panic and flutter away.

AMY

But why, dearest, sweet ogre/witch parents? It would bring me such joy.

132

MARV and LILLIAN
Don't want you to . . . grunt, grunt . . .

MARV guffaws and LILLIAN cackles more.
AMY falls to the floor in despair. She looks up pleadingly.

AMY
But why do you care if I go, dear parents? You've never cared before?

LILLIAN
Now different! Kevin irresponsible troll. Your father's fault. Too indulgent, that ogre.

MARV
You too self-absorbed, ugly witch. Too much care what others think. Too much care about no carbs, low fat. That's why boy child irresponsible and girl child . . .

AMY
Amy.

MARV
Whatever . . . want to escape. Grunt, grunt . . .

LILLIAN
I self-absorbed?! That good laugh. You work too much ogre and read too much newspaper when should pay attention to son!

Sweet Amy continues to beg.

AMY
Please, mean ogre/witch parents, please . . .

133

(big tears spill from girl child's . . . I mean, Amy's eyes.)
It's only a few weeks. There's nothing for me here.

MARV surveys AMY closely, picks something from her hair, and pops it in his mouth.

                                    MARV
Okay, girl child. Make deal with you.

                                    AMY
                              (perking up)
What is it, ogre father? I'll do anything!

                                    MARV
You can go to friend . . .

                                    AMY
Thank you . . .

She rushes to his arms, but the smell holds her back.

                                    LILLIAN
Marv!

MARV scrapes his knuckles across the floor and holds up his green, ogre hand to LILLIAN.

                                    MARV
Wait. There is condition. You pay way. Then you learn responsibility.

                                    AMY
Huh? How I pay? I mean, how can I pay? I don't have any money. You owe me, like, forty-two months' worth of allowance, and you won't let me touch my bat mitzvah money.

LILLIAN
That for college, ungrateful girl child!

AMY
It's Amy.

LILLIAN AND MARV
Whatever . . . grunt, grunt.

AMY
But that's so unfair! What about Kevin? You never make him pay for anything!

MARV
No worry about "actor" Kevin. He dead meat.

LILLIAN
Dead, "lean" meat.

LILLIAN and OGRE MARV guffaw and cackle themselves silly with that one, as they shoo AMY from the kitchen. MARV makes a lunge for the cat with a carving knife.

AMY locks herself in the bathroom, otherwise known as Lillian and Marv's evil lair, with the traumatized cat, and is never heard from again.

THE END

And so, Callie, there you have it. I'm a prisoner, unless I can think of a way to make money.

Amy

PS: Do you think Mr. Lee wants some help in the restaurant? Maybe I can stuff fortunes into cookies?

PPS: Forget about Bucky for a while and write me back IMMEDIATELY.

10/24, 11:15 p.m.

This is SERIOUS!

Dear Callie,

Yes and yes again. I've begged. Right now, my parents are so aggravated (their words, not mine) about Kevin being an irresponsible dropout, they will not change their minds.

And, yes, I've tried to bargain with Kevin, boy screw-up, to lend me some money, but it's a no go. He is too selfish to help me and merely says, "What the hell are you complaining about? I'm the misunderstood artist." (His words, not mine.) "You don't even have any aspirations. You're just a drain on society."

I actually approached Mr. Lee about a waitress job, but he said that since his business is mostly takeout, waitressing wasn't an option. He did have the decency to look sorry for me though, and gave me a free bag of Chinese noodles and a bunch of fortune cookies.

I guess I could go on a hunger strike and starve to protest my parents' refusal to fund me. On second thought, I don't think I could actually pull off the starving thing.

Well, dear friend, it seems as though I will probably

never get to actually meet Bucky, the hunkaliscious pet/
boy or any of your other half-human, half-animal friends.
I am in despair and am going to sign off now. If you don't
hear from me in a few days, call 911 (don't forget to give
them the 212 area code).

Amy

*D*ear Callie,

I have a bit of comical news to lighten our spirits!

Kevin's play about Eleanor Roosevelt actually premiered last night. It seems that the squatters graciously, and for a small fee of fifty bucks, decided to continue donating use of their theater/bathroom and even offered to clean and disinfect the whole place (for another fifty bucks).

If that isn't bad enough, he sweet talked my parents into going to see the show, telling them he wants their support since he's so passionate about this career, blah, blah, blah. So they got all soft-hearted and decided we should all go and give him a chance.

"And who knows," my mom said, hopefully. "Maybe he really does have talent."

As if.

Unfortunately, what Kevin doesn't tell them is that his leading actor got sick. So guess who had to go on in his place in full drag (a gown, wig, heels, makeup, the whole bit) as good old Eleanor? Yes! None other than drag queen sensation, Kevin Finawitz! Or should I say soon to be the "late" Kevin Finawitz.

Well, you can imagine the scene that ensued.

My parents, not known for their even temperedness in public, particularly in weird places where they won't be recognized, start a fight with Kevin right in the lobby during intermission. This was much more interesting than the show. Most of the audience (other distraught family members and general weirdos) then think their argument is some improvisational performance art piece, so when the fight finally ends, people clap and cheer heartily. A few even shout "Bravo," when my mother calls Kevin "a bum."

The argument about Kevin "wasting his life" continued at home with words like "Plebian!" and "Bum!" being thrown around. It was so loud in fact that Lou called from downstairs, advising them to keep it down before someone called the police.

So they're all shouting (a little quieter), and I'm safely sequestered in my room when I hear my mom saying, get this:

"Why can't you be more like Amy? She's a good student and has her head on straight!"

And I, who know a good opportunity when I hear one, come moseying out of my bedroom and plant myself, angelically, in the doorway.

"Did you call me?" I say with as much innocence as I can muster.

Kevin, hip to my tricks, shoots me this really dirty look, and my mom is like, "Amy never gives us any aggravation!"

"Yeah, she's perfect!" Kevin says sarcastically. "Perfectly

boring. She doesn't even have any interests. All she does is hang around and e-mail her friend."

"I do so have interests," I say earnestly. "I'm interested in school; I'm interested in learning about Judaism at Temple Beth Shalom."

Then Kevin looks at me all slanty eyed and suspicious.

"Yeah, right."

"Amy, stay out of this!" my dad scolds.

"Oh, that's perfect!" I say with hurt in my voice. "How come I'm the good kid and I don't get anything."

"This isn't about you, Amy!" he says.

"It's never about me!" I shout, my voice all squeaky and shaky. "I never get any attention! You're so busy with Kevin!"

"Amy, that's not true," my Mom says, looking all guilty.

"It is true. It's like I'm invisible because I'm good."

And then Dad's like,

"Amy, for God's sake, I've got a cross-dressing son here. Can't it wait?"

"I'm not a cross-dresser. I'm an actor," Kevin corrects.

"See what I mean?" I continue. "I always do the right thing and I'm overlooked! All I want is one thing. One thing in this whole wide world. I want to visit Callie. Is that so wrong?"

"All right already," Mom sighs. "You can visit Callie. We'll talk about it later."

"Really? Well, fine then," I sniff a few times for effect and wipe my nose with my sleeve.

And then in a quiet, dramatic moment with just the right amount of flourish (if I do say so myself) I say, "Thanks Mom. Thanks Dad. I appreciate your faith in me. I won't let you down."

"Don't push it, Amy," my dad says. "Mom and I already talked it over and we realized that we were too hard on you. Why should you be punished because Mr. Sensitive Chi, college dropout over here, doesn't know what it means to be responsible? We were gonna let you go anyway."

"But that means not being so excited you let your grades slip this semester," Mom warns. "Slipping grades, no trip."

So then I, who also know when my good opportunity moment is over, quietly slip back into my room.

So, I did it, Cal! Kansas here I come! I'm as good as there!

Amy

10/27, 6:00 p.m.

Yes, I know! I am an evil genius! And I'm super excited too! Can't wait to see you either!! I am so psyched!!!!
PS! Must! Stop! Using! Exclamation points!!!!

*D*ear Callie,

So today, when I walk into social studies, I try and grab the window seat a few seats away from Judy, but then she waves me over and gestures to the empty seat next to her. So, I make this face like, "Wha . . . ? Oh! I totally didn't see that empty seat!"

And I'm forced to sit next to her after all.

Then I'm all cornered into making up some crap about thinking I might have yarn allergies, but Judy deflects with, "My yarn is a hundred percent organic and hypoallergenic."

Yeesh.

In a way, it's a good thing that Judy's unsuspecting, sweet nature keeps her oblivious to people trying to ditch her (people in this case being me, of course).

Fortunately, the "touch me" movement never gathered much steam and has pretty much died down. It's also fortunate that no one seems to remember my connection to Beryl, "the weird, dressed in black religious boy," so I have not, in fact, turned into the next "touch me" diversion.

But here's the really good news: Mrs. Goldstein says

143

that those of us who want extra credit can try and finish our immigrant journal assignment before the Christmas vacation. Each time we turn in an assignment early, she'll leave the next installment in her office box for us to take.

So I'm going for that extra credit. I'll consider it to be my own personal insurance policy, because I totally don't trust that Kevin won't piss my parents off in some enormous way again before Christmas. A stunt from him would surely render a decree of an: "All Finawitz offspring are hereby grounded" trickle-down effect.

Mrs. Goldstein also attached a Post-it to the front of my assignment, which said: "I'm very happy that you have compiled an interesting team to help you. Hope this is encouraging you to get out and about."

Why does everyone in New York think I'm a social freakin' outcast?

Amy

10/29, 9:45 p.m.

*D*ear Callie,

Okay, I've just had another close encounter of the daffy kind with none other than Miss Sophia, who has informed me that there might be a problem with the dream team after all.

Now you might be perplexed as to why I should care. Actually you might be thinking I should be glad that she's not being my BFF, and maybe a few weeks ago, I would have been. But here's the strange thing. I've actually gotten used to having Beryl and Miss Sophia around to help me.

Besides, what would I do traipsing all over Manhattan by myself? Beryl does provide a certain amount of entertaining diversion for me in his old-fashioned weirdness, and Miss Sophia is kind of cute in her little Lord & Taylor ensembles. And who can resist a free Starbucks?

So, this is what happened.

Early this morning, I go to the elevator as usual, but this time instead of pummeling the button for the door to close as soon as possible, I actually hold it for Miss Sophia.

And she's like, "Good morning, Amy. Could it be you've gotten even bigger since the last time I saw you?"

145

So I smile halfheartedly, and give my coat a self-conscious tug across the boob area.

"How is your little friend?" she asks.

"Speaking of my little friend," I say, casually, "I was thinking of visiting her for the Christmas holidays."

"That's nice, dear," says Miss Sophia.

"And I wanted to hand in my completed immigrant journal assignment before the holidays to get extra credit." But then, before I can say anything else, the elevator door opens and in steps Mr. Klein, who gives us both a tight smile and then squeezes himself as far into the corner away from me as possible. Then they have this big, boring chat until we finally hit the lobby and he holds the door open for Miss Sophia and her shopping cart. She clatters out and rolls across the shiny marble lobby floor.

"Wait, wait, Miss Sophia," I call out, rushing after her.

I'll tell you, she can be fast sometimes.

"Morning, Miss Sophia." Lou the doorman holds the door open and tips his little doorman hat.

In a blink, she's up the block, heading toward the corner market.

"Oh, Miss Sophia!" I call out.

"Amy, dear," she turns surprised, as if she couldn't hear me clomping up the street after her. "Shouldn't you be heading off to school?"

"School? Oh yeah, I need to go there," I say. "But I just wanted to ask you . . ."

Then she enters the market with me at her heels, heads

146

for the fruits, and starts pinching them. "Hand me that big orange, would you?" she asks.

"So I was wondering when we could get together again. I'm free after school every day this week, and I'm always free on the weekends, unfortunately," I say piling the fruit into her basket.

"Oh, I'm so excited about our immigrant journal adventure!"

"Good," I say. "So when can we . . . ?"

Then she leans over and takes my hands in hers.

"It means so much that you're including me . . ."

"Great, so . . ."

"You know, dear," she shifts gears, "I'm having a group of my women friends over later this evening for a dinner party. Other retired librarians and teachers. I'm planning a lovely casserole buffet and I have my special items list," she pulls a blue slip of paper from her purse and waves it. "But now that you're here, maybe you could give me a hand with my everyday items list."

She pulls a yellow piece of paper from her purse and waves it.

"Um . . . well . . ." I start.

Then she looks me square in the eye.

"Only if you don't mind, and you won't be late for school."

"It's okay. I don't mind," I hear the voice coming out of my mouth saying, meanwhile the voice in my head is like, what?!

So she hands me the everyday items list and I sprint through the market, grabbing all her old fogy things like oatmeal, applesauce, frozen pureed vegetables, prunes, box of industrial strength denture bond, and a few little frozen entrée dinners for one.

A little sad, really, but the good news is that for one little old lady, she sure has a hearty appetite.

"So what about this afternoon, Miss Sophia?" I run back to her breathlessly. "Can we start this afternoon?"

"This afternoon? I would love that," she says. "We should get right on it."

"Great, Miss Sophia!" I exclaim. "So why don't I meet you and Beryl after school, say about 3:00 back at Starbucks . . . ?"

"You'll need to check with Beryl, dear. He's quite busy all of a sudden," she says, handing me her items to place on the conveyer belt.

Busy?! And what exactly is he quite busy doing? He's not rollerblading, he's not practicing with his band or the lacrosse team, and he's certainly not shopping for clothes.

"As much as I want to help you, I feel very strongly that we should keep Beryl involved. He really does need to get out . . ."

You mean like me, I'm thinking.

"The way you do, dear," she smiles.

"And I'm afraid that if we don't do our best to coax him a little, you know push him gently in the right direction,

148

he'll just avoid the whole thing until it's too late and your assignment will be done."

Then she heads out the door, and we're down the block.

So I'm following her, wondering what I'm gonna tell the attendance lady at school. (I'm sorry I'm late to school. I had an emergency shopping. I was totally out of pureed lima beans and hemorrhoid cream.)

Then Lou looks over his 20/2000 coke bottle glasses and opens the door for Miss Sophia and she enters the lobby.

"Well, can you talk to him?" I ask.

"Oh I already have, but I'm thinking that we'd have more success if you talked to him, Amy."

"Me?"

"Lou, may I have a pen and pad, please?" she asks.

"Here is Beryl's address," she scribbles. "Why don't you get his schedule for the next few weeks and check back with me?"

"You want me to go to his house?" I ask, baffled.

"Well, that's where he lives, dear," she says, patting my arm.

"Why can't I just call him?"

"You can try, but it's Friday and they're probably busy preparing for Shabbat and not answering the phone now."

It was clear that she had her little cashmere heart set on Beryl being part of the investigative team. Since he didn't live too far uptown from me, I decided that I had better go to his house and confront him head-on.

Then before I can say anything else, she pulls her little wagon into the elevator. She gives me the "yoo-hoo" wave and shouts out: "Pay him a visit, dear. Go now before sundown and Shabbat, and let me know and we'll get started and . . ."

And then the elevator door closes.

So right after a very mundane day of school, I catch a cab uptown to Beryl's house.

The cab drops me off, and I climb up the stone steps and ring the bell. Beryl's mother appears at the door. In case you're wondering, she's small and pleasant looking, and I see Beryl around the eyes and nose.

"Hi, Mrs. Plotsky, how are you?" I ask.

"I'm fine. Thank God," she says.

"I'm Amy Finawitz. Miss Sophia's neighbor. She's a friend of my mother and she and Beryl have been helping me with a school project . . ." I ramble.

But she's just eyeballing me in this amused way, and I'm getting the distinct impression that Beryl doesn't get a whole lot of girl visitors.

"Ya know, Beryl's been doing this good deed for us," I continue, "You know . . . a mitzvah."

"Oh, that's right. Beryl told me about you, Amy," she says, wiping her hands on her apron and breaking into a big smile.

"Is Beryl home?"

"Of course. Come in. It's getting brisk outside. We'll go into the parlor, and I'll call him."

I nod politely and we walk through a small entrance-way. Then we turn a corner and enter a room that's completely taken up with this long folding table. I mean like from one end to the other with maybe a few inches on either side. It's flush against a wall that's covered with bookshelves filled with books and religious breakables, like wine glasses and ceramic menorahs.

Beryl's mother squeezes in between the bookshelved wall and the table and starts this little side step toward a room all the way on the other end. Since there's absolutely no other way to get across the room, I squeeze in beside her and start sidestepping too. Suddenly, two little boys that look like miniature Beryls, in starched white shirts and black pants, and one little girl squeeze out from under the table. They start goofing around and shoving each other, jabbering in what sounds like Yiddish.

"Who are you?" one of them demands of me.

"I'm Beryl's fr . . . I'm here for Beryl," I say.

"Is that your name?" he demands. "I'm here for Beryl?"

So then Mrs. Plotsky scolds them gently in Yiddish, and they all pop back under the table. "Come out from under there. All of you," she says in English.

One by one, about five more kids squeeze out behind me, shoving into this weird endless conga line. The china on the bookshelves tinkles precariously behind us.

Then one of the kids says, "So, really what is your name?"

"I'm Amy," I say to him, gazing longingly toward the

other room which is growing farther away, like a door in a horror movie. "What's your name?"

He tells me, but I can't quite grasp it because it just sounds like a lot of guttural "ch's" (like the "ch" in challah bread, not the "ch" in cheese).

And then Beryl's mother points to each kid and says, "Amy, this is Chaim, Menachem, Cham, Chem, Chana, and little Chesed."

Abruptly, one of the little "chch's" screams so loud that I think the china is gonna explode.

"Beryl! Your girlfriend, Amy, is here!"

"Chch" don't shout," Beryl's mother scolds and then smiles at me apologetically.

Then I pass a glance under my cuff at my imaginary watch.

"Um . . . it's getting kind of late. Will we be arriving at the next room anytime soon?" I ask with all the politeness I can muster.

And then Beryl's voice rings out from somewhere upstairs.

"Amy?" he shouts.

"Hi, Beryl, I'm down here," I shout back.

I try to wave, but I lose my balance and tip into the bookshelf, and my heart stops as I hear the tinkling of unstable glass shimmying behind me.

Beryl's mother grabs on to my hand. "Your hand is a little cold," she comments, giving it a motherly squeeze. And I'm imagining that as she's squeezing, she sizing up my ring finger to see if I can wear her grandmother's wedding ring or something.

Then Beryl appears at the other end of the room. He looks like he's a hundred miles away. He blushes and waves and then squeezes between the table and the bookshelves and starts the sidestepping journey toward us.

By this point, I'm too curious to worry about being rude and I say, "So are you having a long dinner party?"

"We usually invite people over for Shabbat on Friday nights," Beryl shouts.

"We would love to have you and your family, if you're free," Beryl's mother adds, eyeballing me in that mother-in-law way again.

Now, can you imagine that? My mother getting all pumped up about her Jewish-osity. And Beryl's mother eyeballing me for Beryl? Way too close for comfort.

"Oh, well," I stammer. "I think my parents have plans. But thanks anyway."

Then another one of Beryl's indistinguishable brothers jabs me with some kind of toy.

"Please don't do that, Chaim," I say.

"I'm Menachem," he sneers. "Get it straight."

"So what brings you here, Amy?" Beryl shouts.

"Miss . . . I mean your aunt Sophia asked me to come by to talk about scheduling time so that we can keep exploring the stuff in Anna's journal. I hope it was okay that I just dropped by," I shout back.

"You're welcome anytime, Amy," Beryl's mother beams.

Oh God.

Finally, one by one the little "chch" children yank themselves out from behind the table and tumble through an entranceway, like they're being expelled from a reverse suction machine. And then I tumble into the other room too.

The children race out the door.

"I'll just be in the kitchen," Beryl's mother says.

Once Beryl tumbles into the sitting area too, we sit across from one another.

"So what's up, Beryl?" I ask.

"I'm fine, thank God," he says.

"Uh-huh," I respond.

"There are some snacks," Beryl's mother shouts out, referring to a plate of pretzels and some apple juice squeeze boxes on a nearby table.

"So, Beryl," I say, pulling a pad and pencil from my coat pocket. "I wanted to set up some dates and times to meet so that we can get moving on exploring Anna's journal."

"I could meet you next Thursday," he says.

"But it's Friday, Beryl," I push. "What about Sunday afternoon?"

"I have to study," he says.

I don't think I need to say that I was losing my patience.

"Well, um . . . I have homework too, but can't you do it later? I mean, I was thinking, if we took a few hours every day, except Friday night and Saturday, of course, we could get moving."

He glances nervously back into the kitchen.

"That seems like a lot of time. My teacher just asked me to do a special tutorial at the Yeshiva. What about Thursday?"

What is it about mild, meek people that makes you want to smack them?

"I'd like to finish my journal response assignment before the holidays," I say.

"Why is that?" he asks.

"Well, I get extra credit if I hand it in early."

"Is that the only reason you want to meet so much?" Beryl asks quietly, averting his eyes and twisting the string thingies on his scarf thingy.

Hello. Awkward moment.

"I just told you, Beryl," I sigh, exasperated.

"Oh," he says, a deep crimson climbing into his cheeks.

"I mean, I'm having fun and everything too . . . ya know . . ." I say.

"You are?" he lightens.

"Yes, but the thing is," I say, leaning toward him, glancing into the kitchen where his mom is and lowering my voice conspiratorially. "My parents have agreed to let me visit my friend Callie for the Christmas holidays. You remember, on Shabbat at my house, my mom talking about her being away for the year in Kansas?"

"Yes, I remember," Beryl says.

"Well, I want to move fast on this assignment and get a good grade so they don't even think about making me cancel my trip."

"Why would they do that?" he asks, leaning forward, lowering his voice too.

I grab a pretzel twist and lean back.

"To punish me because my brother dropped out of college to sing and dance with cross-dressers."

"Cross-dressers?" he says, leaning way back.

"Men who dress like women."

Then Beryl leans forward toward me as if he's examining exotic fish in an aquarium.

"Why would men want to dress like women?" he whispers, glancing nervously toward the kitchen.

"I don't know, Beryl. Maybe they want to annoy their parents, or maybe they just like fashion."

"Hmm," he says. Then he leans back and looks as if he's thinking hard, and then he leans forward again.

"So, if your brother is a cross-dresser, why would your parents want to punish you?" he asks.

"He's not a cross-dresser. He just likes to sing and dance with cross-dressers, and my parents want to punish me because they're twisted weirdos."

"Your parents?!" Beryl looks appalled.

"No, 'your' parents. What are we talking about here, Beryl? Keep up, please."

"Your parents seem very nice," he says, somewhat perplexed.

156

"Yeah, well, that's cause you don't know them that well."

I was edgy. I was tired, and I still had to catch a cab home. I was hungry, and the pretzel twists just weren't cutting it.

Then Beryl looks thoughtfully out the window behind me.

"But . . ." he leans toward me with renewed earnestness. "But what if they're not trying to punish you? What if your parents are trying to teach you something?"

"Beryl," I sigh. "You're reading into this parenting thing way too much. They're not interested in any of this touchy-feely life lessons business. They've given Kevin and me a decent life, and they just want a decent return on their investment. They want us to finish school, find good jobs, get married," I say ticking off the list on my fingers. "And they expect us not to be addicts, or criminals, freeloaders, or . . ."

"Cross-dressers?" he grins.

"Right."

Just then the front door opens, and the house explodes with activity.

"Shalom family," Beryl's father bellows happily.

I hear excited children rush toward him, jabbering a happy stream of conversational Yiddish. Then three of the "chch's" run out from the kitchen into the parlor. "Beryl, come play with us," they call, tugging on his arms.

We both jump up and peer through the doorway over

157

the endless table to the two faraway little figures of the rabbi and his wife.

"Good evening. And who have we here?" the rabbi shouts.

"That's Amy Finawitz, Moshe. Your sister Sophia's little friend. Remember the girl we were telling you about."

"Hi, Rabbi Plotsky," I shout back. "How are you?"

"Fine, thank God."

"Amy, would you like to join us for dinner?" Beryl's mother asks.

"No thanks, Mrs. Plotsky," I say automatically, even though for the life of me I can't figure out why. It was just that third wheel feeling you sometimes get when everyone belongs in a certain place except you. "I have to get home."

Then I squeeze between the table and the bookshelves and start my little side-step shuffle toward the front door.

"Of course," Beryl's mother says. "I'm sure your parents are expecting you."

Yeah . . . something like that, I think.

"Listen, Beryl," I say, somehow managing to pry the little pad and pencil from my pocket and scribble out my e-mail address.

"You're connected, right?" I ask him.

"Connected? To what?" he answers.

"You know, e-mail or I.M. or some Internet, right?"

I glance over my shoulder at him, and it occurs to me that his life suits him perfectly, surrounded by little "chch's"

158

and the deep mahogany colors of a hundred-year-old house.

"Of course we're connected, Amy," he answers. "We're not the lost tribe, you know."

I couldn't help but grin. Good old Beryl has a sense of humor, after all. Then I ball up my little scribbled paper and shoot it down the long table to him. "So e-mail me a schedule of when you're free," I say.

He takes the paper and shoves it into the pocket of his pants.

"Please, okay, Beryl? We need to hurry," I say. "Miss Sophia won't do anything without you."

He glances at me and grins.

Then, having reached the end of the table, I yank myself free and tumble into the entrance hall.

"Goodbye, Amy," I hear Beryl's voice in the distance.

I open the front door and let myself out. The night seems particularly dark and cold. Strangers scurry past me down the street, pulling their coats in tight. The smell of exhaust fills my nose, and the blaring of horns fills my ears. I glance back at Beryl's house with his big, warm, loving from-another-century family. What would it be like to live there, I wonder for just a fraction of a second. Would it really be so bad?

I turn away, quickly hail a cab, and take off for home.

Now Callie, it's late and I'm signing off.

Amy

10/30, 1:34 p.m.

*D*ear Callie,

It's almost Halloween. Wish you were here to do something cool with. Judy invited me over to hang out with her and Claire, rent scary movies, bake orange and black Halloween cupcakes, and take her little cousin trick-or-treating. Little cousin my ass. I'm sure that Judy and Claire are just dying to dress up as princesses and collect free candy.

10/30, 1:42 p.m.

I'm so bored, I'm actually thinking of going. How pathetic am I?

10/30, 1:58 p.m.

Now, here's something that might take your mind off vegetables and half-human lover boys. Oops, I forgot. No more snide remarks.

So I was reading the latest installment in Anna's journal and it was kind of interesting. Anna's mother was fascinated by spiritualism, which apparently was pretty popular back then; you know, mediums, people who talk to ghosts, etc.

Anna also liked spiritualism and was excited about her first Halloween in America. It seems that her family took her downtown to see the great magician Harry Houdini in some Halloween extravaganza. I can only imagine the thrill that Anna felt experiencing Halloween for the first time, all her little shtetl, immigrant senses on undead overload.

Reading her journal brought back so many delightful memories for me! Last year's school Halloween party: you, looking all grotesque as a disgusting flesh-eating zombie child; me, looking snazzy as a decomposing babysitter who gets eaten by zombies and becomes a tangle of muscles and chewed-up flesh. And remember how my costume kept malfunctioning? Fake limbs getting kicked around the dance floor. Dangling eyeball sloshing into the punch?

Sigh. Good times.

10/30, 6:08 p.m.

What do you mean, "if Anna likes Houdini so much, go see Houdini?" Are those organic vegetables destroying your brain cells? Hello . . . Houdini has been dead for years.

10/30, 6:18 p.m.

OMG, you're brilliant. Organic vegetables really are brain food after all! Why didn't I think of that. Of course! Houdini, Houdini fanatics, Halloween! Visit Houdini in-deed!

10/31 (Halloween!), midnight

*D*ear Callie,

So thanks to your brilliant advice, Beryl came through after all and I didn't have to spend the evening with Judy and Claire after all.

Everything started out pretty normal, for Halloween, that is.

It was a fairly mild and dry Halloween evening. The sky had cleared and the moon hung low, throwing a spooky glow over the city. At Starbucks, I took the liberty of ordering three cocoas from the counter people, who were dressed in a variety of costumes. This one guy was dressed as a pirate and thinking he's a riot.

"Hi, three tall hot cocoas, please," I say.

And then he's like, "Arrrgghh, shiver me timbers, mate. Here's your change, you scurvy swabby."

"Whatever," I say.

After a few minutes, Beryl enters, weaves his way through the maze of tables and people. He eyeballs the formation of the chairs, is about to sit next to me, thinks better of it, and sits about two chairs around the other side.

"Hi, Beryl, what's up?" I say.

"I'm fine, thank God. How are you?"

"Fine . . . thank . . . um . . . God," I respond awkwardly.

"So what's up, Beryl?" I ask conversationally.

"I'm fine, thank God," he repeats.

"I get that. I mean what have you been up to? What have you been doing?"

"I've been going to Yeshiva where I study Talmud and Torah. Then I've been coming home where I study Talmud and Torah," he says.

"Wow. You're a wild man."

"I'm a wild man? How so?" he squints his eyes, earnestly.

"Just out of curiosity, Beryl, what exactly do you learn from all that Torah reading?"

"All the lessons you need to live your life as a righteous person who does mitzvot."

"Is that all?" I say.

"What do you mean?" he asks.

"I'm being sarcastic. What I mean is, how can one book tell you all that?"

Then he hesitates for a moment as if he's pondering this question.

"It's a very good book," he finally says.

Fortunately, at that moment, Miss Sophia arrives, this time looking swanky in a red nubby knee-length coat, trousers, and a matching red, nubby hat encircled in fur.

"Happy Halloween, children," she exclaims.

Under her coat, she's wearing a Halloween sweater adorned with flying witches, black cats, and pumpkins.

Her small Lord & Taylor shopping bag is hooked over the crook of her arm.

"Well," she says, "what a wonderful day for an adventure! At my library, we had such a good time preparing for Halloween. And besides, who doesn't love Halloween?"

"I don't love Halloween," Beryl says wryly, sipping his cocoa.

"So," Miss Sophia ignores him and then says excitedly. "I read your e-mail, Amy. I think it's a wonderful idea to visit Houdini's grave!"

"Who's Houdini?" Beryl asks.

"Er, I'll get to that, Beryl," I stall.

Frankly, I didn't know how this graveyard business was going to affect him.

"Excuse me, who is Houdini?" Beryl asks again.

"I just realized that I'm not exactly sure where he is," I say.

"Hmm," says Miss Sophia. "I believe he might be somewhere in Queens."

"But who . . ." Beryl starts.

"Wait a second," I cut him off. "I'll tell you in a minute."

Over at the next table were some goth kids. To the naked eye, they looked as if they were in costume, but I knew they dressed like bizarro ghouls every day. If these kids don't know where Houdini's grave is, then my name isn't Amy Finawitz.

So I head over to their table.

"Hi," I say. "Can I ask you a question?"

"No," snipes the girl with the big kohl-lined eyes and a bone in her hair.

"Get lost, loser," says a boy with multiple nose rings.

"Charmed to meet you too," I say. "Don't worry, I'm not gonna stay. I just have one question. Do you know where Harry Houdini is buried?"

A long few seconds pass as they appear to be processing the question and deciding whether they want to answer it.

"Machpelah Cemetery in Queens," Nose Rings says, taking a bite of some kind of pound cake and then spraying it in all directions. "Every year on Halloween there's a big party there, séances, the works."

"Hey, thanks," I say.

"Good luck, loser," Kohl Girl says.

Then they collapse into convulsions of chuckling and snorting.

I weave back to Miss Sophia and Beryl. He's still looking perplexed and somewhat insulted.

"Got it," I say. "Machpelah Cemetery in Queens."

"Well, we better get going then! I brought sandwiches and extra thermoses of cocoa," she adds, holding up her little Lord & Taylor bag.

"By the way, Beryl," I say. "Houdini was probably the most famous magician in the world."

"Oh, well you might have said that," he mumbles.

Out on the street, some colorfully costumed passersby hoot and holler, "Happy Halloween!"

"Do you really think this is safe?" Beryl asks nervously, as we pile into a cab.

"Machpelah Cemetery in Queens," Miss Sophia instructs the cabbie, who looks at us quizzically, presumably trying to determine if we really are a geeky kid, a religious kid, and an old lady, or merely dressed up for Halloween.

"I mean, going to visit a dead magician at his grave? On Halloween night?! By ourselves?!" Beryl whispers.

"Well, Beryl. With all the Halloween lovers in New York looking for something different to do, I don't think we'll be alone," I say.

"We're not going to desecrate the grave in any way, are we? Because that would be blasphemous."

"Don't worry about it, Beryl." I sigh.

He's such an innocent soul.

After about a half an hour, we drive up to the iron, arched gates of the cemetery and I see a crowd gathered in the distance. And what a strange scene it is. At least two dozen Halloweeners are roaming around, holding lanterns, looking eerie, illuminating the tombstones.

We all pile out of the cab, and Miss Sophia's like, "Excuse me, children, I'm going to see what's going on. You children find us a bench. It's easier for one little person to slip through the crowd. I'll be right back."

Then she walks toward the crowd and is swallowed up in darkness. We hear her calling, "Yoo-hoo" and "Excuse me!" in her small, but determined voice, until that too fades away.

Reflexively, I place my hand in the pocket of my coat where I keep my cell phone. You know, in case Miss Sophia is offered up as some old lady sacrifice, I'll be able to call a cab. I couldn't help imagining her being lifted up in her little red, nubby coat, flipped onto her back, arms outstretched, being carried along to the Halloween god tombstone by the crowd like a kid who jumps into the pit at a rock concert.

Beryl and I make our way to a small bench a few tombstones down and sit.

"Maurice Schwartz, beloved father, husband, brother. Friend to animals. (1901–1980)," I read off the nearest tombstone. "Made it almost to eighty years old," I say, trying to break the mood with conversation.

But it is the wrong topic as poor, terrified Beryl can only stare straight ahead and manage a throat-constricted squeak in response. Then he hunkers down and shoves his hands deep into his coat pockets. The minutes tick by and finally I'm like, "So . . . you spend a lot of time reading Torah. What else do you learn about at Yeshiva?"

"What do you learn about at Hebrew school?" he counters.

"Well, we learn some Hebrew and the right way to act, I suppose, and that everyone should work hard to achieve what they want."

"What do you want?" he asks.

He had me there. The only thing I could think of was a new cell phone. I didn't say that though, knowing that it didn't sound quite right.

"Well, what do you want?" I challenge.

"To be a good person, to do mitzvot, good works, and help others."

And thank you Beryl, for making me feel stupid and selfish.

"That's mostly the heart of what we learn about at Yeshiva, that and learning Hebrew, reading sacred books, learning about the history of Judaism."

"But what about the world and all the people in it? There's a whole, vibrant world out there," I say, extending my arms out wide.

Beryl's eyes scan the graveyard.

"Well maybe not out here. But you get my point."

"No, actually I don't," he says.

God, was this kid maddening, or what?

"I guess what I'm saying is that even Anna Slonovich, who was a lowly female immigrant in a strange country who spoke bad English at the turn of the century, had ambition. And maybe she wanted to live in a house with more rooms than people. Maybe she just wanted to make her own choice about things, ya know, like not have to do something just because it was expected of her. She wanted the American Dream."

"Yes," he nods. "That's true."

"Did I mention that she wanted to write a mystery novel?"

"A mystery novel? Hmm . . . that's interesting. I wonder why," he ponders.

"Well, why not?" I exclaim. "But here you're living in a modern world in one of the most exciting cities in the world and you don't seem to see it or want to make a mark on it."

"You make a mark on the world by doing mitzvot, good deeds," he says.

"Yeah, well . . . okay . . . whatever. But what do you really want to do with your life, like every day?"

"Read Torah and do mitzvot."

"No, really. Deep down. Your secret ambition."

He looks down shyly.

"I won't tell anyone, I promise," I say. "And no one here is listening."

"What do you mean? It's a graveyard. Who would be listening?"

"That was a joke, Beryl, and apparently not a very successful one. I mean it will be our secret. Like, what are you good at?"

He stops and thinks.

"Well . . ."

"Yeah?" I lean closer.

"I'd like to . . . one day . . ."

"Yeah?"

169

"Become . . . a very well respected scholar and teacher," he smiles and then averts his eyes.

"Oh . . . well, there you go then. That's a start. What would you teach?"

"Reading Torah and doing mitzvot."

Doh! Homer Simpson head slap!

"What would you like to do with your life, Amy?" he asks.

"Well, I think, maybe . . . I'd like to be a playwright. I have this teacher, Mrs. Goldstein, and she once told me that I have an unusual perspective on the world."

"Yes, I can see her thinking that," Beryl says.

"Although I don't know what's so unusual about it," I say. "But I would like to finish college and maybe I'd teach to, ya know, make a living. I wouldn't be a bum like my brother Kevin. I'll tell you that."

"The cross-dresser?" he says with a grin.

"Yeah, that's him," I grin back.

And then we're just sitting there, and it's starting to get kind of all uncomfortable as a few more seconds of deadly silence ticks by. Then much to my relief, I see a small person, dressed in red, carrying a flashlight and a Lord & Taylor bag, moving toward us through the darkness. I wave her over to our comfy bench by the late Maurice Schwartz, animal lover.

"So, Beryl, how come your aunt Sophia is such an adventurous kind of gal? Doesn't that seem funny to you?"

170

"Not really," he shrugs. "It's her neshama."

"Her what?"

"Her neshama, her soul. It's who God wanted her to be," he says.

"Well, you're related. What about your neshama?"

"I like to read Torah and do . . ."

"Yeah, yeah . . . I know, but . . ." I lean toward him and grin, "we've been doing some pretty way-out stuff, going on harbor cruises, seeing plays, and now you are hanging around in a graveyard on Halloween night with a bunch of weirdos. Maybe there's some little spirit of adventure in your neshama after all, hmm?"

Then Beryl blushes and he's like, "We are who we are."

"What does that mean?" I laugh. "And that doesn't answer the question of why you're here."

He just stares out the other way, chews his lip, and nervously plays with those little fringe thingies. Then he turns and looks me level in the eyes.

"You know everything," he teases. "You figure it out."

"Yoo-hoo," Miss Sophia cries out just then, and swings the flashlight into our eyes, blinding us both and causing me to see colored spots for the next three hours.

"Well," she plops down, winded. "What a lovely group of people. Ralph will be back shortly to tell us about the schedule for the evening."

"Who's Ralph?" I ask.

But she merely says, "Shall we have our sandwiches,

children?" humming as she extracts the sandwiches and thermoses from her bag and hands them to us along with about forty napkins. We open our sandwiches and begin to munch.

A few minutes later, some big tall guy, dressed up like a female magician's assistant, teeters toward us and waves. And he had the whole bit down: black fishnet stockings, a short black satin dress, a big blond wig, dangerously high heels, and full makeup.

"We're starting in about ten minutes, Miss Sophia," he says in a deep baritone and then turns around and teeters back to his friends.

"All righty, Ralph. Thank you, dear," she waves back.

"FYI, Beryl, speaking of cross-dressers," I say, noticing poor Beryl's slack-jawed shock. "That's a cross-dresser extraordinaire."

"What's about to start?" Beryl gulps.

I take a bite out of the super good sandwich. "Hey, is this havarti cheese, Miss Sophia?"

Miss Sophia nods and dabs her mouth politely.

"With Russian dressing and coleslaw?"

Who knew Miss Sophia could assemble such an awesome sandwich?

"It seems they're not having the séance this year. They're having a wand breaking ceremony," Miss Sophia says. Then she wraps up the other half of her sandwich, takes a sip from her thermos, and places it all back in her bag.

"Er . . . what's that?" Beryl asks.

But before she can answer, Ralph motions us over to the memorial site.

"We're about to begin, Miss Sophia," he says.

We start toward the group, Beryl and I both a little anxious now, my mind flashing back to that sacrificing Miss Sophia image.

"Ralph, may I introduce my little friend, Amy Finawitz," Miss Sophia says.

"Hi," says Ralph, extending a large hairy hand manicured with long red nails. "Nice to meet you, Amy."

"Hi," I say and shake his hand.

"And this is my nephew, Beryl."

"Nice to meet ya."

Ralph extends his hand toward a clearly perplexed Beryl.

Beryl is paralyzed, and time seems to stand still. At first, I think it's because the guy looks so freaky, but then I realize that Beryl isn't sure if he's a man or a woman, in which case, he can't shake hands.

Flustered, he places his hand on his heart.

"I greet you with my . . ." Beryl starts.

I groan under my breath.

"It's a man, Beryl," I whisper.

"Are you sure?" Beryl whispers back.

"It's a costume."

I pop Beryl in the elbow, so his hand reflexively shoots forward. Ralph grabs on and shakes.

"Nice costume, by the way," Ralph admires.

And then, before Beryl can tell him he isn't wearing a costume, Ralph turns on his high, black heels and addresses the crowd.

"Shh, everyone. We're getting ready to start."

Then, some old, serious-looking guy in a suit breaks through the crowd and stands before the little Houdini memorial shrine.

"Good evening, everyone," the man says in a monotone voice.

"It's called a wand breaking ceremony," says Ralph. "That man is the president of SAM, the Society of American Magicians. It's very exciting."

Then the SAM man holds the wand high over his head, waits for a hush to fall over the crowd, and snaps the wand in two.

"ROSABELLE, A-T-P-A-L-T-A-A-T," the SAM man says.

Everyone applauds and ooh's and ah's their approval.

"That was the exciting ceremony?" I say to no one in particular.

Suddenly, Ralph starts jumping up and down.

Cal, you haven't lived until you've had a six-foot crossdresser jump up and down in front of you.

"What does that mean?" Beryl asks.

"What does that mean?!" Ralph gasps jubilantly. "What does that mean?!"

Beryl glances at me with a look that says, "A cross-dresser and nuts?"

"Mary, come on over here. Did you hear that?!" Ralph shouts into the crowd.

From out of the crowd comes another person dressed as a magician's assistant, a clone of Ralph, except petite and blonde with the kind of heavy makeup you could only get away with on Halloween: silver glittery eye shadow, false eyelashes, red circles for rouge, and bright red lips. Not to mention a little purple corset outfit, blond wig, lace stockings, and spiked heels. But this one really is a girl . . . I think.

"Yes! I heard!" she says, also super excited.

Ralph smiles smugly.

"Could somebody please tell us what this means?" I ask.

"It's Houdini's code word," Ralph says.

"Code?" Beryl asks. "What's the code."

Ralph and Mary burst out laughing.

"How could you love Houdini and not know about the code word?"

"I don't love Houdini," Beryl replies dryly.

"Well, then why are you here?" Mary asks, looking him up and down. "Nice costume, by the way."

"It's not a . . ."

"Ah . . ." I jump in. "What my friend means to say is that we admire Houdini. There's a difference."

"There is?" asks a perplexed Mary.

By now, the crowd is making its way toward the gates of the cemetery, and we're being swept along. Miss Sophia is on her cell phone, calling us a cab.

"Well, Houdini thought all the spiritualists who claimed to contact the dead were frauds, and he didn't want his wife Bess to be taken advantage of after he died. So they had a secret code; in case he could contact her, she would know it was really him," says Ralph.

We ponder this for a moment.

"Are you going to the city, Ralph?" Miss Sophia asks.

"Yeah, there are some Halloween parties we thought we'd crash," he replies.

"Well, why don't we give you a lift," Miss Sophia suggests, "and we can talk on the way."

And now you have to imagine this scene!

Mary's looking straight at Beryl and says, "If there's not enough room, I can sit on someone's lap."

Then poor Beryl looks horror struck, like he's going to run back into the cemetery, dig a hole, jump in, and pretend he's dead.

"I think Beryl and his aunt should sit in the front. We'll squeeze into the back," I say, deciding to save the day.

We all get in the cab.

"So, could you tell us what the code means?" I ask.

"You see, Rosabelle was Houdini's pet name for Bess, Houdini's wife," Ralph says. "As far as these letters . . . letters were often used by magicians as a secret code that they passed between themselves and their assistants. So each letter or group of letters stands for a word."

"So here, the message was, I know it by heart," Ralph gushes proudly, "Rosabelle, answer-tell-pray-answer-look-tell-answer-answer-tell."

Then Ralph and Mary smile, clearly satisfied with themselves.

"I understand," says Beryl. "But if this is such a secret code, how come you know it?"

"Well, it only became public information after Bess's death. And besides, with the Internet, is there anything anybody doesn't know about anything?

He had a point there.

"Uh . . . still confused though," I say.

"Oh, sorry," says Ralph. "It's a complicated code for the word . . ."

Mary looks to Ralph for the big finish.

"Believe!" they exclaim together.

"Isn't that awesomely romantic?!" asks Mary. "Houdini's message from the grave is 'Bess, believe.'"

Okay, not really making sense, but we all nod along, as Ralph adjusts his corset top and pushes his foam boobs into place. Beryl turns the brightest beet red I've ever seen and quickly turns back around in his seat.

"Ooh, this is our stop," exclaims Ralph suddenly, lurching forward.

"Thank you, Miss Sophia. Bye kids," Ralph and Mary say. "Happy Halloween!"

"Yeah . . . happy . . ." The cab door slams shut. "Ya know . . . whatever," I reply.

Then we all sink back into our seats. We gaze out the windows, immersed in our own thoughts.

I think about how Houdini's message to Bess was kind of romantic. It seems that, in his head, Houdini believed that no one could communicate from beyond the grave, but in his heart he hoped against hope that he could.

"You know, children," Miss Sophia says. "Houdini was Jewish, just like Anna."

I wonder if that was interesting to Anna. Maybe she felt inspired by him. Like, here's another Jewish immigrant who made his dream of narrowly escaping death through terrifying tricks and torture devices come true.

I look over at Beryl, happily staring out the window, humming a little tune to himself and playing with those fringe thingies hanging out from under his shirt. Then I look over at Miss Sophia, who is now snoozing softly, her chin resting on her nubby red coat.

What did they believe in and hope for? I feel pretty sure that Beryl was hoping for the day when he could be a great teaching scholar. And I bet that Miss Sophia believed that we were all three spiritually destined to be on this little journey together, that the ghost of Anna Slonovich was somehow leading us toward something special, something that only the three of us could find. I hate to admit it, but for one fleeting moment, I had to put my "life is random" theory aside, and wonder about that too.

Finally, we pull up beside Beryl's brownstone. I glance at the clock on the dashboard. It's past midnight now. The house is dark, except for the porch light and for one light in what looks to be an upstairs bedroom. A figure peers out the window and then steps away.

Beryl gets out of the cab, and I suddenly realize that he has probably never been out this late in his life. What will his parents say when they find out where he was? Beryl strikes me as the type of kid who would spill everything, all the way down to the last detail of Ralph's red lipstick.

"Wait a minute, driver," I say.

I look over at Miss Sophia, but she is still snoozing.

"Hey, Beryl."

He turns.

"Are you gonna get in trouble? I mean, it's pretty late, and you have school tomorrow."

"My parents trust me," he says.

"Well . . . um . . . maybe your parents would trust you more if you fibbed a little."

"How would they trust me more if I lied?" he asks incredulously.

"Ya know, maybe you shouldn't fill in all the details of the evening."

He stares at me blankly.

I knew it. Clearly, he didn't understand the fine art of telling half truths and beating around the bush.

I motion for him to move closer, and say, "Beryl, clearly

179

you don't understand the art of telling half truths and beating around the bush."

"What do you mean?"

"For example, if your mother asks, 'Were you in a graveyard with cross-dressers all night?' you could say, 'No, I wasn't in a graveyard with cross-dressers all night,' because, technically, you were not out all night. You see what I mean?"

Poor Beryl just shakes his head and laughs. "You're funny, Amy," he says.

"Yeah, I'm a riot, Beryl," I sigh and lean back into my seat.

"It's all right, Amy. Really," he tries to convince me. "They know we're doing something important."

"Okay," I say, unconvinced.

"Tell my aunt Sophia I said good night," he whispers. Then he grins and is like, "See you next time, Amy. I promise, I won't let you down."

And then he sprints up the steps to his house.

He's all flushed and excited and everything. Despite myself, this kid makes me smile.

And so, Cal, now it's after midnight and I'm signing off.

Happy Halloween to ya, and please don't tell me you spent it under a big, yellow moon dressed as a princess with Bucky pet/boy, dressed as a human, smooching on a big stack of hay, somewhere in a cornfield.

Please don't tell me that, because if you do I'll have to barf, and I would prefer not to barf.

Amy

*D*ear Callie,

So I started my journal assignment about Anna. Thought you might be interested in reading what I have to say. The questions Mrs. Goldstein asked were, "Describe your initial impression of the immigrant whose journal you are reading. What do you think him/her was like? What about he/she do you find compelling?"

So here it is:

I find Anna Slonovich to be a very interesting immigrant. She was independent, spunky, adventurous, and ambitious, probably unlike some of her fellow Europeans who were either too rich or too bone lazy to bother leaving the motherland.

I can relate to Anna because I feel that she might have been somewhat of a social outcast. Even though she seemed bubbly on the outside, a trait usually associated with popular kids, it seems that she was different on the inside; what with her wanting more out of life than to marry Shlomo next door and having oodles of babies. It's like she wanted to break free of society's expectations. Like me, she aspired to be a writer and probably enjoyed observing other people.

Anna also loved New York, especially places like the South Street Seaport, where I imagine she spent many afternoons daydreaming by the briny sea. She also loved Harry Houdini, magician, master of illusion/suicide case. He was a Jewish man who was probably an outcast immigrant himself and very successful at following his dream.

And here's something that's compelling too. In this latest installment, Anna writes that she has some kind of mysterious secret. Talk about exciting! I wonder if she'll write more about this in her next entry.

That's all I have for now. Kind of cool about the secret, don't you think? Anyway, anything you think I should add?

11/3, 3:21 p.m.

No. I don't know if Anna was in a committed relationship. What's with you and committed relationships?! Enough already with the committed relationships!

*D*ear Callie,

In honor of some recently exciting news, I've written a little play, entitled:

MIRACLE ON 79TH STREET!

(A play in one scene by Amy Finawitz)

A news crew has just arrived at the 79th Street Middle School. A young attractive REPORTER with sleek hair and a good nose job is holding a microphone and looking into a camera.

NOSE JOB REPORTER
Breaking news. This just in from the middle school on 79th Street: well-known good athlete and popular hottie, John Leibler, has just made a study "date" (finger quotations in the air) with not so well-known, good English student, unpopular, luke-warmy, Amy Finawitz. This conversation did not occur in the boy's bathroom or any other place where people relieve themselves. Understandably, this unlikely and astonishing event has the whole school buzzing. Or, at least it has the geeky girls buzzing. The other kids couldn't care less.

AMY, our star, walks past NOSE JOB REPORTER.

NOSE JOB REPORTER

Excuse me, Ms. Finawitz, could you explain today's events for our disbelieving viewing audience?

AMY

I would be happy to. I was in the cafeteria when John Leibler . . .

NOSE JOB REPORTER
(interrupting into the camera)
Someone who typically would normally never make a date with the likes of this girl. I mean never, ever, never, ever, ever, never. Did I say never? I mean not in a million . . .

AMY

They get it.

NOSE JOB REPORTER

Sorry. Please continue.

AMY

So I'm sitting with my friends Judy and Claire . . .

NOSE JOB REPORTER pretends to put her finger down her throat and makes fake gagging noises.

AMY

Anyway, we were sitting at the table eating potato logs and minding our own business, when suddenly we were blinded by the presence of a supreme white light, a presence full of hope and unearthly beauty, a true heavenly being.

184

                    NOSE JOB REPORTER
God?

                          AMY
No, John Leibler. So then we all gulp down our potato
logs and look up. Now, John has in the past stopped
by the table to mumble "hi" on his way to the cool
kids, or to compliment my, err, Judy's knitting. But this
time was different.

Dramatic pause.

                          AMY
He pulled up a chair, and sat down next to me.

Many gasps and "huzzahs!" can be heard from the geeky
crowd of girls that have gathered behind them.

                    NOSE JOB REPORTER
As you can see, viewers, the geeky girl population at
79th Street Middle School is in the thralls of a religious
frenzy.

REPORTER pulls a girl from the crowd.

                    NOSE JOB REPORTER
You, there, geeky girl. What's your name?

                          JUDY
Judy Sweeny.

                    NOSE JOB REPORTER
Judy Sweeny. And you were a witness to this remarkable behavior?

                          185

JUDY

Yes. Yes, I was.

NOSE JOB REPORTER

You heard it here first, folks. Remarkable. Please continue, Amy. Then what happened?

AMY

Well, first he made small talk . . .

One of the geeky girls in the back faints.

GEEKY GIRL
(popping up from back)
Does this mean we can go out to dances now?

REPORTER shoves the girl back.

NOSE JOB REPORTER

Small talk?! Like what?

AMY pulls out a paper.

AMY

I memorized it, and then wrote it down. May I?

(AMY gestures to the camera)

NOSE JOB REPORTER

Please . . .
(she mouths to camera)
Astonishing!

AMY

(clears her throat)
Well first, he said: "Hey."
   Then I said: "Hi."

Then there was an awkward pause. Claire giggled, and I kicked her hard under the table.

Then he said: "Did you finish the book for the English final?"

Then I said: "Yes. Did you?"

Then he said: "I looked it over."

Then Claire said: "What does that mean?"

Then I shot her a warning look, and she quickly shifted her legs away from me.

Then he said: "Do you think maybe you could help me study for the next test? If I don't pick up my grades, my parents are threatening to pull me off the lacrosse team."

Then I said: "Uh . . . okay."

Then he said: "Maybe I should come to your house?"

Then I said: "Uh . . . okay."

Then he said: "How about this weekend? On Sunday at about 1:00?"

Then I said: "Uh . . . okay."

Then he said: "Great. Thanks. See ya."

Then I said: "Uh . . . okay."

The NOSE JOB REPORTER is fast asleep in a nearby chair. The CAMERA GUY jolts her awake.

NOSE JOB REPORTER

Huh? Oh sorry, is she done? Well you heard it here first, folks. A miracle and it isn't even Christmas. And now for the less astonishing news of the day, a lady in Illinois has inarguable proof that aliens exist . . .

And we FADE OUT.

THE END

So there you have it, Cal. I know you're probably fantasizing that this is the beginning of a relationship, that I'll wear his lacrosse shirt, we'll walk down the hall holding hands, get married, have children, grandchildren, move to assisted living together, etc. But I think we better pull in the reins. He just needs me to study. That's all. Really. He doesn't like me in that way. I'm sure of it . . .

What do you think I should wear?

Amy

11/5, 5:07 p.m.

What's this? You're upset because Bucky pet/boy has been wandering around, sniffing other girls' hands? I thought he really liked you and you guys were talking on the phone and he was walking you to class. Didn't he ask just you to some hee-haw carnival or something?

You're not very experienced in these boy/girl matters. Is it possible you're overreacting?

11/5, 5:19 p.m.

All right! All right! You're not overreacting!! Sheesh! Don't take my head off!

11/5 5:23 p.m.

Ah, so it's the old, ex-girlfriend let him off the leash, sees him romping around you and wants him back scenario. This sounds suspiciously a lot like the plot for *Night of the*

Undead Babysitters movie we saw on the indie cable network last year. Remember how nice girl, Maxine, liked Jim, but then Lilah, secretly an evil undead creature of the night got wind of it and wanted him back?

Well, first of all, assuming that Bucky's ex-girlfriend, unlike Lilah, is not some evil undead creature of the night (she isn't, is she?), just do what Maxine did.

11/5, 5:29 p.m.

No, not chop off the other girl's head and bury it in a hallowed grave! . . . I said let's assume she's not some evil undead! Honestly, you worry me sometimes.

11/5, 5:34 p.m.

Flirt with someone else in front of Bucky, that's what. There must be tons of half-human boys with pet names like Bo and Bruiser and Rover (well, maybe not Rover) out there in the heartland. Just find one and flirt. Then leave Bucky in the pen to think.

11/5, 5:42 p.m.

Hey, I'm just making stuff up here as I go along. What the hell do I know about boys? And what do you mean, ask Kevin. You mean brother from another planet who looks better in a dress than I do? I don't think so.

D*ear Callie,*
Life is crazy.

No, that's not a fortune cookie, but it should be. Or maybe it's just my life that is crazy. I'll tell you what happened and you decide.

It's Sunday morning, and I'm getting ready for John Leibler to come over. And so I'm trying on everything I own, aiming for that casual, not too dressed up, not trying too hard look.

And of course, after about a hundred hours of trying things on, I decide on the safe, but comfortable, jeans and red sweater with the cool, white interweaving.

Then I take out the crochet thingies that I borrowed from Judy and place them casually across the dining room table, like I'm working on some project, since it seems that John likes to make small talk about knitting. We'll call this small talk, plan A.

I also take out Anna Slonovich's journal, since John also seems to like to talk about the immigrant assignment and plop it askew next to the crochet thingies.

While doing this, my mind wanders to Anna's diary and

190

the secret mystery treasure she mentioned. According to the latest journal installment, she, her brother, and her parents originally lived in Kentucky during the Civil War. Sadly, her little brother died during this time, but she doesn't say why or how. Kind of intriguing and, since John Leibler is such a history buff, I thought this might be good ice breaking conversation, or plan B, just in case the knitting topic runs dry.

So, at about 12:00, Kevin gets a phone call, and after he hangs up he's, like, all excited about something; humming and picking up around the living room.

I sense danger on the horizon and I start following him around. And I'm like, "So, Kevin . . . why so chipper?"

And he says, "I'm having an actors slash producers meeting."

"Oh, you found a rehearsal space?" I fish.

"Yeah," he says. "Here."

Gulp.

"Tomorrow?" I say, straining to keep the desperation from my voice.

"Today," he replies, folding some newspapers that were left on the coffee table, and then not knowing what to do with them, putting them on the side table.

"Later?" I squeak. "Like, after, say 3:00?"

"No, in about ten minutes," he says, heading into the kitchen, where he begins pulling glasses from the shelf.

"Wha . . . so fast?" I squeak, glancing desperately at the clock.

"They were at the subway. I was just giving them the address," he says, dropping little chinklings of ice into the iced tea.

"I'm sorry, Kevin," I say in the most authoritative voice I can muster. "This afternoon's not good."

"Yeah, and who made you boss?" he asks, piling a bag of veggie chips on a plate.

"Kevin, someone's coming over to study," I stammer.

Then my father shuffles through the kitchen, unshaven, his hair on end, in his frayed bathrobe and favorite slippers, you know the black backless ones that look like they came from a mental ward and slap his feet when he walks. He's got the entire Sunday paper tucked under his arm.

"Amy's got a date." My father grins at me, peeling a banana and shoving it into his mouth.

"Oh, a date." Kevin grins.

"It's not a date," I seethe. "He's a classmate."

"Well we won't get in the way of your date, or, excuse me 'classmate,'" Kevin says, making quotation marks in the air.

"Kevin, we need to study," I strain, trying a different tactic. "We need quiet."

"Well, I need a place to discuss business and rehearse."

"But can't you do that later?" I ask.

"Everyone's free now," he says casually.

"Everyone's always free!" I shout. "You're all freeloaders!"

Probably not a very good tactic. He glares at me hard. "You are so plebian," he drawls snootily.

192

"I'm not plebian!" I yell.

What's plebian? Remind me to look that up.

"Kevin, we need to study," I say. "Some of us have to do that because some of us are still students."

"I'm a student of the human condition," he replies.

"Oh for God's sake, Kevin, you're a freakin' dropout!" I scream.

This wasn't going well. Not even a little bit.

"Yeah, well, at least I'm doing something with my life. I have a passion for something," he says. "What do you have a passion for?"

He had me there.

"Hey, I may not be doing something important, but at least I know that I have no talent!" I say.

That didn't come out quite right.

Then my father heads into the living room, and Kevin and I both follow him, frowning helplessly while it takes him about nine seconds to spread his newspaper all over the couch, drop his banana peel on the floor, and stretch his mental ward slippered feet across the coffee table.

"Ma!" Kevin and I shout at the same time.

So then my mother comes out of her room, fully dressed and ready to bolt. And she's like, "I have a volunteers Sunday brunch/meeting at the museum. The monkeys of Shekfmeksmfeklgooney Island are endangered."

Then she pecks Kevin on the cheek. "Have a good . . . meeting," she manages to say. Then she turns to me, "Have a good date," she pecks my cheek and grins.

"It's not a date," I sigh.

Then she turns to my father.

"Marv, collect your things, get dressed, and go to the den," she instructs.

He groans and starts picking up his crap, when, at just that moment, the doorbell rings. And before anyone can scream, "Stop the mental ward guy!" he opens the front door. (He sure shuffles fast in those slippers.)

Much to my shame and despair, there standing in the hallway is John Leibler.

"Hello, Mr. Finawitz," John says to my father, the mental patient.

"Amy, your date's here," my father says, and shuffles toward his bedroom.

Only then did I realize that he had a piece of toilet paper stuck to the back of his robe, floating gently behind him like a tail.

Kevin makes like he's coughing, but he's really saying: "Toilet paper." Cough, cough. "On your butt."

And my dad's like, "Huh? Me?"

He turns around like three times trying to catch the end of it, until he finally grabs it and rips it off.

"Thanks, Kevin. Nice meeting you, Joe," he says to John, waving the toilet paper in a goodbye gesture.

And then I'm like, Floor, please, swallow me now. And I don't even have the courage to glance at John, who's probably completely mortified.

"Nice to meet you, John," my mother grins as she slips

past him. Then she grins at me over her shoulder and mouths, He's cute! "There's fresh papaya juice in the fridge, kids," she sings and then disappears out the door.

"Oh yum." Kevin rolls his eyes. "I gotta pour me some of that." And he heads toward the kitchen.

"Hey," John says stepping over the threshold.

"Hi, come on in. Um . . . wanna sit over here?" I say, gesturing to the dining room table.

"Sure," he says, brushing past me and dumping his backpack on the floor.

Man, I never noticed how good he smells, like clean, like good soap. All I ever smell when I see him in the cafeteria is that intermingling of meatloaf, pizza, and apple brown Betty. And of course the hallways and classrooms just smell like feet.

"Your family's nice," he says.

"You're kidding, right?" I snort.

"What?" he says perplexed.

And then I remember that other people have normal families who they probably like, so I say, "I mean, yeah. They're okay."

So then he spies my planted knitting stuff and he's like, "So what are ya knitting now?"

"I'm making a sweater."

Then he holds it up and it's just this weird piece, like twenty feet long.

"Oh," he says. "It's nice. I like the colors. It's kinda long though."

195

Damn that Judy, I thought. I never really looked at it before I dumped it on the table. What the hell did she give me?

So then I mumble something about the latest style, grab it, roll it into a ball, and put it on the plant table behind me.

Okay, knitting talk didn't go well. On to plan B.

"Did I tell you that my immigrant has some kind of secret mystery?"

"Huh," he says, trying to discreetly glance at his watch.

"Yeah, I'm not sure what it is yet, but before she came to New York, she lived in Kentucky during the Civil War." That's kind of cool . . . ya know . . . historical."

"Em . . . Nice . . . ," he says unenthusiastically. "Okay, well, I brought the book."

He proudly produces a completely unread-looking *Catcher in the Rye* from his backpack.

So much for plan A and plan B.

"Good," I say. "Did you like it?"

"Well, I haven't actually read the whole thing yet. Ya know, I kinda . . ."

"Looked it over. I remember."

"Right," he says.

So then he sits down, takes out a pen and pad, clicks the pen, and holds it expectantly, like a dog waiting for a savory treat.

"Well," I begin. "So Holden is like . . ."

"Wait, wait," he says scribbling. "Holden . . . okay."

"Well, Holden is a really funny character."

"Who's Holden?"

"I thought you said you looked this over?"

"I did," he says.

"Oh, well, Holden's the main character, and he's really irreverent . . ."

"Wait . . . wait . . . main character . . ." he says aloud as he scribbles fiercely. "And he's what? Irreverent?"

"Yeah, you know, like offbeat. He's sees things differently from other people in a way that's ironic."

He holds up his hand.

"Is irreverent one 'r' or two?"

Then I have this rush of exasperation. Like, you might be hunkaliscious and smell good, but are you kidding? So then I reach for the pen. "Here I'll write it."

He hands me the pen, but brushes across my hand as he gives it to me. Then he flashes this awesome, 100-watt smile that's so bright I'm practically blinded, and that's it. I'm jelly.

"I know I'm a little dense when it comes to this book." he says smoothly and leans in, so my senses are overwhelmed with the scent of cleanness. "But it's really awesome that you're helping me. If there's anything I can help you with, just let me know."

You can marry me, I think.

"I'm happy to help," I rasp instead.

"Okay, so Holden . . . he's irreverent." John breaks the connection and glances back at his paper.

"So, what's the plot? He'll ask that, right? On the test? They usually do."

"Yes, but the book's less plot, and more about tone," I explain.

"Tone?" he asks quizzically.

"By that I mean . . ."

"Wait," he holds up his hand. "Holden and tone . . ." he says aloud as he writes.

At that moment the doorbell rings, and Kevin races past us and opens the door. A great chorus of "heys" and "hi's" swell up as four guys, four girls, and three people of indiscriminate gender burst into the room.

Both John and I snap our heads around.

Two of the girls immediately catch the scent of John and he, of course, catches them catching his scent. Smiles all around.

"Ah . . . John?" I prod.

Excited conversation bursts out around us. One of the people of indiscriminate gender plops down on the piano stool in front of our upright and begins banging out a medley of show tunes.

"There's no business like show business!" a few of them wail.

"Wow, you didn't tell me you were having a party," John says.

"It's just my brother and his wacky friends." I laugh nervously.

Then one of the girls, slim, dressed in funky, sexy black, slinks over. "Hi, don't I know you?" she asks John.

I groan. Hello . . . oldest line anywhere.

"I think I know you too." Another actress girl converges.

"Maybe," John flashes back.

Man, these people were killing me.

"Don't you have a sister who goes to NYU?" first artsy girl asks.

"Yeah," John says.

"Camille, right?" artsy girl two asks.

"Yeah, right. She's in the School of the Arts. She wants to be a designer."

"We go there too," the artsy girls coo. "We're in the acting program."

Smart, artsy girls, no less. Could this get any worse?

"Oh yeah. That's cool," John flirts.

"Um, John," I interrupt.

"Hmm? Oh, yeah . . . we're studying for some test," he says.

"You must be Kevin's little sister?" artsy girl one asks me, emphasizing the "little" with a bit of snotty in her voice.

"Listen John, if you want to study . . ." I say gesturing toward the books.

"Oh yeah," John remembers. "Gotta learn about Harry."

"Holden," I correct him.

Then artsy girl one draws in this big, dramatic breath. "Holden Caulfield?! *Catcher in the Rye*?! I love that book!"

"Yeah, me too. It's one of my favorites," John exclaims.

What?!

Then she hooks his arm in hers and leads him toward the piano.

"He's really irreverent, don't you think?" John says.

Double what?!

"Oh my God . . . so true!" artsy girl one exclaims.

"What other books do you like?" artsy girl two asks.

"What do you like?" he asks them.

"Ooh . . . I like Kurt Vonnegut and Dickens and Jane Austen. How about you?"

"Love 'em," I hear John say as he's being led toward the living room.

"Ooh, aren't you just gonna be cutealiscious one day?" I hear one of the gender benders say to John. "Sit here."

"Well, I really should study. Amy?" John cranes his neck over the crowd and shoots me a look of transparent insincerity.

Just when I think things can't get any worse, the doorbell rings.

My dad emerges from the bedroom and has, thankfully, changed into real clothes. Unfortunately, he is still wearing his mental ward slippers.

And guess who's standing on the other side? None other than Miss Sophia, wearing a winter white nubby coat this time and a little white fur hat, looking like one of

200

Santa's little helpers, and Beryl, dressed in his usual black, looking extraordinarily like he's visiting from another century.

Before I even have time to groan with despair, my dad shouts, "Amy, your friends are here!"

"No business I know!!" the singers end with a big crescendo, and then the whole room falls silent. All eyes swing toward the pair standing in the threshold.

I sink slowly behind the table, but am spotted, nonetheless.

"Yoo-hoo, there she is!" Miss Sophia crows. Then she and Beryl sidle past my father and climb over the group of actors slash producers draped around the living room, and head straight for me. "Yoo-hoo, Amy!" she calls out again. "You forgot our date."

"Our date?" I croak, pulling up from the floor, feeling every eye in the room on me.

"You know, dear. To explore Anna's journal. Beryl and I were waiting for you at Starbucks, and you were so late we thought we'd come get you."

Suddenly, I feel as though I'm in a weird movie where the main character finds herself in a strange room with people who are all in on a secret plot against her and the camera angles go wonky and people's faces go in and out of focus and she imagines everyone is laughing at her.

Then I really do hear a snicker from across the room, but I'm too mortified to look up to see who it is. I pray silently that it isn't John.

"Are you a performance artist?" one of Kevin's actors/producers asks Beryl.

"A what?" Beryl responds.

Then suddenly, reality snaps back into focus like a rubber band. I hear Kevin's friends start talking amongst themselves again and attention is diverted from me.

"Well, it's time to go," I say, leading Miss Sophia by the arm with one hand and Beryl's sleeve with the other. We make it to the door. I grab my jacket and pea hat and almost make it out the door when I hear a voice.

"Hey, Amy. Where you going?"

Crap.

I turn to see John Leibler.

"You gonna introduce me to your friends?" he asks.

I squint at him for a moment trying to determine if he's making fun of me, but he actually looks sincere.

"Miss Sophia and Beryl," I mumble as quickly as I can. "Well, gotta go."

"What?"

Miss Sophia stops and turns around.

"Hello, young man," she extends a white gloved hand. "I'm Miss Sophia."

"Hi, Miss Sophia. I'm John Leibler," he says, shaking her hand.

"What a good looking young man you are," she says. "And very charming. You must be our little Amy's boyfriend."

God just kill me. Kill me now and make it quick.

"He's not my boyfriend. We were just studying. Well, time to go," I say, trying desperately to leave.

"Funny, you don't look like you're studying," Beryl says, his face stony, his blue eyes blazing out from his marble paleness.

Then John extends his hand to Beryl.

"Hey, I'm John," John says.

But Beryl just stares at John suspiciously as awkward seconds tick by.

"I'm Beryl," he finally says.

"All righty then," I say, coaxing my little dream team out the door. "See you later."

"Wait," John persists.

Then probably for the first time in my life, I pray that John will go away.

"What is it, John?" I demand, through bared teeth.

"Well," he says, suddenly looking strangely abandoned. "Are you leaving? I thought we were studying."

Was he kidding or what?

"Hey, how 'bout *Fiddler on the Roof*?" someone cries out.

"If I were a rich man, yudda, dudda, yudda dudda . . ." they sing.

Then a few of the girls/boys do a strange dance like Tevye, with shades of Madonna.

The piano stops abruptly. Artsy girl one nudges the piano player. She mumbles something in his ear, snickers, and glances over at Beryl. Then after a chain reaction of nudges, glances, and some nervous snickers, the singing comes to an uncomfortable stop. All eyes flit to Beryl, who thankfully, seems oblivious.

I turn back to John. "Well, you sort of wandered off," I say.

"I did?" John answers, like he really doesn't know what I'm talking about.

How does he do that? I wonder. How does he get away with saying things that are clearly stupid and nobody calls him on it?

"I was just talking about books, ya know. That girl seems to know a lot about Harold. Probably not as much as you, though." He winks.

"Holden," I say.

"Holden, right. See what I mean?" he says, giving my arm a playful tug.

"Should we go now?" Beryl asks, with just the slightest tinge of irritation in his voice.

"Where are you going?" John questions, coyly.

"We . . . um . . ." I stall.

"Well, we should go," I say. "I'll type up my book notes for you, John. Okay, well bye-bye."

I grab my book bag with Anna's journal pages inside.

"We're taking a fascinating journey through New York to experience the life of a Jewish immigrant," says Miss Sophia to John, who, unbelievably is following us!

"Cool. Hey, did I ever tell you my cousin is Jewish?" John says.

"Yeah . . . well gotta go," I say.

"I have an immigrant journal too, but it's bogus. I was telling Amy just the other day in the bathroom that I really connect with American history."

"In the bathroom?" Beryl repeats stonily.

This was not going in a good direction.

"Hey, Johnny, come sing with us," artsy girl two calls out from across the room.

"Yes, join us," one of the boys/girls calls out. "We need a baritone."

"Sounds like you're wanted on stage 1," I quip. "So . . . bye." I turn for the door again.

Then I finally get us all out the door and almost make it halfway down the hall when I hear, "Hey wait!"

I turn and John is trotting after us, pulling on his jacket and his backpack over his shoulder.

"Listen, maybe I could help," he says. "Amy said something about her immigrant being around during the Civil War and having some sort of secret mystery too."

This was bad.

"Mystery?" Beryl glances at me and raises his eyebrows.

"As far as secrets go, I'm pretty good with clues," says John. "I play Sudoku sometimes and I usually win."

"Isn't Sudoku a game you play by yourself?" asks Beryl.

"Well, yeah . . . but you don't always win . . . yourself I mean. Sometimes you lose to . . . yourself."

We all ponder this for a moment.

"I also like mysteries. I must have seen that old Sherlock Holmes movie like a hundred times. What's that one with the dog and the fog in England somewhere?"

"You mean *Hound of The Baskervilles*?" I ask.

"Yeah, that's the one. Well, I always guess it right."

"But if you've seen it a hundred times, wouldn't it follow that you'd guess it right?" Beryl challenges.

"I meant the first time, dude," John says with just a tinge of snarkiness in his voice. "The first time I saw it, I guessed it right."

"I see," Beryl responds. Then he turns to me with icy eyeballs. "Amy, you never said anything to me . . . to us," he says, in what seems like an afterthought as he glances over at Miss Sophia, "about a mystery in Anna's journal."

"It's a new thing, Beryl. I just read. I'll tell you about it later."

This was exhausting! Now Beryl was insulted and had his shorts in a bunch, which I was going to say out loud, but thought better of it at the last minute.

"Hmm . . ." Beryl purses his lips.

Then Miss Sophia presses the button for the elevator and it whirs open.

Suddenly I feel all eyes on me, until Miss Sophia and Beryl step into the elevator.

I face John so they can't see me. "It won't be very interesting," I whisper gesturing to the dream team behind me. I even roll my eyes and make a "can you believe it" face to emphasize how ridiculous the whole thing is. "I'm kind of doing them a favor."

Believe it or not I feel a little guilty as those words are leaving my mouth.

Then John glances over my shoulder at Beryl and Miss Sophia. "I don't know. They look nice," he says.

Was this guy kidding or what? Couldn't he see that they were geekier than I was?

"It sounds kind of cool. Something different," he says. "Besides, we can talk about Holden on the way."

At this point, the elevator doors start to ping loudly, and John hasn't budged. It's clear that he isn't taking "no" for an answer.

"Well, why don't you come with us," I finally say.

"Cool," he exclaims and jumps in.

Miss Sophia smiles up at him. I can feel Beryl's angry eyes boring into the back of my neck as the elevator doors slam shut.

But, for now, Callie, I will leave you in suspense. It's late. I'm tired, and I'm going to bed. It gets worse, trust me. More tomorrow.

Amy

11/15, 6:01 p.m.

Dear Callie,
Yes, yes, I'll tell you the rest. Don't have a cow. And I wish
you were here too, not only for your company, but to secretly take pictures of John Leibler and me together like
celebrity paparazzi. I can just see the caption under the
photo in the newspaper now:

JOHN LEIBLER AND AMY FINAWITZ (?!)
Hunkaliscious John Leibler on mercy date
with geekaliscious Amy Finawitz.
Old Lady and unknown religious kid in tow.

We decide to stop in briefly at Starbucks.

Of course, being Sunday, there are a lot of kids from
school there and, of course, John knows almost every single
one.

While John is socializing, Miss Sophia buys her usual
hot cocoas for us all.

"Oh thanks, Miss Sophia," John says. "This is awesome, but you didn't have to buy us drinks."

"You're welcome, dear," she leans over and pats his
hand. "But I always provide the refreshments."

"Always? Really?" John says. Then he glances over at Beryl and me and kind of raises his eyebrows like we're both gold-digging ingrates taking advantage of poor little Miss Sophia.

I open my backpack and pull out three copies of Anna's latest, keep one, pass them to Miss Sophia, who then passes one to Beryl.

John starts dragging his chair over toward me, but Beryl quickly scrapes his chair over to John.

"You can share with me," he says.

"Hey wait, anybody hungry?" John asks, distractedly.

"Well, I brought along some sandwiches," Miss Sophia says, rustling through her Lord & Taylor shopping bag. "I remembered how Amy loves my sandwiches, so I brought along a few extras, piled especially high."

Oh God.

And John is like, "Oh whoa, you don't have to feed me too. I'll just buy a sandwich here."

"But I have plenty, dear," she insists.

"Nah, I'm a real big eater," he responds, patting his slim, washboard flat stomach. Then he stands and weaves his way toward the counter, taking the opportunity to stop every three seconds to schmooze with someone new.

"Just start without him," I sigh.

Then I fill Beryl and Miss Sophia in on what I know so far.

Miss Sophia reads a bit from the first page:

" 'I am the most excited after today's most exhilarating

day! Papa took me to Coney Island, where we rode the Wonder Wheel! We saw for miles. We were so high, and the world below us looked so small. And just like life, things seem big, then small, important and then not, close then far. Like life and death, everything is how you perspective it.

" 'My mind can't help thinking to thoughts of my brother, Yacov, who would have been a young boy by now if he had lived. Oh, how he would have loved Coney Island!' "

"Oh, dear that is sad," Miss Sophia says. "But Anna is right, your perspective shapes your attitude toward life."

She glances out the window momentarily and then smiles.

"I too have fond memories of the Wonder Wheel and Coney Island. Every summer my family and I would take some trips to Coney Island. I used to ride the Wonder Wheel all the time!"

"I've been to Coney Island," Beryl says proudly.

"What's a Wonder Wheel?" I ask.

"It's a wonderful Ferris wheel, at least 150 feet high," Miss Sophia reminisces, her eyes gleaming.

Did she say Ferris wheel? Did she say 150 feet high? Man, I hate those things.

"Shall we go?" Miss Sophia practically jumps out of her seat.

"You want to go there?" I stall. "Isn't it a little cold for outdoor activities?"

"Amy, Anna would have wanted us to ride the Wonder Wheel. We have to go," Beryl states matter-of-factly.

So we all start collecting our stuff, when I catch John's eye across the room. Taking the cue, he weaves his way back to the table.

"What's up? Did you solve the mystery?" he asks.

"I'm afraid we just started, John," Beryl says.

"Oh," he looks disappointed. "So where we going?"

"Coney Island," I answer.

"Coney Island? You mean way out by . . . Coney Island?" John asks.

"It's Brooklyn, actually," Beryl replies.

"Brooklyn . . . wow," John considers this. "That's kinda far."

Then he looks back to the cool crowd. The boys are shoving each other playfully, joking, and showing off for the girls. The girls, so slim and fashionable, are tossing their hair and smiling.

I watch John's eyes dart from his clan and then back to us. He can't mask the look of conflict on his face. They are the big dark, alpha monkeys. The kings of the jungle. The monkeys you didn't mess with. We are the less significant monkeys. The rhesus monkeys. The tiny mahogany ones with the long tails, that chatter at the zoo and throw poop at each other.

And at that moment, I knew I had lost a battle I wasn't even fighting. What was I thinking? The study date with John was just that, an appointment to study. He only left

211

Kevin's party because he was bored or needed me to help him.

"Hey John!" some girl calls from across the room, breaking my reverie. "You have to see this."

"Are we ready, children?" Miss Sophia asks, scooping up her clutch and her shopping bag.

"Did you get yourself a sandwich, dear?" she asks John.

"A sandwich?" he repeats absently. "Oh yeah. I mean. No. I forgot."

And then, against all reason, these words come out of my mouth:

"So, you want to come with us?" I ask, trying to sound as casual as I can.

"Uh . . ." he stalls.

I can practically hear the gears spinning in his head as he ponders his options: king monkeys, rhesus monkeys, king monkeys, rhesus monkeys . . .

Beryl sighs with irritation and shifts his weight. "We should go," he says.

I guess to Beryl, I was the cool monkey.

Should I be flattered? I don't know. I used to think that no matter how fast you climbed, your rung position never changed. But here was a revelation. Somehow, I had been elevated beyond my bottom rung status by a monkey who was lower down the ladder than me. So maybe it wasn't a ladder after all. Or maybe it was a circle, like the track at the gym. If you're slow enough, you look like you're first and it looks like the other people are slower than you.

Maybe Anna was right about the circle of life stuff and her metaphor about the Ferris wheel. Maybe everything was a matter of perspective, with just a few simple truths.

And maybe there was hope for me yet.

Then again, just because a monkey is climbing up your behind, doesn't necessarily mean you've gotten any closer to the top.

Somehow I had the strangest impulse to chatter and scratch my behind.

"Sure," John smiles at no one in particular. "I'll come with you."

Beryl nervously clears his throat and starts for the door.

"I'd like to do something different today," John announces casually.

Well, I'll be damned.

And with that we all tumble out into the street. Miss Sophia hails a cab and we pile in. First Beryl, then John, then me! Miss Sophia sits in the front.

I can't help but smile like a happy little monkey, shoulder to shoulder with John Leibler and his good smell, as we race off to Coney Island.

Maybe I really will learn to knit a sweater.

Amy

*D*ear Callie,

Well, I don't think it's time to knit just yet, and yes, yes, I'll tell you the rest. A girl's gotta eat, ya know. Well, this girl does, anyway.

Firstly, you might be wondering what we could possibly have to talk about in an approximately fifty-minute cab ride all the way to Coney Island. And the answer is pretty much nothing, since none of us has anything in common.

Mostly, we ended up listening to Miss Sophia having a conversation with the cab driver about the proliferation of potholes and endless and very loud highway reconstruction.

Finally we unfurl our stiff bodies from the cab and tumble out into the Coney Island amusement park.

"This place hasn't changed in fifty years," Miss Sophia squeals, delighted at the sight.

I don't know if you've ever been to Coney Island, Cal, but it's big. There are rides and amusements everywhere, obnoxious tinny music and the brinish smelling ocean is just across the way.

And then there is the famous Wonder Wheel, large

214

and looming, with the words, "Wonder Wheel and Thrills" written on the side. It's the first thing you see, jutting out from miles away.

So we make our way over to it, and there's a line of people snaking out from the monstrosity, waiting to board. Miss Sophia buys us tickets and plucks an information pamphlet from the ticket line.

"Oh, we're in luck, she says. The Wonder Wheel is usually closed in November, but they opened it this weekend for some special Coney Island commemoration activities."

"Oh, great . . . luck. Err . . ." I stall, "It's really huge."

"Hey, it will be awesome," John assures us.

"Did you know, children, that the wheel itself stands 150 feet high and holds 144 people at once?" she reads.

Before I know it, it's our turn to board. John swings into the seat with the grace of a star athlete.

"Come on!" he urges.

"Err . . ." I repeat.

Beryl, flush with excitement, maneuvers around me.

"Hey, Beryl, dude. Sit with me," John insists.

Beryl climbs in, and they pull the seatbelt over themselves. A pimply teenage attendant checks their seatbelt, pushes a lever, and their seat creaks up a few feet. An empty seat presents itself to me, squeaking and creaking in a mocking, sadistic way.

"Have you ever been on a Ferris wheel this big, Beryl?" I ask.

"I've never been on any Ferris wheel," Beryl says.

"And you're not afraid?"

"Yes, I am," he replies bluntly.

"So, how come you didn't want to sail on the *Ambrose*, but you're so eager to ride this huge, old Ferris wheel?"

"That was because I can't swim," Beryl whispers, blanching slightly and leaning toward me, away from John, presumably in the hopes that he wouldn't hear.

"Oh, but you can fly?" I shoot back, sarcastically.

Beryl just leans back and shrugs, feeling, I'm sure, that God wouldn't let him plunge 150 feet to a very splattery death.

Then, with the assistance of the pimply attendant, Miss Sophia steps spryly onto the metal grating and plops happily onto the seat.

Then it's my turn. John, Beryl, and Miss Sophia all stare at me, looks of cheery expectation on their faces.

Was I the only coward who didn't see the fun in swinging through the clouds on a rusty seat on a ninety-year-old ride?

The woman behind me clears her throat impatiently.

"Don't worry, dear. It's perfectly safe," Miss Sophia says, skimming her pamphlet. "It says here that the only accident was in July 1977, during an electrical storm. But riders on the Wonder Wheel were brought to safety because the owner hand-cranked the Wonder Wheel down. Can you imagine, hand cranking a 400,000-pound Ferris wheel to the ground?"

I look over at the pimply teenage attendant. He's picking stuff out of his ear and examining it.

I was a dead girl.

"Come on, Amy. It'll be fine," John coaxes.

So then I, with my heart in my mouth, step off the platform into the metal chair and almost lose my balance.

"A little help here," I demand of pimply teenage attendant.

"You're kidding, right?" he snarks.

"Do you work here, or not?" I snap.

He holds out his arm reluctantly and I, clutching onto him for dear life, trip my way on.

He pulls the metal seatbelt tightly across us.

"You cozy now?" he drawls sarcastically.

To which I respond by giving him the dirtiest look I can muster.

Then the ride jerks forward, pushing us ever upward.

God, if you let me live, I promise to be a good person, I pray silently.

After only a few minutes, we're pretty high up, and I can see the ocean waves in the distance.

"Did you all remember to use the bathroom?" Miss Sophia asks.

And thank you for that, I'm thinking. Now in addition to obsessing over crashing hundreds of feet to my death, I'll be obsessing over having to pee.

"Ahh . . . and doesn't the ocean look beautiful this

time of year?" says Miss Sophia, a happy, contented expression on her face. "Just look at those waves. So rough and wild. Churning and breaking."

She sways, causing the little swing to rock back and forth. "Churning and breaking, churning and breaking . . ."

I can feel that egg salad I had for lunch working its way back up my esophagus.

And then as if reading my mind, John is like, "Listen if you need to hurl, wait till the ride stops or it'll fly in everyone's face. Right, Beryl? That happened to me once a long time ago."

"You threw up on a ride?" Beryl asks.

"No, it wasn't me. It was my friend. Man, was it gross."

Help me, God, I thought. Please, don't let me puke on John Leibler. I'll do anything you ask for the rest of my life.

"Maybe this would be a good time to talk about Anna's journal," I croak, swallowing down my bile.

I take the journal from my backpack. "So, Anna says that in Kentucky, during the war, a few bad guys who happened to be Jewish were accused of stealing cotton. So General Grant said that all the Jews were guilty and had to leave their homes. So I guess that means that Anna and her family were exiled too. But then she says that when the truth was upheld, the families were free again and people could go home. But they were so heartbroken that they didn't want to stay in Kentucky anymore and decided to move in with relatives in New York."

We all ponder this for a moment.

"Oh, and then she writes that something set them free," I continue, "and hints that this is related to the secret mystery. I wonder what that something was. Beryl, any ideas?"

"Oh, you're including me now?" Beryl suddenly gets all icy again.

"Of course I'm including you, Beryl," I sigh.

Beryl looks out toward the ocean and to the naked eye seems to be thinking, but, frighteningly, I know him well enough now to see that he's probably thinking and sulking.

"So, all the Jews," I say, "were accused of something because of a couple of criminals. And they were kicked out of town? How is that legal?"

"Hmm . . . Ulysses S. Grant," ponders John, "I've read a lot about him. He was popular for some things, but he was kinda slick, sort of a double dealer, and then whenever he got caught doing something not quite legal, he blamed his staff, that kind of thing. He got away with a lot of slippery stuff, too."

John twists around in his chair and says,

"So let's say there was some black market stuff going on, like there would be during a war. Ya know, people selling something to both sides, making profit from items that were hard to get."

"And General Grant blamed all the Jews," I say.

"If this is true, children, it's the first I've heard of this incident, and I was a librarian for thirty years!" says Miss Sophia.

"That's so cool," John says.

We all shoot him a perplexed look.

"I don't mean about kicking people out of their houses because they were Jewish or the little kid dying, but I mean about us discovering some little-known piece of history. That's cool."

"But how could a general have the authority to actually banish people from a town?" asks Beryl.

We all ponder this for a moment.

So what set them free? I wonder.

Then suddenly, Miss Sophia pulls a tissue from up the sleeve of her jacket and dabs her eyes.

"It's all so exciting!" she says, tearfully. "Discovering a piece of American history. I wish that my Arthur was here to share this adventure with me . . . with us."

Beryl pulls a wad of tissues from his backpack.

"It's all right," Beryl comforts, leaning toward us. "Here's another tissue, Aunt Sophia."

Then John pulls a mint from his backpack.

"Here you go," John says. "It's refreshing."

I don't have anything in my backpack except a pad, pencil, and a linty half-wrapped Butterfinger bar. I give her arm an extremely awkward pat.

Much to my relief, the Wonder Wheel finally whirs back to the ground, and I find myself staring into the face of the pimply attendant. He leans over and unlocks our seatbelt.

"Want to go around again?" asks John.

Pimply boy stops unlocking the seat and grins at me with a twinkle in his eye.

I shove the metal bar up myself. "Uh . . . I don't think so."

Then I stagger off and climb down the platform, stomping up and down a few times, enjoying the solid ground beneath my feet. Salty cold air blows up from the ocean, and I take a long, deep breath.

The rest of the dream team piles out behind me.

At this point, we're all feeling a little excited. We find a bench and Miss Sophia breaks out her awesome sandwiches. It's kinda sweet the way she thinks to feed us all the time. Beryl seems to have gotten over feeling "dissed" and begins to fill John in on what we've uncovered so far and where we've gone. John continues to seem sincerely interested.

At one point, he turns to me and says, "Why didn't you tell me any of this, Aim? You know I'm a history buff."

And I'm thinking, maybe because we're not friends and you outrank me socially?

But instead I smile and say, "Glad you're having fun."

After we eat, Beryl and John decide to "boy bond" by riding death-defying rides and playing arcade games. Neither one of them seems particularly interested in me anymore (not that either of them ever really was). Then Miss Sophia gets it in her head that she and I should "girl bond" by walking around the carnival grounds on a quest to taste all the carnival foods that she remembers from her youth. And boy does she have a tin stomach. It doesn't take her long to scarf down two corn dogs, cotton candy, a caramel apple, buttons, shoestring licorice, and an ice cream cone, all of which she insists I taste and share.

And then something strange comes over me, probably prompted by a sugar buzz overdose. Somewhere between jaw breakers and fried dough, I start to feel, well, for lack of a better word, spiritual. I look out into the happy faces of the carnival crowd and my thoughts wander, once again, to Anna.

"Miss Sophia," I say, licking the sticky, crystallized cotton candy from my fingers. "Do you think Anna would be happy we're reading her journal? Do you think it was sort of, I don't know, meant to be that we're doing this . . . and, like, meant to be that we're doing it together?"

"Well," Miss Sophia says. "I think there's a reason for things."

"Okay," I say. "Well, then why do awful things happen? Like Anna's family getting exiled from their home, losing their son, and they didn't even do anything wrong . . . doesn't that seem random to you?"

"Well, Amy," Miss Sophia says, stopping to buy us two big, blue Slurpees. "I don't know about the mysteries of religion, but I'll tell you what my bubbe used to tell me . . ."

Uh oh, not another "made from love" bubbe story.

"Bubbe always said that God connects us."

"Meaning?" I say.

"God puts people in our lives to fill in the blanks."

"What blanks?"

"The blanks in our lives."

"I'm not following," I say, as we walk down the slope of the boardwalk and make our way back toward the arcades, where we spy Beryl and John hopping around in front of some "fish for the duckie" game.

"For example, do you know what Beryl would be doing today if he wasn't here with us?" Miss Sophia asks, taking a long blue slurp of her drink.

Just at that moment, Beryl wins something. He and John slap each other five and Beryl grabs the prize, a bug antennae hat with attached oversized glasses and coil spring eyeballs. He pulls it on his head, then bops up and down causing the eyeballs to go boing, boing, boing. He and John practically split a gut laughing.

"Uh . . . probably not that," I say.

"If Beryl were home," Miss Sophia slurps, "he'd probably be in his room, alone, maybe feeling lonely, quietly bent over some solemn book. Instead, he's out here in the salty air, laughing and having fun with friends."

"If I were home, I'd probably be alone with my cats watching one of my television programs, planning my little dinner of chicken and green beans for one. But instead, I'm here," she says, spreading her arms out wide and giving me a Slurpee flash of totally blue teeth, "having a wonderful, exciting time, munching on treats, riding the glorious Wonder Wheel, and being with you lively wonderful children!"

And what would I be doing if I were home? E-mailing you, Cal? Knitting with Judy and Claire? Nothing?

Just then, John sneaks up behind me, and shoves a bobbly clown head on a stick in front of my face.

"We won you something," Beryl says proudly.

"Wow," I say. "Thanks."

Well, it isn't John's lacrosse sweater, but it's something. I wonder if I can somehow pin it to my jacket, without looking like I needed anti-psychotic drugs.

Finally, it's time to go. Miss Sophia hails a cab, and we all climb back in, in the same order as before.

"Where do you live, dude?" John asks Beryl.

"I'm uptown," Beryl answers. "Washington Heights. 160th Street."

"Then you get dropped off first because Anne and I live close together," John says.

"Well," Beryl ponders uncertainly, as his eyes shift toward me. "I suppose that makes sense. It all depends on what route we take."

"Washington Heights, 160th Street," John instructs the cab driver, cutting Beryl off.

"Hey," Johns turns to me, "I think Miss Sophia's asleep."

I lean forward and, sure enough, her head is tilted gently on her shoulder and her chest is rising and falling in even rhythms. I move her ever so slightly so she'll be more comfortable (also, so a short stop won't send her thumping over into the cab driver's lap).

I sit back in the seat, enjoying the cleanness of John's smell mixed with the sea saltiness wafting off his hair.

As the cab pulls onto the parkway and the horizon turns to streaky lines of red and blue, I wonder if maybe Miss Sophia and Bubbe are right. Maybe God's not really saying "talk to the hand;" maybe he has a hand in what we do. As for Beryl and Miss Sophia, maybe we were meant to be on this little adventure together. Maybe I'm helping to fill in their blanks. And here's a really strange thought: maybe even John has blanks. Maybe he likes to feel smart. Is it possible that maybe he gets bored sometimes being Mr. Perfect, top monkey?

"So, do you want to talk more about *Catcher in the Rye*?" I turn to John.

"Nothin' else to do. Sure, why not?" John says.

An enthusiastic response to literature if ever I'd heard one.

So talk I did. I talked about Holden and tone and plot and irreverence, and John was pretty much listening and nodding. Whether he heard any of what I was actually saying is anybody's guess.

Beryl perked up and seemed totally way more interested than John, peppering me with questions about the book, like what's the story about, why is Holden so unhappy, where is he going, and why does he fight so hard against fitting in?

"But why doesn't Holden have purpose?" Beryl struggles to comprehend.

I lean way over John to answer him.

"That's the whole point," I argue. "The author wants us to understand that life is a pointless journey of isolation."

At this, Beryl couldn't have been more appalled. He just keeps shaking his head and nervously twisting the fringes around his waist. "I understand that's the author's point of view, but I think he's misguided, and what I don't understand is why your teacher had you read it."

"Because it's important literature," I insist.

"Maybe Holden's problem," states Beryl, seeming perplexed "is that he has no faith. If he had faith and purpose then perhaps he could have found contentment."

"I don't know, Beryl. I don't think J. D. Salinger thought . . ."

"Dude, I hear that. That's like so awesomely insightful," John suddenly interrupts. "Like I love lacrosse, right? It gives me purpose."

"Yes," Beryl considers this. "I can see that. Sportsmanship develops character."

"And Miss Sophia," John continues, lowering his voice to a whisper. "She's, like, really old and probably lonely and has been, like, dismissed from society. But these outings give her purpose."

"I don't know, John," I interject. "Just because she's an old woman doesn't mean she's totally lonely. She seems pretty vital . . ."

"Yes, that's true, John," Beryl cuts me off.

"And Amy, here," John continues. "She has . . . um . . . what gives you purpose, Amy?"

Now, that's a loaded question, I'm thinking. I guess the only answer is visiting you, Cal, but that sounds too pathetic to say out loud.

"Knitting," I finally say.

Then both Beryl and John nod solemnly like I had just said, "developing world peace," because they probably think that knitting is some transcendental, nurturing dorky, girl thing, and as far as they can figure I'm a dorky girl.

"Uh, okay, well that's good," says John. "Knitting is important. You can make warm sweaters and stuff for people. Clothing the naked and stuff like that. Oh sorry, Beryl. I'm not supposed to say naked, right?"

"It's all right," Beryl assures him.

"But I don't think that's what *Catcher in the Rye* is really . . ." I try to say.

"And like you," John says to Beryl. "You're, like, a really purposeful person, praying a lot and stuff and doing good deeds. That's wickedly awesome. Right, Amy?"

"Oh yeah . . . pray . . . good deeds . . . awesome," I mutter. Once again, I had become completely irrelevant in my own life.

Finally, we arrive at Beryl's house.

There's a light in the bedroom again and a woman's shadowy figure appears momentarily behind the drapes. So Beryl gets out and then looks back through the window, first at John and then at me. An ambiguous expression crosses his face, like he's not sure what he's feeling.

"Bye, dude," John says. "Good to meet ya. Keep it real."

"Yes, nice meeting you," Beryl nods his head up and down a few times.

"Bye, Beryl," I say. "See you next time at Starbucks Detective Agency."

"Will you be joining us again, John?" he asks, hesitantly.

Now, that was a damn good question. I turn to John and hold my breath.

"Hey, yeah. Sure. Maybe. Ya never know, right?" John hedges.

What a definitive answer!

"Oh," replies a perplexed Beryl.

Then he catches my eye again, blushes, quickly turns to go, and makes his way up the stone steps. The front door opens and a warm light sprays out into the darkening street for just a millisecond, before the door closes behind him.

The rest of the way home, John chats, mostly about lacrosse and school and himself. I smile and nod and try to look interested until I think my face is gonna crack. And then the cab stops to let him out, just a few blocks from my building.

And as he hops from the cab, he flashes me his famous 100-watt smile, and I can't help thinking that maybe John is just a little too "sexy for his shirt."

Totally fried. Signing off. More later.

Amy

11/24, 4:38 p.m.

*D*ear Callie,
Enjoy Turkey Day! My grandparents are actually coming to Manhattan for it! My grandmother says she's packing brass knuckles and Mace. She says if my mother tries to make Tofurkey again she's getting takeout from Mr. Lee's (me too).

Amy

11/24, 4:42 p.m.
I hope your aunt and uncle buy a turkey and don't have to actually catch it and kill it with a hatchet or anything because that would be mondo disgusting.

11/24, 4:46 p.m.
In what way does writing about turkey and Thanksgiving feel like I'm pressuring you to come back to New York? Where is this coming from? You're saying that you didn't think that your desire to stay in Kansas would hurt my feelings? You thought I would understand?

Of course it would hurt my feelings and I wouldn't understand! Isn't that obvious? If you weren't my best friend and I didn't feel that your soul was in mortal danger, I would be very angry with you. But I know that somewhere deep inside, the little New Yorker in you is crying for help, so I will try. Could you just keep your damn Davy Crocket coonskin cap on till I get out there?

11/30, 3:05 p.m.

Dear Callie,
For now, I will try to keep you stabilized by describing the next installment of my adventure.

Since the Christmas/Hannukah holidays are approaching, everyone's dragging bags of stuff through the lobby. This puts Lou in a pissy mood because he has to let them squeeze into the people elevator (instead of the freight), but he keeps an obliging face, because it is tip season after all.

But the worst part are the pine trees. Today there was this big forest in the elevator, and I was practically getting my eyes poked out by pine needles. And I was forced into a "cheery" once a year conversation with Mr. Klein who managed to choke out a "How are you?" even though he didn't wait for an answer and lunged out of the elevator as soon as the doors pinged open. Bah humbug!

So anyway, I'm clomping through the lobby in my toasty, cool, Himalayan boots on my way to meet Beryl and Miss Sophia when Lou calls me over, looks down his nose over his big coke bottle glasses, and hands me this note. It says:

231

Dear Amy,

I'm afraid I'm feeling under the weather, so I will be unable to accompany you today. Stay warm and good luck.

Best wishes,

Miss Sophia

PS: I'm afraid that it is unlikely that Beryl will be able to accompany you either.

What?!

I hightail it back into the elevator and two seconds later, I'm knocking on Miss Sophia's door. After about half an hour of her unbolting the locks, she opens it. She is wearing a silkish pink bathrobe ensemble, including worn-out pink slippers; you know the flat kind with the wafer thin, white rubber bottoms. Her hair is wrapped in a turban, and her nose is red from sniffling.

"Why hello, Amy. Come in," she says, opening the door, holding out her pink foot to keep a cat from escaping. "Didn't you get my note, dear?"

"Yes. How are you feeling?" I ask. "Do you need anything?"

"It's just one of those bronchial things. I'll be fine," she says.

"Miss Sophia, you said in your note that you don't think that Beryl will be able to help me today. Is he mad at me?" I fish.

"I can't imagine why he would be," she sneezes.

"Is he sick too? Is it a holiday?"

"Not that I know of," she replies.

This was turning into a mystery all its own.

"Well, so why can't he meet with me?" I ask.

"Well, you would be unchaperoned, of course," she says matter-of-factly.

"Are you kidding?"

"No, dear," she sniffles. "I'm afraid I'm not. You know he's very modest."

"Is he waiting at Starbucks?" I ask hopefully.

"He must be, dear. I tried to call the house, but his mother said he had already left."

I glance at my wrist. Damn, I need a watch.

"All right," I say. "I'm gonna try and catch him. Feel better."

I sprint, as best as one can sprint in Himalayan boots, all the way to Starbucks. I pull open the big glass door and it's like walking into a great wall of coffee aromas, music, and steaming red holiday cups.

Gruffly, I elbow my way through the crowd, craning my neck over short people, and through armpit spaces of big people, until finally, I spot Beryl. He's in a corner by the window, reading a small black book. He's deep in concentration, looking stark in his black pants and coat, with just the smallest bit of bright white peeking out from his lapel. His milk pale skin shines luminously against the crowd wearing bright colors.

"Beryl," I call out. "I'm so glad I caught you. I hope you weren't waiting a long time."

"Maybe a little while," he says, looking up from his reading, his eyes round and faraway.

"Your aunt can't make it," I say.

"Oh?" he says, his eyebrows going up.

"She's got a cold. She's all right. But listen," I say, trying to talk fast before he has time to respond. "I figure that maybe we could talk about Anna's mystery and see if there's another clue. There's a free table over there. Why don't we sit down?"

"Just us?" he says uncertainly.

"Looks that way," I chuckle.

"Well . . ." He bites his lip.

"I'm gonna grab that table before someone else does," I say, rushing over to a small table. I quickly move the seats as far away from each other as I can, and then sit down. He comes over but just stands uneasily, shifting his weight ever so slightly from one foot to the next.

Then some annoying man comes by and is like, "You using this chair?"

"Sorry, yeah," I say, placing my hand on it. "Beryl, you need to sit."

"Amy, I know this will sound strange to you, but for us to be together unchaperoned is something we don't do," he says, still not sitting.

"But we're just talking. We're not dating or anything," I blurt out.

"Yes, of course," Beryl says, blanching red, and quickly averting his eyes. "But it's still not done."

"Why not?" I ask.

"It's not proper," he says.

"Hey, you using that chair or not?" Annoying Man returns.

I glance up at Beryl, who looks down and shuffles his feet.

"Fine," I snark at Annoying Man, releasing the chair. "It's yours." I look back at Beryl. "Beryl, we're surrounded by people in here."

"Yes, but we don't know any of them," he says.

"Strangers are just people we haven't met yet," I say, recalling a recent fortune cookie.

Beryl glances at the door.

Great. Where the hell was I gonna find a chaperone?

And then it hit me. John Leibler! He could come with us. That would not only solve my problem with Beryl, but it would give me an excuse to spend time with John.

At this point, I know you're probably thinking that I'm insane, Cal. I know you think that John is way too into himself, and, ya know, he kind of does what he wants when it suits him.

But he did seem to like being part of the detective agency last time. And he did seem to like Beryl. And besides, desperate times call for desperate measures.

I turn to Beryl, and I'm like, "I'll tell you what, Beryl. I know someone who would make the perfect chaperone."

"You do?" he asks skeptically. "For real?"

"No, not for real. He's fake. I'm gonna make a sock puppet, wear it on my hand, and call it a chaperone."

Beryl chuckles and readjusts his yarmulke.

"Come on, let's go," I say.

So we make our way out of Starbucks and start up the street toward school. I figure, if I hurry, I can catch John at pre-spring lacrosse practice which, according to the million signs hung around the school, is every day at 4:00 in the gym.

I try to make fast tracks in my fat boots, and Beryl picks up his pace to keep up. Already it's almost 4:00, and I don't need to tell you that, this time of year, the light fades fast. And we hadn't even looked at the journal yet. Who knew where it was gonna send us?

"I don't mean to irritate you, Amy," Beryl says, clearly sensing my irritation.

And then I feel all guilty and I'm like, "Look Beryl, I know it's not your fault that you're religious."

"What do you mean?" he asks, looking pepped up like we're gonna have this big theological conversation.

"I mean you didn't ask to be born into a religious family. You could have been born into a more normal family, like mine . . . Well, maybe not like mine. But like somebody else's," I say, moving aggressively down the street.

"Another family?" Beryl asks.

"I don't mean a better family, necessarily. Your family seems pretty nice. I just mean not so strange, more . . . contemporary."

"I like my family," Beryl says, thoughtfully.

"I'm sure you do. But maybe that's just because you're used to them," I counter.

"Well, I am used to them, that's true. But I think I'd like them anyway," he says.

"Okay, whatever," I say.

"Well, if you had a choice, wouldn't you choose your family?" he asks.

That was a good one.

"My family?!" I bark a laugh.

"Oh, I forgot." He grins mischievously. "Cross-dressers and twisted weirdos."

Finally, I can see the school looming ahead. We run up the steps, bolt through the front door and down the hall.

We rush to the gym, where sports-type sounds are emanating from the other side of the thick, double doors; you know, all those hoots and hollers and squeaking of sneakers on the gym floor.

"By the way," Beryl says. "What are we doing here?"

"You'll see," I respond, cryptically.

So I pull open the door, thinking we can slip in unnoticed, but it seems that a lot of people hang out in the gym after school; team girlfriend wannabes, sporty kids on teams shouting team stuff. A few people gawk at Beryl, so I usher him into a shadowed corner.

"I don't think I'm so strange, Amy," Beryl says, out of nowhere.

"You don't?" I ask, spotting John among the other sweaty, running boys.

"Well, maybe I look different," he reluctantly admits.

"Maybe?! Beryl, you must know that if you look different, that other people perceive you as different."

The coach blows a whistle and the players stop playing. I can't keep my eyes off John, who looks so totally cute in his lacrosse outfit, with his hair matted down by sweat, leaning over and puffing and swearing and stuff.

"Well, I do see other people gawk at me sometimes," Beryl says.

The coach blows the whistle and the game begins again.

"And I know that your brother's friends were making fun of me when they sang that song from *Fiddler on the Roof*," he says quietly.

"Yeah, I'm sorry about that Beryl," I say, feeling ashamed. "Why didn't you say anything?"

"Other people's perceptions are their own."

At that moment the coach blows his whistle, the practice stops, and there's John, the center of attention, smiling that 100-watt smile at his teammates. He must have scored a goal, or hit the ball, or whatever. Everyone is congratulating him.

"Yeah! All right!" they slap each other five.

I catch John's eye but am too shy to call his name. All I can manage is one of Mrs. Goldstein's 'gas' smiles and a small wave that's more like a finger wiggle.

Then Beryl finally catches on.

"Is this your chaperone?" he asks perplexed. "John?"

John looks at me like he's never seen me before in his life and gives me an odd head bob.

"Do you really think he wants to come with us?" Beryl asks.

"Why not?" I retort. "He did before."

Beryl ponders this. "That was before, Amy," he says quietly.

"Oh Beryl, you're just being . . ." I wanted to say jealous, irritating, boring, but instead I say, "out of touch."

Then John starts moving across the gym toward us, and suddenly I realize that I have no idea what to say to him.

"Look Beryl, John got a real kick out of coming with us last time. Remember, he got into this whole discussion about purpose and Holden Caulfield?"

"I remember." Beryl shakes his head thoughtfully. "But let me ask you something? Did you have your English test yet?"

Across the room, John stops to talk to Horrible Susan.

"Uh, yeah," I say distractedly. "We did have the test, as a matter of fact. I got an A."

"I'm not surprised you got an A," Beryl says. "But how did John do?"

"Uh, I think he got a B+ or something, Beryl. Why?"

"So, he doesn't need to study anymore, right?" Beryl questions, in that irritating way he has sometimes.

"Well, not about *Catcher in the Rye*," I say.

239

Then John is moving toward us again, in "slo mo" like he's in a commercial for something that smells really good.

"I see," Beryl responds, "and when's your next test?"

"Not for a while." I turn angrily. "Beryl, I know what you're implying."

"You do?" he asks calmly.

"Cut it out, okay?" I say, my eyes flaring red. "John and I made a connection. Maybe not 'he likes me, like I'm a girl' connection, but he's definitely my friend."

"He is?"

"And, by the way, he's your friend too."

"He's my friend?"

John is intercepted again by wannabe Jennifer from math class.

"Amy . . ." Beryl starts.

"Beryl, I mean it. Stop it," I hiss.

"What should I stop?" He stares at me.

"Stop implying that I'm a delusional idiot," I growl.

"Don't be upset. I'm just trying to look out for . . ."

"Well, don't," I snap, way too loudly.

And then, like a hundred heads turn in our direction, and I give them all a little embarrassed smile and motion for Beryl to take a few steps back with me into the shadow of the bleachers.

"You said you needed a chaperone, so I'm finding us a chaperone," I say.

"Is that all?" he asks, with an expression that looks like a mixture of pity and hopefulness. "Honestly?"

"You know what your problem is?" I seethe, completely losing my temper and poking at his skinny, concave chest with my finger.

"I . . ." he stammers, kind of stunned, "don't know."

"You're not part of this world. You don't understand how the social scene works. Friends help one another, and John Leibler is our friend!"

Then I turn, and there's John Leibler standing in front of me, and the blood completely rushes out of every inch of my brain.

"Heh, heh, hello John," I say, forcing myself to smile.

"What's up?" he says, looking at me weirdly. "You guys okay?"

"Us? Oh yeah, we're fine. I . . . we . . . just wanted to ask you something."

"Oh, okay. Because I hope you're not having a little lover's spat," he grins.

My jaw falls open so hard that I feel it bash against the floor. Beryl lowers his head, and I swear I can hear him choke back a laugh.

"Ach," I sputter, choking on my own tongue. "We're not . . ."

" 'Cause you guys are really cute together. I'm not kidding." John winks. "Hey, Sue, be there in a minute." John waves to Horrible Susan. He turns back to us and says, "You guys coming to the lacrosse game this weekend? It's on a Sunday, so that means you're free, right?"

"We? Well, Beryl is busy, aren't you, Beryl?" I say

through gritted teeth. "And because I'm single and I don't have a boyfriend, I'm never busy . . . I mean, I'm always free . . . I mean . . ."

"I'm free," Beryl interrupts, poker faced. "Why don't we go to the game? . . . honey bunch."

If I could have, I would have swallowed my own head.

"Cool." John nods.

And then Horrible Susan ambles over.

"We're all going out now, John. Whatcha doing?"

She looks Beryl and me over with amused disdain.

"Oh, Sue, this is Amy and her boyfriend, Beryl."

Kill me, God. Please. Do it. I'll even lie down and give you a head start.

"Hi," Horrible Susan bleats, trying to hide a snicker.

"Well, gotta go," John says. "I had an awesome time the other day, you know, that whole investigation thing. Oh and thanks again, Amy, for helping me with that test and old, irrelevant Holden."

"Irreverent," I mutter, completely mortified.

"Yeah, whatever. Hey, you're the best." Then John points his finger and bends his thumb like he's pretend shooting me and gives me that 100-watt smile. He turns to go, but stops and turns back, "Hey, didn't you want to ask me something?"

"Ask you something?" I croak.

"Yeah, you said you came to practice to ask me something."

"I . . . uh . . ."

242

"Johnny, let's go," Horrible Susan prods.

"Wait a minute," John says. "What do you need, Aim? Just say the word."

"Ah . . ."

"We just wanted to thank you for helping us the other day," Beryl jumps in. "And we wanted to know if you found my . . . um . . . tefillin."

Oh God.

"Your what?" John asks.

"My tefillin. It's a little box with straps. It's a prayer box. I think I left it in the cab."

"Um . . . no," John says, looking perplexed. "But if it turns up I'll let you know."

"Thank you," Beryl replies.

"Hey, try calling the cab company," John shouts over his shoulder as he moves toward the door. "But I wouldn't say tefl . . ."

"Tefillin," Beryl helps.

"Yeah, whatever. You better just explain what the thing looks like."

"Thank you." Beryl waves.

Then John gives Horrible Susan a quick kiss on the cheek, meets up with his lacrosse guys on the other side of the gym, and disappears into the boys' locker room.

I spin around on Beryl, lightning daggers shooting from my eyeballs.

"You lost your tsifilli!? What the hell is that?"

"My tefillin," he corrects me. "It's the little box . . ."

"You couldn't just say you lost your pen or pad or sweater like a normal person? You had to say tifiline??!!"

"Tefillin."

"Stop it!" I hiss. "Like they didn't think we were freaky enough?"

Then I bolt out the gym doors and up the hall.

Did you ever get so angry, Cal, that tears just start rolling down your cheeks and you have no control over them?

Well that's what happened to me at that moment. So I'm trying to get away from Beryl, clomping down the hallway in my hot sweaty boots, wiping away these uncontrollable tears with the sleeve of my jacket, and I can hear Beryl running after me. I throw open the school doors and race/clomp up the street. And it's dark and cold already, and my cheeks are starting to freeze over. And I swear, I must have looked so crazy that everyone just jumped out of my way.

"I'm sorry," Beryl pants, catching up to me and hands me a tissue, which makes me even angrier.

"I'm going home now, Beryl. Why don't you just go home?" I say.

"Well, wait a second. Maybe we can go sit on a bench," he suggests pointing to the benches that line the outside of Central Park.

"What? Sit on a bench together? Unchaperoned?"

"Well I didn't say I would sit directly next to you," Beryl grins.

Then he just sits down. And for some reason, I sit down too, a few feet away of course.

I put on my gloves and my little pea hat, and Beryl buttons up his coat. We sit there in silence for a few minutes, watching the people scurry past. Some big Santa on the corner starts ringing his bell for the Salvation Army.

Another few minutes go by, and my tear flow has dried up and iced over, and then Beryl says, "I'm sorry about what happened at school, Amy."

"You're not gonna say I told you so, are you?" I fish.

"I wouldn't do that," he replies.

"Well, maybe you do know the world more than I gave you credit for. That must give you some satisfaction. Especially since I guess I was mean to you, and then I was humiliated."

"Hey, I'm the religious one. I don't feel satisfied when people are humiliated. Especially if it's a friend."

"Well, thanks for not laughing at me."

Beryl smiles and pushes his hands deep into his pockets.

"I guess I made a fool of myself with John, huh?" I say sheepishly.

"I don't think so. A person with a trusting heart is never a fool."

"Thank you, Beryl. That's a very thoughtful sentiment," I say. "It sort of sounds like a fortune cookie I once read."

"Actually, it's a quote from Rabbi Zekiel Hymanski, a respected scholar from the twelfth century."

"Hmm . . . no kidding. Well, I guess people in the twelfth century had problems too."

"I'll say," sighs Beryl.

Then we both sit in silence for a few seconds.

"Look, Beryl. I really would like to visit my friend in Kansas," I say, turning around to look him in the eye. "And you know that I need to finish this assignment so I can get a good grade so I can visit her.

"And besides," I say, giving my icy nose a swipe. "I need to help Callie."

"May I ask what's wrong with her?" he asks.

"Let's just say that she's having kind of, like, an emotional crisis."

And then he looks at me as if he's really listening. No pretense. No ego. Just listening.

"See, Beryl," I look around furtively, "I think that she's been abducted by aliens."

"What?"

"And they left her body empty, like a shell. I think they filled it with an alien soul, who likes hayrides through pumpkin patches and twangy music and people who say things like 'dang' and organic lettuce and a half pet/half boy named Bucky. And worst of all, this alien likes to go to dances and actually dance."

So then Beryl is completely confounded. He blinks a few times, and then just starts to laugh. But not a chuckling laugh, a good hearty laugh. He actually throws back

246

his head so far while he's laughing that he has to put one hand on his head to keep his yarmulke from falling off.

The way he's laughing is so funny that I have to laugh. And it's so infectious, I'm crying and laughing and so is Beryl. I can only imagine how we looked, this religious kid and geeky girl laughing and crying on a park bench.

Then Beryl finally catches his breath and wipes his cheeks and is like, "No, really, Amy. What's wrong with her?"

The laughing kind of slows down.

"I don't know, Beryl. She just doesn't want to come home."

"Oh," he says.

And then I'm like, "We were best friends and she's . . . I don't know . . . moved on."

"I'm sorry, Amy," he says.

And then I say, "I don't think she wants to be my best friend anymore. I miss that. I miss all the things we did together, all the things we talked about, all the things we didn't have to talk about. I don't think I'll ever have a friend like her. And I can't believe it. And it makes me feel like I'm nobody, like I was left behind."

So Beryl stares out for a few seconds, and we're both lulled into quiet by the big emotional moment of all that crying and laughing. And all the people are rushing by, colorful and cheery, with their big shopping bags. The

Santas are ho-ho-ing and ringing their bells. Then a light snow starts falling, quiet and delicately white.

"Maybe I can help you," Beryl says.

"But we don't have a chaperone."

"I was taught that the most important thing is to help other people."

"I'm listening."

"Well, if Aunt Sophia doesn't get better soon, maybe I can justify being with you unchaperoned if you were my . . . my mitzvah project. You know, officially."

"You mean, like, I'm this pathetic creature who needs charity?"

"You said it. I didn't," he responds.

"Well, it could work," I ponder. "I mean, I've never really needed charity, but I've always been pathetic."

"Then I'll ask the rabbi. I think it could be okay if we follow certain rules," he says perking up. "Yes, I think I can help you and your little alien too."

"That would be great, Beryl. I appreciate it."

"It's my pleasure," he says.

He looks down, but I can see a shy smile tugging at the corners of his mouth even under the dim lamplight.

That wacky Beryl. He gets on my nerves sometimes, but he's a damn good listener and a pretty good guy too, I guess.

Then we sit awkwardly for a few seconds.

"Well, we can't do anything tonight."

"Okay, I guess I'll go home now," Beryl remarks, standing.

"Okay," I say, trying to wipe my nose discreetly with the back of my gloved hand.

"I'll e-mail you and let you know what I find out," he promises, and he turns to go.

"Bye," I wave at his back.

Then he blends into the dark city and disappears.

And so, Callie. There you have it. The whole story, so far. Now, it's late, and I'm signing out. Until next time . . .

Amy

PS: Can't end without a fortune cookie thought, though, which is this:

FOOT: A DEVICE FOR FINDING FURNITURE IN THE DARK.

You can't make these things up.

12/1, 4:16 p.m.

Dear Callie,

What do you mean, I made you sound like a nut job to Beryl, implying that your body is being inhabited by an alien? I'm quite sure he doesn't really think you seriously have been abducted by aliens. It was just a figure of speech, like, "Oh, she's just little Miss Sunshine" or "What a clown." When you use expressions like that (which I totally never do), it doesn't mean a person is really an inhumanly hot solar ball or that they're a member of the circus. It's not literal.

As far as the other part, yes, I know you feel bad that you hurt my feelings and that you're not trying to leave me behind. I know that "you just want to experience new and interesting things."

What better place to do that but in New York City, where new and interesting things happen every day? Why, just the other day Mr. Lee said he was adding an unusual Mandarin shrimp dish to his menu and he was going to make it super spicy! That's new! And what about my friendship with Beryl, a religious kid?! That's a really new thing! You could be experiencing new things all day long with me (your best friend), Judy and Claire (your weird friends), and even John Leibler (my imaginary friend).

And speaking of John Leibler, I was so mortified by my last encounter with him that I'm intent on avoiding him at all costs. Normally, this wouldn't be a problem because he doesn't really know I exist anyway, but it might be harder in English and social studies for obvious reasons. Yesterday, in social studies, I sat in the back next to Judy and spent those free moments before class started chatting her up about the "thread arts" until my eyes glazed over.

But today I had a wee problem.

So, I'm bustling down the classroom aisle, passing the brainiacs, the cool kids, making my way back to the "thread arts" section of the room, and I'm all relieved because John isn't even there yet, when I hear none other than Horrible Susan call out (what she thinks) is my name.

"Annie!"

That's me, in case you didn't know.

"It's Amy," I say, stopping in front of her desk.

"Oh yeah, right. Amy, so how's your little immigrant journal thing going? This assignment must be so way fun for someone like you."

"It's going fine," I say and keep walking.

Then she's like, "Your boyfriend is totally cute. Oh, by the way, John told me you guys went to Coney Island. I know because we were supposed to go to the movies that day," she says with just the slightest edge in her voice.

And I'm thinking, great, now I'm on Horrible Susan's bad side. What else could go wrong?

"Amy has a boyfriend?" Horrible's best friend, Miranda, pipes in, but with a tone like it's the most astonishing thing she's ever heard.

"Oh, yeah, and he's cute," says Susan. "Except he's very religious looking, you know, like the ones who go to that school on 82nd Street. What's his name again, Amy? Bertok? Berlie?"

"Oh my God," exclaims Miranda. "One of those kids in black? They don't go out or have fun or do . . . anything, right?

"Trust me, Susan," I say, shooting them both dagger looks. "Beryl is not my boyfriend. And, by the way, John and I had an awesome time at Coney Island."

And, yes, I really did say that!! Score one for the dorky girl!

So then Horrible gets this twisted expression on her face, "harrumphs," and swings back around in her seat.

Of course, I'm totally sure she's out to get me now, but what difference does it make? What's she gonna do? Ignore me more?

At that moment the bell rings, John Leibler glides in on cue and sits down next to Horrible Susan, putting her back in her usual phony cheery mood.

I plop down next to Judy, who is not only oblivious to the whole scenario, but immediately whips out her cloth ruler and starts measuring my arms. Apparently, her mother has forbidden her to knit herself another sweater, so she is circumventing the mandate by making sweaters for all her friends. And seeing as how I'm getting even more of the big social freeze out than usual, I'm gonna need it.

Amy

*D*ear Callie,

I haven't heard from you lately. Hope all is well in the heartland, and you haven't been swept away by a snow drift. Feels weird to not get the latest on Buckyliscious and the other dog people. Seriously, pardner, I'm waiting to hear from you.

Anyway, Beryl e-mailed me back almost immediately, and it seems that he's gotten the green light from the powers that be. So now I am officially a "mitzvah project." You can call me M.P. for short. We met today after school.

I have been to visit Miss Sophia a few times, and she is recuperating but still has a nasty cough, so the doctor wants her to keep laying low for a while. She's made me promise to report back all information to her.

So, here's the latest in the saga. Ironically, it's an early dismissal day for both me and Beryl, so I meet him at Starbucks with an eager determination and an empty bladder. He finds the largest table in the place for just the two of us.

I shuffle in and sit down, but before long, I sense that there's a strange awkwardness between us. It seems that the camaraderie we had established a few days ago, laughing and crying and fighting, has left us both a little shy to be alone with each other. I couldn't help but wish that Miss Sophia was with us.

"Hey, Beryl," I say.

"Hello, Amy," he says.

"How are you doing?"

"I'm fine, thank God. And you?"

"Fine."

"Good."

"So."

"Well."

Then the moments tick by like hours until I break the ice.

"I guess we should look at the latest journal installment," I suggest, rummaging through my backpack. "I haven't read it myself yet."

"Oh, yes," he says, reaching for the copy I e-mailed to him.

"Let's do it," I say.

Then I get all embarrassed that maybe "let's do it" sounds lewd or something and I'm like, "I mean let's look at the journal."

"I know what you mean," Beryl says.

"You do?" I exclaim. "Why Beryl, that's amazing. We're actually communicating?! We should celebrate. Oh, Barista!" I pretend to call out. "A round of cocoas for the house. Make them ventis!"

Then Beryl chuckles, and at least the ice is broken.

"Okay," I say and start to read from Anna's journal:

"Today I went to the most beautiful of places, the Metropolitan Museum of Art! I saw a painting by a woman artist, who is very famous American who lived in France, who likes to paint women with children. But this painting is different. It is one of a woman attending a special task! It made me think of our family secret . . ."

"And the Met's only a few blocks from here. Come on, let's go."

I drain the last of my cocoa, secure my little pea hat, and we head off to Fifth Avenue and start walking uptown.

The thing that makes this supernaturally coincidental is that one of my favorite books just happens to be *From the Mixed-up Files of Mrs. Basil E. Frankweiler!*"

Beryl shrugs.

"Mixed-up Files . . . ? The Metropolitan Museum?"

He shakes his head and shrugs again.

"Anyway, I love the Metropolitan Museum, don't you?" I say, as we start walking uptown.

Beryl nods, but avoids eye contact and nervously starts twisting his fringe thingies again. And then it hits me.

"You've never been to the Metropolitan Museum, have you?"

"No," Beryl answers.

"Oh," I say. "Well, are you allowed to see art?"

"Well, I can't see that it would be a problem," he replies.

But at that moment, I'm imagining all those nude statues and nude paintings, magically springing to life, and upon seeing Beryl, running frantically through the halls, like, bumping into each other in a desperate search for clothing.

And of course, since Beryl is the Jewish George Washington who refuses to tell a lie, I could just envision how he would explain it all to his parents when he got home. To commemorate that event, I've written a short play entitled:

BERYL PLOTSKY'S EXCELLENT ADVENTURE

(A play in a few pages by Amy Finawitz)

WE FADE INTO: The PLOTSKY dining room. They are having Shabbat dinner. They are all sitting at the super-long dinner table, along with all the "CH–CH" CHILDREN and a variety of friends and relatives. MRS. PLOTSKY is passing soup around the table.

MRS. PLOTSKY
So Beryl, where did the assignment with that pathetic mitzvah project/potential daughter-in-law, lead you today?

BERYL
We went to the Metropolitan Museum of Art.

RABBI
Oh, that's very interesting Beryl. I've always been meaning to go there. What did you see?

BERYL
Oh, lots of beautiful art: magnificently carved statues, relics from ancient civilizations, and some of the world's most expressive and luminous paintings.

                    MRS. PLOTSKY
Why, Beryl. That's lovely . . .

                       BERYL
And lots and lots of naked people.

                RABBI and MRS. PLOTSKY
Sputter, cough, sputter . . . WHAT??!!

We hear the sound of loud CLANKING and CRASHING as
spoons drop into bowls and bowls crash to the floor. The
"CH-CH " children nearly faint from giggling.

                       BERYL
That's right. And different kinds of naked people too.
There were fat naked people and skinny naked people,
naked people standing up, naked people in repose,
naked people dancing and playing instruments, naked
people with animals, naked people . . .

A few of the GUESTS GASP loudly. MRS. PLOTSKY falls over on
the long dinner table into a dead swoon. RABBI PLOTSKY is so
mortified that he is completely unaware of the hot soup that
he has ladled into his lap.

                       BERYL
Yeah, it was excellent. Oh, by the way, they're having a
totally rockin' exhibit next month: nudes in photogra-
phy. Can I go?

WE FADE TO BLACK.

                     THE END

After a few blocks, I see the majestic museum looming before us. The enormous flags announcing the latest exhibits billow in the wind.

We make our way to the bottom of the million steps up to the front door and weave around all the people lounging on them. We shuffle through the doors, like Alice climbing into the tiny rabbit hole. Then—bam! We bounce into that cavernous room, so busy and alive with the buzzing echoes of dozens of voices, a cacophony of accents and the vibration of thousands of shoes tapping along the polished floor.

I observe Beryl out of the corner of my eye, scanning the place, trying to make sense of it.

"It's like Grand Central Station," he says, making the best comparison he can.

"You see, in the book, *From the Mixed-up Files of Mrs. Basil E. Frankweiler*," I say, "this brother and sister run away to the Metropolitan Museum and live there for about a week, and the girl doesn't want to go home until they find the answer to a secret mystery. Callie and I used to talk about how cool that would be."

"How can you run away to the museum?" Beryl asks.

"Well, think about it. There are plenty of places to hide. There are beds, bathrooms, a cafeteria . . ."

"I don't understand. You wanted to live in the museum?"

"Not live there forever or anything. Just stay for a few days," I say.

"You wanted to vacation in the museum?"

"Not vacation really. Just, like, hide for a while, to teach the grownups a lesson . . . about taking us for granted."

"You wanted to punish your parents by hiding in the museum?"

"Not punish really, just . . . we thought it would be fun. The kids in the book had fun."

"You wanted to be like characters in a book?"

"Oh, forget it," I groan.

"All right," Beryl says nervously, glancing at his watch. "But I have to be home by sundown for Shabbat."

"Oh, okay," I say.

I had completely forgotten that it was Friday and this evening was Shabbat. So, Beryl and I collect our museum buttons and ascend the grand staircase.

"We're looking for a painting by a woman who usually paints women and children," I say. "But this painting is of a woman alone who's doing something in the painting."

"Yes, attending to a task," Beryl says.

"Listen, Beryl," I stop and turn to him, realizing I can't avoid this any longer. "You do realize that there are a lot of paintings and statues of nude people in the museum."

"Yes," he says, solemnly nodding his head in a perfunctory way. "I anticipated that."

"And you're okay with it?"

"Of course. It's art, and art is a spiritual manifestation of the creative aspect of the soul."

"Okay," I take a deep breath. "If you say so."

So we begin our journey through the paintings, breezing through the Impressionists, the Romantics, the American paintings, the European paintings.

I try to scramble quickly by the pictures with explicit nudity, however. And when Beryl isn't looking, I pop ahead around corners to make sure we aren't heading into a room with really big nudes.

But, surprisingly, Beryl took most of the art in his stride. He kept his eyes moving along and, only once or twice, I saw them linger over some naked picture, causing the slightest red to crawl into his cheeks. I suspect that Beryl kept telling himself that we were on a mission, and that he was responsible for me, his pathetic mitzvah project/loser.

Finally, I find an empty bench in the Modern Art section, a room I deem as "safely modest" because most of the art is just a series of colorful blobs, splatters, and lines.

"I don't see our painting yet," he says.

At this point, it's getting late, we're tired, and the countdown to Shabbat is hanging over our heads.

"Beryl, this museum is just too damned huge. Oh sorry, should I say darn?"

"It's all right, Amy," he says. "I'm not offended by your swearing."

"I mean, we need some help. Finding one particular painting without even knowing the artist's name is like finding a needle in a haystack."

And by that time, I was wishing that I had worn sneakers instead of my cool Himalayan boots, which were anything but cool, as my feet were completely roasting off my ankles. And speaking of roasting, I was starting to get hungry.

Then Beryl turns to me, looking all anxious and kinda hungry himself, and he's like, "It is getting late, Amy, and I have to be home for Shabbat. Why don't we just come back another day?"

"Look, Beryl, I know Shabbat is important to you. Your family gathers around and you eat awesome food and thank God and it's all comforting and happy. Seriously, I get it. I'm not making fun of you."

"I know that, but I still have to be home for Shabbat," he persists.

"But Beryl, we're in one of the most famous museums in the world, and you want to rush out," I wheedle, trying to keep the mood light. "Aren't you enjoying the beautiful art?"

I gesture to all the white canvases smattered with dots and blobs.

"Yes, of course . . . but I have to be home for Shabbat."

"Well . . . Beryl . . . I thought we'd been through this. I need to finish this assignment soon, so I can visit Callie and . . ."

"Amy," he interrupts, with maddening calm. "Did it ever occur to you that God has another plan in store for you and your friend? Maybe she was meant to stay in Kansas for a while, and you were meant to stay here?"

"No. That didn't occur to me. I have to help her because I am the voice of reason," I screech. "And she is mentally insane!"

"That may be so," he says evenly. "But I have to be home for . . ."

Then I grab his arm and pull him into an unpopulated corner next to some idiotic painting of, like, a hundred Campbell soup cans in a row and I say, "Beryl, we need to find a woman artist who paints pictures of women and children. And what happens if you're not home in time for Shabbat? What happens if Shabbat starts at about 4:30 and you're home at 4:35 or something?"

I'm completely out of line, but I just can't stop myself. And a few people stare and then scurry by us as my voice gets squeakier and squeakier.

"Will God come down and smite you? Geez, Beryl, my family rarely celebrates Shabbat and when we do, I'm sure we do it wrong. But God doesn't hate me . . . well, maybe he doesn't like me that much, but I don't think it's because I don't celebrate Shabbat. Look, do you really think that, with all the crap in this world, God cares if you're twenty freakin' minutes late for Shabbat?!"

And then Beryl just stares at me, all red, his eyes buggering out in a shocked and unattractive way, and I'm breathing fast and my face is all hot. And I'm thinking, holy crap, what did I say? Beryl is gonna have a stroke and die, and I'm gonna have to explain why.

I hang my head and let out a long breath.

"Look, Beryl. I'm sor . . ." I start.

But before I can finish, some happy, birdy-looking older woman comes by.

"Excuse me," she chirps.

We both turn to her, and she's like, "Excuse me, I couldn't help but overhear."

And I'm thinking, oh great, now this bird lady is gonna lecture me about screeching in the museum or about being disrespectful to God and poor Beryl. But instead she says,

"You're looking for a woman artist? Who primarily paints women and children?"

"Uh, yes, that's right," I reply.

"Well, that's Mary Cassatt."

"Mary Cassatt?" I repeat. That name sounded vaguely familiar.

"Yes. She did lovely work. Sometimes the museum has one or two of her paintings," Birdy Lady says, leafing through the little catalogue she's holding, "Ah, here. You're in luck."

"The paintings are here?!" I exclaim.

"I'll show you," she says sweetly. "It's right this way. You must have passed her work and didn't even know it."

So we all backtrack a few rooms, Beryl staying as far away from me as he can.

"Wait, I think this is it!" I exclaim.

And sure enough, there it was, a painting of a woman alone, sitting at a desk. There was a letter in front of her, and she was licking an envelope.

"Oh yes," says Bird Lady. "That painting's called, *The Letter*."

I take in as much of the picture as I can and quickly jot down some information in case we need further reference. Then we rush downstairs toward the exit.

Once out the main entrance doors, we thank Bird Lady and bid her goodbye. Within seconds, Beryl and I are once again unchaperoned.

"Well, maybe God's not so pissed at me after all," I say. "He temporarily eliminated Miss Sophia from our investigation, but sent us her doppelganger instead."

"Her what?" Beryl glares at me.

"Her doppelganger. Her otherworldly double."

"Why would God send an otherworldly double to the museum?" he asks.

"Oh forget it." I sigh.

We head down the steps toward the street and scramble to pull on gloves and hats. The sidewalks are packed up with people doing their "going home shuffle." Horns blare as traffic starts backing up.

It had to be at least close to 4:45 and, even if Beryl

caught the fastest cab in the world, he would surely be late for Shabbat.

"So," I say, "what do you think Anna is trying to tell us? Are we supposed to know who the woman is, or are we supposed to discover who she was writing to, or maybe we're supposed to discover what she's writing about."

"Amy, sometimes the point is right in front of your eyes, and you don't see it."

"What do you mean?" I ask.

"The letter. Don't you see? Anna must have hidden away a very important letter."

"You're right," I say. "A letter. But where could it be? How do you hide a letter for a hundred years, and how can we find it? And how is a letter a secret treasure, anyway? It had better be a damned important letter after all this."

"I need to go now, Amy," Beryl says.

"Oh, yeah," I feel myself blush. "I'm keeping you from . . ."

But then I'm too ashamed to actually say the word Shabbat.

"Well, see you next time," I mutter, but as the words are leaving my mouth, I get a premonition that next time will be a long time coming.

Then Beryl's hand is up and he's hailing a cab. Within seconds, one screeches to the corner. He opens the door, but still hasn't said a word.

"So, see you later?" I ask, more than say.

He turns around. He doesn't look angry anymore. Instead, he looks pale and small and lonely in his thick black coat, and I think I see just the slightest tinge of hurt flash across his eyes. And I feel bad. Then he gets into the cab, closes the door, and disappears into the night.

And so, Cal, it's the end of another day. I still have not heard from you. Does everyone hate me now?

Amy

12/4, 9:39 p.m.

*D*ear Callie,

What do you mean, you've given it a lot of thought and you're disappointed that I'm being so insensitive? Have you and Beryl been e-mailing each other behind my back?

Amy

12/4, 9:45 p.m.

I'M selfish?! You're the one who's selfish! Did it ever occur to you that I am actually being a super good friend by pointing out that the choices you're making are stupid? Best friends know their friends best. That's why they're called best friends!

12/4, 10:00 p.m.

Excuse me, you're forgetting one important thing here! I'm the one who's been abandoned. I'm the one who has to go to school alone, to confirmation class alone, to hang out with dorks alone. I'm the one who has to eat Chinese food alone. You're the selfish one, not me!!

12/4, 10:11 p.m.

Fine. Whatever you say. If you hate me so much, why do you even care what I think? And by the way, you've gotten

268

me so worked up, I'm, like, feeling totally nauseous. Are you happy now?!

12/4, 10:17 p.m.

No, I didn't eat too much crispy orange flavor beef. And no, I don't always eat that when I'm upset. For your information, I just had a nice bowl of wonton soup, which is very light. I'm nauseous because you've upset me. Now I'm going to have to drink that chalky, white, bubbly stuff that makes me want to hurl. God, you are so thoughtless!!

*D*ear *Callie,*

Yes, I got your e-mail about your being upset with me about not understanding your dilemma of whether to stay in Kansas. But exactly how am I making things difficult for you? I am not asking you to chose between Bucky and me (or even the organic earth and me). If you still do "heart" New York and really want to come home, then why are you letting pet/boy keep you on a leash? Just who is the pet in this relationship? And let's face it, there are plenty of vegetables that are more than happy to grow in New York soil.

Look, let's not fight. You know how hard it is for me to stay angry. How about this? From now on, I'll try and think more positively. Don't laugh, it's true. This entire change of perspective is based on a recent fortune cookie. It read:

THE WORLD WILL CHANGE IF YOU THINK POSITIVELY.

And so I shall.

Well, now, I'm off to school where I continue to try and avoid all contact with people. Wish me luck.

Amy

Dear Callie,

Well, I have officially decided to abandon my resolution to think positively. For one thing, it's way too hard. And another, I am a negative, sarcastic person by nature. According to Kevin, these are two very hard personality characteristics to overcome without years of therapy, and even then the success rate is dismal.

I imagine that, on this point, he's probably right.

Anyway, Judy was very excited about my "date" with John Leibler, you know, Coney Island forever ago. So much so, that she already started crocheting a sweater for her delusional fantasy date with John's friend, Mark. I had to break the news to her that a setup with Mark was about as unlikely as Christmas in July, and the news rendered her sullen and odd. During lunch, she stared at Mark with a hangdog expression, and scarfed down two plates of potato logs, a large slice of Sicilian pizza, chips, a shake, and a Hostess snowball, complaining all the while that she'd lost her appetite entirely.

As for John Leibler, I continue to avoid him like the plague. My routine of getting to social studies early and

271

leaving late has been successful and, in the cafeteria, I keep my head in a book as much as possible. It is remarkably distressing how few people notice that I've made myself inaccessible. Even Horrible Susan is ignoring me now, more than usual.

12/8, 6:20 p.m.

*D*ear Callie,

What do you mean I'll never change? What do you mean I don't understand you anymore and that makes you sad? What, are we, like, not friends now?

Amy

12/8, 7:10 p.m.

Cal? Are you there? You can't be serious. You're just gonna shut me out?
Fine. Whatever.

12/8, 8:52 p.m.

You gonna write back, or what?

Dear Callie,

Okay, I give. I've been doing a lot of thinking these last few days and in the spirit of the coming holidays, plus the latest fortune cookie which says: Life without a best friend is like moo shu pork without that tart, black, gunky sauce, I've decided to re-evaluate my attitude and try to unclog my inner chi. I've even written you a play entitled:

FRANKEN-AMY

(A scary, but uplifting story of transformation
in one act by Amy Finawitz)

SCENE: A dark, gloomy laboratory (pronounced "la–bore-a-tory") with dusty tables and cobwebbed corners. All around are bubbling test tubes and cauldrons filled with smelly liquids puffing out white fog. A storm rages outside.

As we begin, AMY FINAWITZ, our heroine, is being dragged across the "la-bore-a-tory" by a hunched boy who bears a strong resemblance to the pimply faced attendant at Coney Island. AMY kicks and bites, but he overpowers her, mostly with his breath, and straps her into the electric chair.

274

                    PIMPLY BOY
    (with great sarcasm)
    Comfy?

                       AMY
    I'm so gonna get you fired.

                    PIMPLY BOY
    Good luck. My uncle owns this place.

Suddenly, a MAN in a white coat, who bears a striking resemblance to Mr. Klein from 8B, approaches her.

                       AMY
    Mr. Klein? Don't kill me. I swear I'll stay out of the elevator, even if I have to walk the twenty flights of stairs.

With a malevolent expression, the MAN shakes his head no and gestures to his lapel, which reads IRVING FRANKENSTEIN.

                       AMY
    You're Irving Frankenstein? Hey, haven't I seen you on the Temple Beth Shalom confirmation class wall of fame?

                      IRVING
    (defensively)
    Err . . . no. That must have been my brother, Neal. Neal Frankenstein. He's a dermatologist.

                       AMY
    And what are you?

                      IRVING
    A respected scientist, of course.

                       275

AMY
(unconvinced)
Uh-huh . . . Hey, listen, you're not gonna hurt me, are you?

IRVING
Hurt you? Of course not. I'm going to help you. First, I'm going to kill you, then I'll use the electromagnetic currents from this lightning-sensitive hat here to unclog your inner chi so that you become a more loving and understanding person. Then, if we have time, I'll bring you back to life.

AMY gasps in horror.

IRVING
Don't be alarmed. It's a common outpatient procedure.

AMY
I'll scream and my family and friends will come and rescue me.

IRVING
(raising his eyebrows)
Your family? Are you serious? They probably don't even know you're gone, no offense.

IRVING throws back his head and laughs, a long maniacal, disturbing laugh. PIMPLY BOY joins in and they both laugh for, like, fifteen minutes.

AMY
All right already. I get it.

276

IRVING

My dear girl. Don't you see? You don't have any
friends anymore.

AMY

Yes, I do.

IRVING

No, you don't.

AMY

Yes, I do.

IRVING

No, you don't.

AMY

No, I don't.

IRVING

Yes, you do.

AMY

Ha!

IRVING

Enough! You vile girl! Can't you get it through your
head! No one likes you. You're selfish, insensitive. You
don't consider other people's wants or needs. Pimply
faced nephew, bring me the electromagnetic, electron
changing ionizing coil distributor!

PIMPLY BOY

Huh?

277

IRVING

(exasperated)
The plug.

PIMPLY BOY

Oh.

PIMPLY BOY drags the plug over to IRVING, who attaches one end to the metal hat that hangs over her chair and the other to an outlet marked "lightning bolt." AMY struggles as he secures the hat onto her head. He flicks the lightning bolt switch.

LOUD, CRACKING THUNDER fills the room. BOLTS of lightning shoot from the open ceiling, down the wire, into the hat, and through AMY'S vibrating head.

IRVING

(laughing and screaming like the nut he is)
It's alive! It's alive!

He throws the switch off and removes the metal hat from AMY'S head. AMY takes a moment to regain her composure and flatten out her hair.

AMY

Just barely alive, you . . . You . . .

AMY is furious and struggles to insult them, but cannot get the words out. IRVING clasps his hands together in glee.

Suddenly, a dozen little bluebirds swoop down from the ceiling and encircle AMY'S head, singing a pleasant, tweety song. AMY turns and smiles compassionately at IRVING.

                    AMY

Why, you poor misunderstood man. You can't help it if
you were raised by parents who mocked your weird
ways and were rejected by the kids at school for being
a psycho. You can't help that.

                    IRVING
(whining)
No, I can't.

                    AMY

You just want to be loved. That incident with the cat
was an accident, as was that unfortunate experiment
with Grandma.

IRVING sobs loudly now.

                    IRVING

Yes! Yes!

                    AMY

And you, pimply faced boy. DNA helix formations are
very complicated. You can't help it if your spirals
twist in the wrong direction. You both have a friend
in me.

PIMPLY FACED BOY stops examining his ear wax and sobs into
his sleeve.

            IRVING and PIMPLY FACED BOY
You like us! You really, really like us! And we like you
too!

                          AMY
Yeah, so could you, like, release me from bondage
now?

                         IRVING
Oh sure.

IRVING unstraps her. She places her hand to her chest.

                          AMY
My inner chi . . . I feel it opening in my chest,
warm and fuzzy, like a piece of blue sky pulsating beneath my thorax. I feel like I actually sort of understand my friends now. For example, maybe Beryl likes
to be religious. Maybe it gives him peace and happi-
ness.

AMY pirouettes around the room, knocking over most of the
apparatus and igniting the window shutters in the process.

                      AMY (cont.)
And now I really understand my best friend, Callie.
I know now that she needs room to explore different parts of her personality and her neshama. She's
discovered that she likes the great outdoors. She
likes meeting new and exotic, half-human people. She
feels strongly about environmental issues, and when
she sees organically grown vegetation, she yearns to
pick it.

IRVING and PIMPLY FACED BOY join the pirouette.

                      AMY (cont.)
I must go now and show off my new, unclogged chi.

                          280

Goodbye for now, and thank you for not electrocuting me!

PIMPLY BOY blow-torches the door open. AMY dances through, into the damp, moonlit night.

THE END

So anyway, if you haven't figured it out, that was my demented way of saying sorry. I guess "best friend" doesn't actually mean that I know what's best for you. I guess it probably means I should have your best interests at heart.

And there's something else too. While I'm having these *Oprah* moments of self-exploration and spiritual enlightenment, I've realized that I've spent much of my life being just a tad insensitive. So, just maybe, unlike that poor emu from the PBS documentary, my life is not just a random journey that will end with being devoured by dingoes. Perhaps I am being divinely directed in my quest to turn from change into a dollar.

And I hope you save this e-mail because I will never again in my life be so free about expressing my feelings (unless, of course, it's bitter disillusionment).

Amy

12/11, 11:32 p.m.

So, we're good?

Okay, enough corny stuff already. It's time to get moving! To take the bull by the horns! To move onward and upward! To get cracking! (Having said all that, I'm tired and I'm going to bed. More tomorrow.)

Dear Callie,

Well, my premonition about Beryl was right. GOR (geeky girl, old lady, and religious kid research agency) was alarmingly close to becoming GO. And GO was even closer to becoming G.

Here's what happened:

The week was rolling to an end and I hadn't heard from Miss Sophia or Beryl. I was actually starting to miss Miss Sophia and her inane questions.

I started to get a little worried and e-mailed Beryl. Here's what I wrote:

Hi, Beryl, it's Amy. I was wondering if you know where your aunt is. I hope she's okay. I also hope you're okay. (And then I'm still feeling guilty, and I'm trying to be all light and everything, hoping he still isn't pissed and so I add,) Hope everything worked out with Shabbat the other night and your parents weren't too angry that you were late. Totally awesome deduction at the museum, by the way. We should call you 'Sherlock' Plotsky—ha ha!

Anyway, please write back soon!

283

(Then I put one of those obnoxious smiley faces on the bottom that I hate so much.)

See ya soon! ☺ Amy."

Not surprisingly, I didn't receive a response. In the end, nobody likes a kiss ass, especially not someone like Beryl, who, unlike me, would never stoop so low as to be one.

So finally, I ask Lou if he'd been shopping for Miss Sophia lately and if he knew if she and her cats were okay. He says loudly so as to be overheard by any tenants walking by, "You must be mistaken, Amy. I don't shop for the tenants or care for their pets. That would be inappropriate, even if that person, privately, gave me a large holiday gratuity."

And then I roll my eyes and am like, "Okay . . . well, have you seen her, even though I know you weren't making inappropriate shopping deliveries for secret large gratuities."

Then he continues to ignore me.

"Happy holidays," he repeats, while opening the doors for all the grownups. Talk about a kiss ass.

Then finally, I'm like, okay, don't answer me, and I start to walk away. But then he calls me back. "Wait, Amy. I just remembered."

He opens his little desk drawer and pulls out an envelope. It's addressed to me:

Dear Amy,

I am feeling much better, so I am going to Florida for a few days to visit my youngest son. I hope you aren't worried about me. I asked Lou to let you know where I am going.

I will be coming back on Friday and have been invited to Moishe's home for Shabbat dinner. Chaya has asked for you specifically, and all the Plotskys are hoping you can join us. Meet me in the lobby at 4:00 and we can take a cab uptown together.

Miss Sophia

PS: Dress warmly and use the bathroom. Traffic is heavy at that time of the evening.

I can't help but groan out loud. Talk about divine retribution. I dissed Beryl and Shabbat, now I'd have to partake in a Shabbat/interview for potential daughter-in-law ceremony myself.

So, on Friday afternoon I meet Miss Sophia in the lobby. She's looking smart in a plaid coat ensemble, white, with black, red, and blue checks to be precise, a matching French beret, red leather gloves, and a red vinyl purse and boots. Overall, I'm thinking she fairs a solid nine and a half out of ten on the Lord & Taylor best dressed older ladies list. She would have scored a ten, but I would have gone for the blue leather gloves. I'm just saying.

I think I was looking pretty smart for a change too. I

dug out the black skirt I wear for chorus concerts from the back of the closet and paired it with a white fuzzy sweater. I wore my black boots with the stumpy heel for the klutzy fashionista. Then I topped it off with my brown parka and snug pea hat that makes my hair look like it's been pressed in cellophane.

We head out into the street, she yoo-hoos a cab, and we climb in. Loud holiday music blares from the cabbie's radio.

"Where to, girls?" asks the cabbie.

Girls. It cracks me up when men say that to flatter women who clearly haven't been girls for, like, a hundred years.

"Washington Heights. 160th Street, please," Miss Sophia says. "My you've gotten bigger since I last saw you, Amy," says Miss Sophia leaning back in her seat, giving me the once over.

I just sigh and reflexively pull the buttons of my coat snugger across my boobs.

"How is your little friend?" she asks.

"I'm planning to visit her soon," I reply.

Miss Sophia nods and pats my knee.

"It will be good for you to get out some more, Amy," she winks.

Again with the getting out. Remind me to tell my mother to stop telling the whole building that I'm this pathetic shut-in.

"Don't worry, Amy. I'm not insulting you. It's good for

286

everyone to get out and mix it up sometimes, especially those of us who are a little stuck in the past," she says, presumably referring to herself this time . . . I think.

Then she changes gears and is like, "Oh, cabbie, can you turn that music up?"

"Sure thing, hon," he says.

Hon. That's even funnier than girls.

"It's so cheery, isn't it?" she says, leaning back and humming merrily along with all the Christmas tunes.

"You and your grandmother goin' to a Christmas pardy?" he asks.

"Yup," I say.

You know how we always just go along with cabbie conversation for two reasons:

(a) It's easier.

(b) We've both spun quite interesting lives by just following a cabbie's assumptions.

"Oh, this big, young lady isn't my granddaughter," chuckles Miss Sophia.

"No?" he says, squinting into the rearview mirror. "She looks just like ya. Got your eyes."

Of course. Mine are brown and almond shaped and hers are azure blue and round. Perfect sense. And that's another reason why I never argue with cabbies.

"Oh, no. Amy is my neighbor," corrects Miss Sophia. "And we're going to a Shabbat dinner at my brother's house. Do you know what that is . . . um, Tony?" she says, peering over at his ID that's taped to the dashboard.

"Shabbat? That's like the day 'a rest and prayer, for Jews, right?"

"Yes, that's right," Miss Sophia replies pleasantly. Then Miss Sophia launches into this long story about Judaism, and I feel like I'm back in Miss Goldstein's class, wishing I had a copy of *Hip and Hebrew* to doodle in.

So, finally, after Miss Sophia and Tony become good chums, agreeing that despite our religious differences, in the end we're all just people, we disembark from the brotherhood mobile and arrive at Beryl's house.

Mrs. Plotsky opens the front door, and I'm immediately hit with a wave of warm air and delectable smells.

"Shabbat shalom, everyone!" Mrs. Plotsky greets us.

"Shabbat shalom, Chaya," Miss Sophia says, hugging Mrs. Plotsky.

"Hi, Mrs. Plotsky. How are you?" I ask.

"Fine, thank God. And you?"

"I'm okay, I guess," I say.

"Chana, take their coats, please," she instructs her.

Then she turns to us and says, "Come in, please. What a cold night. You must be freezing."

So we pass through the entranceway, and I peer anxiously into the long table room on my right, already set with terrines of food. The bookshelves that line the walls are alight with candles of different sizes and shapes.

"Sophia, I know that you and Beryl and Amy will probably want to talk before Shabbat. Why don't you settle in the parlor," Mrs. Plotsky says.

Suddenly, terror grips my heart as I imagine sidestepping between the table and the bookshelf toward the parlor. I'm envisioning myself shaking the table so badly that all the food slops out of its bowls and I fall back into the bookshelf, setting my hair and sweater on fire in the process.

But before I can move, Mrs. Plotsky directs us to another room on the other side of the entranceway, avoiding the long table room all together. And, why, I wonder, couldn't Beryl and I have sat in this room the last time I was here?

So we go in and there's Beryl, his back to us, looking slim and ghostly in his starched white shirt, plinking out the same few notes over and over on a small upright piano in the corner.

I'm going to visit the ladies' room. I'll be right back, children. The latest journal entry that you e-mailed me is in my purse. Why don't you take it out and get started?" Miss Sophia says.

Then she disappears around the corner, and it's, like, all awkward. Beryl glances over at me and then turns back around to the piano again.

"Hi, Beryl," I say. "What's up?"

"I'm fine, thank God," he says.

"I figured as much," I say, sitting down.

Then he plays plink, plink, plink on the piano.

"So . . . um . . . listen. I get the feeling you're mad at me," I say.

"I'm not mad at you," he replies, turning to me.

"Well, great. I'm relieved to hear that. So let's get started then, okay?" I say, picking up Miss Sophia's red vinyl purse.

I try the clasp but, what a surprise, it's locked tight. I turn it over a few times, trying to determine the best way to break into it.

"I am a little disappointed, though," Beryl says softly, continuing to plink on the piano.

"Disappointed?" I echo. " 'Cause I made you late for Shabbat last week? Look, I'm sorry about that."

"It's not really that. Never mind," he sulks.

"Uh . . . okay," I reply, preoccupied with trying to un-clasp Miss Sophia's inscrutable purse. "What is this, glued closed or something?" I start shaking the purse upside down.

"Don't you want to know why I'm disappointed?" Beryl asks sullenly.

And I'm thinking how rude would it be to say, "Uh . . . not particularly," so instead I say, "I don't know, Beryl. I can't read your mind."

Then he sighs and shrugs.

Plink, plink, plink, he continues.

I fish a paperclip and a pencil out of my backpack and try to open the purse surgically.

"You think she has a secret code to open this thing or something?" I ponder.

I put the purse on the coffee table and wave my pencil.

"Wingardium Leviosa!"

No response.

Plink, plink, plink goes the piano.

"Get it, Harry Potter? Wingardium Leviosa? Did you read . . . ? Never mind. Do you have a pliers?"

Plink, plink, plink.

And then I start tapping the pocketbook clasp gently against the table.

Plink, plink, plink . . . Plink, plink, plink, plink, plink, plink . . .

I'm hitting the purse against the table to the rhythm of plink, plink, plink.

"Beryl, don't you know any songs?" I finally exclaim. "Even 'It's a Small World' would be better than plink, plink, plink."

Then he pauses for a moment, and I think he's gonna say something . . .

Plink, plink, plink.

"All right, all right, I give! Why are you disappointed?!" I shout, slamming the purse hard against the table.

I hear footsteps. Mrs. Plotsky pokes her head in. "Are you children all right?" she asks, looking anxiously from me to Beryl.

So then I'm all smiley and say, "We're fine, Mrs. Plotsky . . . um . . . thank God."

So she smiles broadly, and I'm imagining her envisioning me in Grandma Plotsky's wedding veil. "Good," she says, and disappears around the corner.

I stand by Beryl.

"Okay," I sigh. "Why are you disappointed?"

He raises his finger, poised for plink, plink, plink, and I place my hand menacingly on the piano lid.

"Don't even think about it," I warn.

"Well if you must know, I'm disappointed with how you think of me," he says. "I know how you must see me. It's pretty much how everyone sees me."

He had me there.

"You mean people see you as someone who's religious? Well, Beryl, you kinda are," I say.

"Yes, I am, but not like you think. It's not like all I do is follow old-fashioned rules. I have interests."

I hide my grin. "Like what? Wait, don't tell me, let me guess. You like plinking on the piano."

"Very funny," he says.

"No, really. Like what?" I repeat, suddenly pretty curious.

"I like music," he says.

"Yeah, I can see what. What's your favorite tune? The plink, plink sonata?"

So he shoots me this almost-dirty look. "No, I like regular music. Contemporary music," he says.

"Really?"

Now he's totally piqued my interest. What could he mean by contemporary?

"I like the Beatles," he says.

I had to hide my grin again. At least he didn't say Beethoven. "Well, that's mighty interesting, Beryl," I say.

"You think that's stupid," he responds, suddenly defensive and churlish.

"No, I don't. Really. I like the Beatles too. But, do you know any more recent music, like do you listen to the radio or watch TV?" I ask.

"Not too often," he says offhandedly.

"Are you allowed to listen to the radio or watch TV?" I pry.

"I'm allowed to do what I want," he says defiantly.

"Really?"

"This isn't Siberia. I'm not in exile, ya know."

"Okay. Don't get huffy."

"But it's not encouraged," he admits. "It's not really considered a higher spiritual pursuit."

"Yeah, my parents don't think so either," I say.

"They don't?" he brightens.

"Look, Beryl, most parents don't want their kids watching TV all day."

"Oh," he says, thoughtfully, as if he's just learned something revolutionary.

"But seriously, Beryl, what brought this on? I thought it didn't bother you how other people see you."

"It doesn't bother me how other people see me," he glances shyly sideways at me in what seems like a mildly flirtatious way.

Uh-oh. This wasn't going in a good direction.

He turns back to the piano. Plink, plink, plink, he starts.

"Sorry, nervous habit," he says, quickly pulling his hand away.

Then we're both grinning and chuckling. But, after a few seconds, there's this uncomfortable silence again.

"So, hows about we try and blast Miss Sophia's purse open and see what little Anna has to say about this secret treasure?" I suggest, changing the subject.

"Good idea," he says.

He gets up, walks over to the couch, picks up the inscrutable purse, and examines it.

But before he can do anything, one of the little "ch-ch's" come charging through.

"Hi. How are you?" I sing-song insincerely.

"Fine, thank God," he squeaks. "Do you like Beryl?"

Beryl blushes bright red, and I can feel the heat rising in my face as well.

"Menachem," Beryl warns. "That's not polite. Go play with Chaim and Chesed."

"Well, does she?" he insists.

It was clear this kid wasn't leaving without an answer.

"Beryl and I are friends," I say.

Clearly he isn't satisfied. He squints skeptically at me. "Well, Beryl likes you, but he says you like someone else." Then he breaks into a torrent of giggles.

I couldn't help but wonder if anyone would miss this kid if I killed him.

"Menachem!" Beryl scolds, physically leading him from the room, accosting him with a stream of Yiddish, presumably advising him to mind his own business. Unfortunately, that just sends Menachem into more spasms of giggles as he's ejected from the room.

Then I can't figure out who I'm more embarrassed for: me or Beryl. However, since I've now opened my inner chi and am much more sensitive, I can recall that it wasn't that long ago when I felt humiliated in front of John Leibler and feel empathy for Beryl.

So, now Beryl and I are alone again and we're both mortified. There's this terrible dead silence that seems to last for forty hours, and I'm thinking, where the hell is Miss Sophia?

"Where the hell . . . I mean, I wonder where your aunt Sophia is?"

Suddenly, it seems like the perfect opportunity to mend fences and show off my recently discovered, totally sensitive self with the new and improved energy flow component. (This model comes fully loaded!)

"Look, Beryl," I start. "I've been thinking about it, and I kind of get why Shabbat is so important to you."

So then he just stares at me expectantly as the seconds tick by.

"Oh, you want more?"

"That would be nice," he says.

"Well . . . um . . . I guess Shabbat is a time to show God that you're grateful for all the things he's given you and all the good people in your life."

"Yes?" he prods.

"And . . . um . . . ya know, it's a chance to pay respect to God, who asked you to put aside some time during the week to pray and reflect on your life's purpose."

"Yes?"

"And . . . um . . . it's a time to be with family. So you have to follow certain rules about when it starts so you're all on the same page. So at sundown you're home and not out, like, buying new tefillin, or something. But mostly, I should have recognized that it was important to you and been more understanding."

"Yes?"

Is this sensitivity stuff exhausting or what?

"That's it, Beryl. Let's not get crazy here. I'm done."

Thankfully Miss Sophia appears around the corner.

"Well, children. Did you solve the mystery yet?" she asks.

"If you mean the mystery of opening your purse, no we haven't, Aunt Sophia," Beryl says.

"Oh, maybe it's stuck."

Then she takes her purse, turns the little clickety-clack lock a few times and it opens.

But just at that moment, Mrs. Plotsky's voice rings out from the other room.

"Everyone! It's time to light the candles! Come now, everyone! Into the dining room!"

"But wait, we didn't get a chance to look at Anna's journal," I say.

"It will have to wait, Amy," says Beryl. "Patience is a virtue."

"Great, now you're starting to sound like an embroidery sampler."

"What?"

"Never mind," I sigh.

By this time, all the "ch-ch" children had already shimmied into their places and were standing behind their chairs, gently shoving each other and giggling, struggling to maintain a façade of politeness.

"All right, children," Mrs. Plotsky scolds gently. "It's time to light the candles."

Mrs. Plotsky strikes a match and lights two tall candles, while chanting a prayer in Hebrew.

And as I stare into the small flames my mind swirls. What an interesting little journey this has been so far. It's been cool exploring New York in Anna's shoes, or lace-up boots, as the case may be.

But the most astonishing thing of all has been hooking up with Miss Sophia and Beryl, two people I never wanted to spend time with. And now I actually consider them to be . . . well . . . for lack of a better word . . . I don't know . . . friends.

"Amy . . . Amy?" I hear Mrs. Plotsky's voice sounding far away.

I feel Miss Sophia gently patting my arm. "Amy?"

"Huh? Oh . . . I'm fine, thank God," I blurt out.

The "ch-ch" children convulse into loud giggles, and I realize that I've somehow made an ass of myself.

"My mother's asking you if you want to light Shabbat candles," Beryl says, biting his lip to keep from laughing.

"Ah . . . I'm good," I say, awkwardly.

The rabbi clears his throat and gestures to the candles. Miss Sophia does the speed reading version of the prayer and says, "Amen."

"Amen," everyone repeats.

Fortunately, the service portion of the meal is short and it's time to eat. Then Rabbi Plotsky asks us to talk about a mitzvah that we could perform in the near future.

Beryl talks about emulating Rabbi Akiva ben something-or-other from the sixteenth century. Miss Sophia says that she was making her dead bubbe happy by helping us children with our mission and helping us fill in our "blanks." Then she winks at me across the table and everyone is like, "Huh?" but they just move on.

She's all right, that Miss Sophia, I think. I make a mental note that, the next time she cooks one of her bubbe's "made from love" smelly recipes, that I will actually taste it instead of lopping it onto the windowsill when her back is turned.

And what did I say, you might wonder? I said that I would soon be visiting my friend in Kansas, who I initially thought was mentally unbalanced through no fault of her own, but recently realized is just exploring different aspects of her neshama.

All the Plotskys were very excited by this and shot me such gigantic "what a great daughter-in-law she'll make" smiles that it made me super nervous.

After dinner, and some delicious desserts, Miss Sophia and I said our thank-yous and goodbyes, bundled up, and headed out into the dark, frosty night.

So, even despite some periods of discomfort with Beryl, which I'm hoping will blow over, all in all, it wasn't a bad evening.

Amy

*D*ear Callie,

And speaking of awesome things, you gotta hear this.

Today, I'm heading into social studies class and I bustle to the back, as usual, when I see that Judy's seat is empty. Mrs. Goldstein is late, so I'm just hanging out pretending to be engrossed in reading *American History and You* when, out of the corner of my eye, I see John Leibler making his way toward me. I glance up and guess what?! He plops right into Judy's chair!

"Hey," he grins.

"Hi," I croak back.

"Listen, I just wanted to say thanks for helping me with the test on *Catcher in the Rye*. I aced it. B+."

"Um, that's awesome," I say.

Then we both glance up, like that instinct when you're being watched, and believe it or not, Horrible Susan is glaring at us. But the minute she catches us looking at her, she spins around and starts chatting up Jim (that kid with the flat head) in this phony, over-the-top way.

Then John turns back to me and is like, "So, because I got my grade up, my parents are letting me stay on the lacrosse team."

"Congratulations," I say.

Then there's this big, awkward silence for a few seconds and, finally, Mrs. Goldstein ambles in, so John stands up.

"So, um . . . thanks," he says.

And then he lightly touches my shoulder! On purpose!

"No problem," I say, feeling my face turn beet red and a big surge of adrenaline shoot through my body. I was so happy that I was almost oblivious to the superior look Horrible shot me when John took his rightful place in the seat next to her.

But wait! It gets better!

"Anyone have any new interesting stories or insights concerning their immigrant journal?" Mrs. Goldstein asks.

I glance up and she, presumably reacting then to my beet red face, like some kind of lighthouse activating her to talk to me, says:

"Yes, Amy? Anything you'd like to share?"

Then, unbelievably, before I can even open my mouth, John Leibler starts talking all about Coney Island and how cool and awesome it was.

Then he turns around in his seat, smiles, and winks at me!

So, Mrs. Goldstein gives him this very pleased gas-smile supreme and says that now she can't wait to read my essay. It promises to be very exciting and informative, blah, blah, blah.

I'm so astonished that I give John my own version of a gas-smile supreme.

Then to top off an almost perfect moment, Horrible looks totally pale, like she swallowed a big pit or something, and is scrutinizing John. It's as if she's thinking, Don't you know you're not supposed to share your bananas with inferior monkeys?

So what does it all mean, you might wonder? Was John being grateful about the B+? Was he just being nice? Or was he brownnosing Mrs. Goldstein? Hmm . . . it's a mystery all its own. You decide.

Amy

12/14, 3:01 p.m.

*D*ear Cal,

So, it's Saturday night and, pathetically, I don't have anything to do and I refuse to spend another non-school moment with Claire and or Judy. I decide to take a look at
the last, and latest, installment of Anna's journal. Hmm . . .
kind of interesting. Believe it or not, I actually find myself
looking forward to discussing it with the "dream team."

At 12:30 on Sunday afternoon, I arrive at a very crowded
Starbucks where Beryl and Miss Sophia have staked out a
table and are sipping hot cocoas out of red holiday cups.

"Yoo-hoo! Amy! We're over here!" Miss Sophia calls
out, just in case I didn't see them; like there are so many
tables occupied by old ladies and religious kids with red
hair.

I weave my way toward them, grab a seat and take out
the journal.

"So after Anna and her family had that seriously awful
experience in Kentucky, they moved to Brooklyn. 175 Garfield Place in Park Slope, to be exact. I looked the address
up last night. And here's the cool part: Anna writes that
she helped her mother hide a special letter in the basement
in a box under the stairs."

"It is a letter!" Beryl exclaims. "I knew it."

"Then she says that the letter is the Slonovich secret treasure, and it was written by someone of great character. And then . . . that's it," I say, looking up. "So, we're screwed. Ooh, sorry, Beryl."

"I agree with you, Amy. What are the chances of the letter still being there after all these years?" Beryl says. "We are probably . . . what you just said."

"Wait a minute, children," Miss Sophia says calmly. "I took the liberty of doing some checking up on our Anna Slonovich," she says.

She removes a few more papers from her purse. "I was a librarian, you know, for . . ."

"Thirty years," Beryl and I say in unison.

"I suppose I do say that a lot," she grins.

"Anyway, what I found out is this: Anna Slonovich grew up and eventually did became a mystery writer. She wrote about twenty dime store novels, plus a children's book called, *The Honest Letter* Anna married, but didn't have children. She spent many years traveling in Europe, where both she and her husband died unexpectedly. She probably never had time to clear out her possessions. And maybe no one else knew about the letter."

"So you're saying that the letter could still be hidden in that house?" I ask. "But what if the house isn't there anymore?"

"Park Slope is considered to be a historic district. So not only is the house still there, I'm sure, but it's probably pretty much the same as it was so many decades ago," says Miss Sophia triumphantly.

"Wow," I say.

I lift my hot chocolate, but just as I'm about to take my first sip, Miss Sophia bursts in, "So, children, shall we head to Brooklyn?"

Beryl shoots up and adjusts his backpack. Miss Sophia stands, adjusts her little teal colored fur-lined hat, which, I might add, harmoniously accents her teal coat and boot ensemble, and they're ready to go.

I stand too, take a couple of gulps and before I can say, "Ouch, that was hot," I turn quickly and run smack into none other than John Leibler. But I mean literally run smack into him, so that I spill hot cocoa down the front of his awesome brown leather jacket.

"Oh my God," I exclaim. "I'm so sorry!"

Then I'm searching desperately for a napkin and grab one that looks somewhat clean from a nearby table and start wiping the front of his coat. He's totally grossed out and gently moves my hand away and is like, "Uh . . . hang on."

He gracefully weaves over to the napkin/condiment area, grabs a couple of napkins, and wipes his coat down himself.

"I want to talk to you," he shouts in my direction. "Don't move."

As if.

I see Beryl and Miss Sophia through the glass window, outside on the curb. Miss Sophia is trying to hail a cab, and Beryl is glancing over to the door as if he expects me to pop onto the street any second.

Then John weaves his way back to me, flashing that 100-watt smile at everyone in his path, and they all just part out of his way, like the way Moses must have parted the Red Sea.

I bet that Moses probably also had a lot of charisma and a 100-watt smile, just like John. I mean, seriously, if Moses was bald, paunchy, and had falafel in his teeth, us Jews would probably still be building pyramids and writing in hieroglyphics.

The thought strikes me as so absurd, it's inspired me to write a little play entitled:

YOU WANT US TO GO WHERE?!

(A play in a couple of lines by Amy Finawitz)

SCENE: The outskirts of Egypt. The brutally hot desert, home to icky, furry spiders and thorny cacti.

MOSES, the Jewish savior, stands before the JEWISH SLAVES. He rubs his protruding belly, pulls his only two long strands of hair over his shiny, bald head and belches. He steps forward and stumbles on the hem of his long white robe.

MOSES
Come, Jewish people! Leave slavery and oppression behind, and follow me into the desert! By the way, does anyone have any antacid? That falafel gave me gas.

306

JEWISH SLAVES
(grossed out)
Uh, sorry, Moses. You're, like, a nice guy and everything, and we don't like slavery any more than the
next person, but you want us to go where? Oh, and by
the way, you have a little falafel in your teeth.

The JEWISH people shuffle back to slavery.

THE END

The point is this: even when you know that sexy people
aren't really better than other people, you're more willing
to follow them to strange places.

Anyway, I'm standing there, glued to the spot, and
John says,

"I was hoping I'd find you here. Anything new with
the mystery, Miss Sophia, and your boyfriend, Beryl?"

"He's not my boyfriend," I say flatly.

"He's not?" John asks. "But you two look like you really
like each other."

"Well, there's like and then there's like, John," I reply.

He considers this for a moment and nods like I just
explained the theory of relativity. "So I guess that makes
you a free woman, huh?"

And I'm like, Oh my God, is he flirting with me?

"I guess so," I say coolly.

"So," John continues, "does Beryl know there's a difference between like and like?"

"Sure. Of course. He's actually . . . engaged to some religious girl named . . . er . . . Sarah," I improvise.

"Engaged?!" John exclaims. "Isn't he a little young to be engaged?"

"Well, sort of pre-engaged. You know how the super religious are," I say, darting my eyes around to see if anyone is listening to this crap that I'm totally making up.

Then John looks at me all skeptically, with the slightest bit of a grin, and I know I've gone too far but it's too late to go back.

"No, not really. Beryl's the only super religious person I know," he says.

"Amy!" I hear my name across the room.

And there's Beryl standing at the door, gesturing for me to hurry, and I can see out the window that Miss Sophia has flagged down a cab. Then Beryl spots John. His face falls, but he manages a lukewarm wave.

"There's the man of the hour now," John says. "I should congratulate him on his pre-engagement."

Beryl starts politely shouldering his way through the crowd toward us.

"No, no," I stutter, grabbing on to the sleeve of John's awesome jacket as Beryl closes in on us. "He's . . . um . . . very self-conscious about it."

"Why?"

"It's private. Liking someone is a private thing," I say, sounding ridiculous even to myself.

"Really? Since when?" John chuckles.

"Since . . . Moses. Moses told the Hebrews that 'like' is private."

"Moses?" John says in amused wonderment.

Then before I can think up another idiotic way to put my foot in my mouth, Beryl pops up beside us.

"Hello, John," Beryl says.

"Hey," John extends his hand.

"Congratulations, dude," John says.

"Ah, we should go," I say panicked, trying to corral Beryl toward the door without actually touching him.

"For what?" Beryl answers, totally perplexed.

"For being so close to solving the mystery," I jump in. "Oh, there's Miss Sophia holding that cab. We should go now."

Then John grins at me and I can see, of course, that he's having a hell of a good time pulling my chain. "For . . . um, ya know . . . that thing," John says slyly, watching me squirm.

"What thing?" Beryl asks.

"Ya know the thing that Moses wants you to keep private."

"Moses wants me to keep something private?" Beryl furrows his brows in befuddlement.

"You know, the girl. The one you like."

Beryl looks at me questioningly. "I don't know what . . ."

"Sarah. Is that her name?" John says.

"Come on now. We can't keep the cab waiting, Beryl," I urge.

"Who's Sarah?" Beryl asks.

"Like and like, huh." John leans toward me and whispers, serving me good. This was ridiculous.

"So, where you all heading to today?" John persists.

"We're going to Park Slope," Beryl says. "175 Garfield Place, to be exact."

"I know that area. My cousins live in Park Slope," John replies. "But 175 Garfield, what's there?"

"That's where we hope to find the secret letter," Beryl says.

"That sounds awesome," John responds.

I glance out toward Miss Sophia. She's involved in what looks like a happy, animated conversation with a lady I recognize from the building.

Suddenly Beryl isn't in such a hurry. Beryl fills John in on the details about our trip to the museum and about the letter we hope to find. And before I can stop him, Beryl's verbal diarrhea becomes all about me, you, and my quest to rescue you from brainwashing aliens.

I'm standing there, mortified, and John is fascinated, but not in a sympathetic way, more in the way a person is fascinated by disgusting sea life at the aquarium. And Beryl and John are, like, separated at birth, laughing and talking like old chums, and all the while John is interjecting comments like, "I know Callie from school, but I didn't know she was mentally unbalanced."

And "So Amy wants Callie to come home that badly? Even if she's happy in Kansas?"

Finally, John's like, "But how are you gonna get into the house and get the hidden letter, if you don't know who lives there?"

"Well, we hadn't gotten to that yet," Beryl ponders. "We thought we'd just explain our situation to the home-owner."

"Well, there's a way to talk to people so they kind of, ya know . . . do what you want."

"You mean like manipulation?" I snark at John, my face warm and flushed.

"Not like manipulation, exactly," John says. "More like persuasion."

"What's the difference?" I ask, unzipping my overheated parka, shifting my backpack onto my other shoulder.

"Manipulation and persuasion? Let's just say, it's like the difference between like and like," John says, with a glint in his eye.

"Hmm, that's interesting," ponders Beryl. "What do you think, Amy?"

"I have no opinion on the matter," I say, feeling my armpits getting clammy. "We better go. See you in school, John." I wave over my shoulder, excusing myself through the crowd, with Beryl at my heels.

"Not if you work so hard at avoiding me," John replies.

I stop dead in my tracks and turn around.

This was beyond belief. Did John really notice that I was avoiding him? And what did he care anyway? And after treating me like a leper at the lacrosse practice, was he actually wanting to come with us to Park Slope? Even if John's "blank" was boredom and a desire to be more, at that moment, I couldn't believe that his perfect life could be so boring that he'd want to go with us again.

"Can your perfect life be so boring that you'd want to come with us again?" I blurt out.

"What?" says John, looking stung.

"Amy," Beryl says, disapprovingly.

Then there's this uncomfortable pause for a few seconds and John is like, "Okay, well, I'm outta here."

Then he opens the door and bolts through it.

Crap. When am I gonna learn to think first, edit my thoughts, and then speak?

So I quickly push on the door and Beryl and I tumble out of Starbucks. A delicious blast of cold air slaps me in the face, bringing me to my senses. I suck in a deep cool breath.

"Yoo-hoo, children!" Miss Sophia calls out from the corner. "I've got a cab."

"Just tell her to keep her beret on," I bark at Beryl.

Then I start clomping up the block after John in my Himalayan boots. I don't think I need to tell you that John's super fast and I'm super slow.

"Hey, John, John!" I call out, knowing full well that he hears me, but is refusing to stop.

Finally, he stops abruptly.

"What's up, Amy? I promised I'd show up at a soccer game," he says tersely, shoving his hands deep into his pockets.

"But it's Sunday," I say.

This was remarkable. I had somehow insulted John Leibler.

"We still play. In the park." He shrugs. Then he glances over my head.

"Oh," I say, and suddenly I have no idea why I had chased him down the street. "Well, good luck with that."

Then we both stand there, the chill air causing clear liquid to run uncontrollably from our red, frozen noses.

This was the most awkward moment of my whole life. Hiding in school wasn't gonna cut it after this. I was gonna have to drop out completely.

"Well, I gotta go," John says.

Then a voice emanates from my throat that I vaguely recognize as my own.

"Wait! Listen, John," I call out. "Why don't you come with us? We could use your help."

"No thanks," he calls back over his shoulder. "See ya."

I open my mouth again, but nothing comes out as I watch him sprint onto the opposite street corner and disappear into Central Park.

Then I just stand there for a few moments, overwhelmed by this uncomfortable feeling, like the one you get when you hit your funny bone, or like when you reach for something with your fingertips and accidentally push it farther out of reach.

It's the feeling that a significant opportunity has presented itself and you have screwed it up.

Forlornly yours,
Amy

Dear Callie,

Sorry to leave off so abruptly. Just thinking about that part of the day makes me feel kinda sad, but things did pick up from there.

Anyway, so after John Leibler left me standing on the corner, I wearily galumph the few blocks back to Miss Sophia and Beryl, who are already sitting in the cab.

"Isn't that handsome young man coming with us again?" Miss Sophia asks. "He was so helpful last time."

"He had something important to do," I lie, although it wasn't quite a lie, because the thing he had to do was get away from me.

"Uh-huh," replies Beryl, skeptically.

"Not uh-huh," I snark. "He really did. There's some soccer game in the park."

"Cabbie, take us to Park Slope. 175 Garfield Place," Miss Sophia instructs the cab driver.

So after about forty-five minutes and a pretty quiet cab ride, we finally arrive in Park Slope and you know, it sort of looks very turn of the century, with all the quaint brownstones and tree-lined sidewalks that are covered with dustings of snow.

"Oh, it's just as I remember it," gushes Miss Sophia. "It's so beautiful here during the holidays. Isn't it just like stepping back in time, children?"

The cab makes a few turns and pulls up in front of a large reddish-colored brownstone.

"Here we are, lady," the cabbie says.

"Thank God, there are lights in the window," Beryl whispers to me, as we emerge. "We didn't consider that maybe nobody would be home, and now I'm not so sure that just explaining our situation to the homeowners will prompt them to let us in."

"Hmm, you know you're right, dear. I was so excited about finding the letter that I hadn't given enough thought to our strategy."

Stumped, we all contemplate this for a second.

"We need a plan," I say.

"We need a common acquaintance," Miss Sophia says.

"We need a miracle," Beryl says.

What we really need is John Leibler, Mr. Power of Persuasion, I think to myself.

Then before I can actually say "Mr. Power of Persuasion," there he is bounding around the corner, all bright eyed, flushed, and glowing, once again looking like some gorgeous model moving in slow motion toward the camera in a fresh-smelling deodorant commercial.

I swear to God, I'm not kidding.

John spots us, and his smile hits my eyes like a flashbulb.

"John?" I sputter.

"Hey," he says, coming upon us, slightly out of breath.

"Hi, John," Beryl remarks, perplexed.

"Oh, look, it's that handsome young man," Miss Sophia exclaims with delight.

"What are you doing here?" I demand.

"Amy . . ." Beryl warns, as if I was gonna insult him away again.

"I mean that in a good way," I clarify. "What are you doing here?"

"I came to help," John shrugs. "I thought you might need it. Besides, you know I like history. And did I tell you that my cousin is . . ."

"Yeah, yeah, we know. He's Jewish."

"Besides," John says, grinning. "Life was too perfect. I was bored."

And you know, it hit me, Cal. John is probably the most inscrutable guy I've ever met. Was he really that bored? Was he intrigued that I insulted him? Was he that intrigued about the mystery? Is he seriously passionate about history? Is it possible he likes me? And would I ever really know the answer to any of these questions?

But then I really looked at him, past the hunkalisciousness, past the awesome smell, and what I saw was an okay guy who spends a lot of time thinking he's "all that." Then, believe it or not, the next question that popped into my head was . . . Do I really care?

"Well, you came at a very serendipitous time, young man," Miss Sophia says, interrupting my thoughts. "We

317

need an especially attractive and persuasive person to get these homeowners to let us look around their house."

"How did you get here?" I ask.

"The subway. It comes straight from the city to the park, a couple of blocks that way," he says, gesturing toward the street intersection.

"How did you know that?" Beryl asks.

"I have another cousin who lives right around here. So, have you knocked on the door yet?" he asks, gesturing to the brownstone.

"We just arrived," Beryl says. "We've been trying to think of a good strategy to approach the situation."

"Allow me," John says, gently moving us out of the way. "You guys stay down here for a second."

Then he puts a smile on, straightens himself up, heads up the steps, and rings the bell. It was kind of fascinating to watch him in action, like an actor preparing for a scene.

The door opens, and a tall man appears. John starts chatting with him, then gestures down to us. We all smile as pleasantly as we can, trying to give off a normal, we're not thieves, psychopaths, or nut jobs look. Then, much to our surprise, John is invited in and the door shuts behind him.

"Damn, he's good," I say.

"These homeowners are very trusting," Miss Sophia remarks.

"Either that, or they're going to murder him," Beryl says.

"Beryl!" I exclaim with a laugh. "That's a very inappropriate thing to say!"

Beryl shrugs.

A few minutes later, John emerges and trots down the steps, a satisfied expression on his face.

"Well?" I ask, expectantly.

"Give them a minute," John says confidently.

A man, with a baby on his hip, pokes his head out the door.

"We'll be upstairs if you need us. The basement is through the kitchen."

"Will do," John replies.

"There's a fresh batch of oatmeal cookies on the counter. Help yourselves," he says.

We all stare at John in amazement.

"They were nice, huh?" he says enigmatically.

"Good job, young man," Miss Sophia beams. "I knew you were the right boy for the task."

"That was very . . . inspirational," Beryl says.

"That was awesome," I exclaim. "How did you do that? Are they gonna let us use their car too?"

"It was nothing," John shrugs. "They liked the whole idea of some historical secret letter hidden in their house."

"No really," I say, starting up the steps after him. "You have, like, a gift or something."

Miss Sophia pushes open the door, and she and Beryl walk in.

"I knew you were good with people in school, but this

is something else. This family is letting perfect strangers into their house and offering us food, and . . ."

"Amy, before you go on," John holds up his hand. "It just so happens that they know my cousin. The one who lives by the park. They're friends with his parents."

I think about that for a minute.

"Even so. What are the odds of them knowing your cousin. That's pretty lucky."

"Hey," John chuckles, as he enters the house. "I'm a lucky guy, and luck goes a long way."

And, dagnabit, I think he's right.

So, Cal, it is now past midnight, and I'm fading fast. But before I sign off, I will give you my original fortune cookie thought for the day:

You can accomplish a lot with luck—luck plus a religious kid, an old lady, a geek, and a hot guy.

Amy

Dear Callie,

Okay, so I know you're dying to hear the rest. Back to the adventure at hand:

We're inside the house, and we all look around.

"What do we do now?" John asks.

"Let's find the basement," I say.

We walk through the kitchen, past a plate of oatmeal cookies, and sure enough there's a slim door on the far wall. I open it and find myself looking down a long narrow staircase descending into what looks like a dark, dank pit.

"Creepy down there," I say peering anxiously into the hole.

"But a perfect place to hide something," says John.

"Yeah, like a body." I shudder.

I try the light switch, but it doesn't work.

"We'll need a flashlight," Beryl says.

"Hang on, children."

Then Miss Sophia disappears around the corner and, within seconds, she reappears carrying a small yellow flashlight.

"This was in my bag. I think it belonged to the nice

man dressed in high heels that we met in the graveyard," Miss Sophia chirps. "I must have forgotten to give it back."

"You met a cross-dresser in a graveyard?" John asks.

"Don't ask," I say.

"All right, are we ready?" Beryl says.

Miss Sophia hands him the flashlight.

Beryl takes a deep breath and descends into the blackness with only a thin beam of light to guide him.

In single file we follow him down.

"How far down do these stairs go?" I ask, brushing totally gross cobwebs from my shoulder.

"I'm at the bottom now," Beryl says.

He's flush up against a furnace. He swings the flashlight around the room and then under the dark staircase.

"Wait, I think I see something," he exclaims. "I think I've found it. There's a little door."

Beryl stretches way over, pulls open the door, and points the flashlight inside.

"Well, what do you see?" John asks.

"I think . . . I think, there's a box in here, but I can't reach it. Amy, you're smaller than I am. See if you can crawl under there and grab it."

"You're kidding, right?" But reluctantly, I crawl under the stairs and reach into the black hole trying to remember when I've had my last tetanus shot. "Okay, everyone. This is now officially way totally gross."

I grab a small box with a little key attached to it by a

chain. I pull it out as quickly as I can and carry it to a nearby laundry table.

Excitedly, everyone gathers around.

"The box looks airtight," John observes.

"Let's just hope it was airtight enough to keep the letter from decomposing," says Beryl.

"Well, this is the moment of truth," I say, gesturing to the box. "Miss Sophia, would you like to do the honors?"

"Oh no, dear. I'm too nervous. You open it."

So there we are, the most unlikely dream team. We hold our breath.

I place the key in the lock and turn. It clicks and the box pops open.

"Awesome," says John.

Inside is a somewhat yellowed envelope.

"Oh my God. There's really a letter in here!" I say.

Carefully I pick up the envelope and read the address:

"Mr. and Mrs. Boris Slonovich,
142 Mead Street,
Greensburg, Kentucky."

"Wow. Look, the address is Kentucky. This must be Anna's parents."

"Who's it from?" John urges.

I turn it over.

"The White House!" I say, astounded. "The name above it is: President Abraham Lincoln."

"Oh my!" Miss Sophia says, in a small trembling voice.

"Open it up, Amy," Beryl says, excitedly.

Carefully, I open the envelope and pull out a piece of delicate, ivory colored paper. The note is handwritten in dark black ink in thick loopy penmanship. On the bottom is a gold seal.

"My goodness," exclaims Miss Sophia. "That's a gold presidential seal!"

"Well, come on, what does it say?" urges John.

I start to read.

January 15th, 1865

Dear Mr. and Mrs. Slonovich,
It has come to my attention by way of a Mr. Cesar Kaskel of Paducah, Kansas, with assistance from Congressman Gurley of Ohio, that a grave injustice has been perpetrated against you, your family, and your class in the form of a proclamation, called General Order 11, signed on December 17, 1862, by General Ulysses S. Grant.

The proclamation mandated the expulsion of "the Jews as a class" on foot, without privilege or rail transportation, from Northern Mississippi, Kentucky, Western Tennessee, and Kansas, within twenty-four hours without trial or hearing.

Upon learning of this shocking abhorrence, I immediately ordered that General Order 11 be revoked. I have been informed that, since this time, you and yours are now safely back within your homes and communities.

I believe that to condemn a class is, to say the least, to wrong the good with the bad. I do not like to hear a class or nationality condemned on account of a few sinners. I draw no distinction between Jew and Gentile and would allow no American to be wronged because of his religious affiliations.

Furthermore, I was deeply saddened to hear of the death of your child during your grievous period of exile. This time of war that afflicts the nation has yielded many casualties and stolen many young lives. Please accept my deepest sympathies.

Abraham Lincoln

We stand in silence for a few moments, then John lets out a low whistle.

"That is off the hook!" he says.

"Amazing," Beryl exhales, shaking his head in disbelief.

"But wait, could this be the only letter?" I say. "Is that why none of us have ever heard of this?"

"I never heard of it," says John.

We all turn to look at him.

"I *am* a history buff," he says.

"Well," says Miss Sophia, "since President Lincoln performed a presidential function by revoking General Grant's mandate, there must be an official letter on file somewhere in the government's library. But perhaps since the matter was such a public disgrace, it was never made very public."

Then Miss Sophia pulls a tissue from up her sleeve and mews softly into it.

"Are you okay, Miss Sophia?" I ask, awkwardly placing my arm around her shoulder, hoping she isn't gonna keel over and wondering how we'll get her back up the basement steps if she does.

"Yes, I'm fine," she says bravely. "But it's all so monumental."

"Yeah," I say, feeling a bit choked up myself.

"We have uncovered a very important piece of American history. You should be proud of yourselves, children. I'm proud of you," Miss Sophia says, misting up again.

Then she spreads her arms out wide and looks at us expectantly, and I'm, like, praying that it isn't a cue for a group hug. Fortunately, John and Beryl, clearly being of similar mind, just smile, nod, and take one step back.

"I feel less blank already, Miss Sophia," I say.

"Blank?" asks Beryl.

"I'll explain it in the cab home," I smile at Beryl.

"It's very irreverent," says John, which actually makes me smile.

And, Cal, I have to tell you that I can't help thinking that this odd little group are now my friends. Who would have thunk it? Coincidence? Divine guidance? I guess I'll never know for sure, but I gotta believe that this is all too weird to be totally random.

"Now you have something really interesting to write about for your class assignment, and soon after that you'll be visiting Callie in Kansas," offers Beryl.

"That's really wicked," says John. "You must be psyched."

"Actually, I am," I say.

"I feel psyched . . . thank God."

And you know what Callie? I really do.

Amy

*D*ear Callie,

Thought you might like to read my latest, and last, immigrant journal assignment for Mrs. Goldstein. Here it is:

Anna Slonovich came to America as a young child and had a full and interesting life. Initially, she and her family emigrated to Kentucky, where they experienced bigotry and ultimately the tragic death of her brother. Undaunted, they then relocated to New York City, where Anna delighted in experiencing the many interesting sights, sounds, and attractions that New York has to offer. She lived in small quarters surrounded by a big family, but didn't follow a traditional path for a girl of that time, ultimately achieving her dream of becoming a mystery writer.

Also, Anna left her own little legacy in the form of a special "treasure"—a letter from Abraham Lincoln, indelibly marking a place for herself in the annals of American history.

I liked Anna and felt she was somewhat of an outsider

in her world. I admired her adventurous personality; how-ever, I couldn't quite relate to her optimistic cheeriness, even though I tried.

Overall, I enjoyed this assignment and actually kind of miss having adventures with my little "dream team" of immigrant journal companions: Miss Sophia, my neigh-bor; Beryl Plotsky, her nephew; plus special cameo ap-pearances by fellow student John Leibler.

However, we are talking about meeting once a month to find more historical places around New York to ex-plore. I think that would be fun.

So Cal, what do you think?

12/24, 10:02 a.m.
What do you mean you think I should try alternately dating both John Leibler and Beryl?! That's all you got out of this? And BTW, I think you're crazy!

12/24, 10:03 a.m.
And stop grinning. I can feel you grinning through the computer screen.

12/24, 10:05 a.m.
You totally are. I know you are. Fine. Don't admit it. TTYL.

Okay, quick! Make a wish!

Because it's 11:11! Everyone knows that you make a wish when it's 11:11!

I don't know who said it. It's common knowledge. Sheesh! Just make wish!

Your wish is that I would get there already? OMG, you're so corny! You're also too late. It's 11:13. But your wish might come true after all. My dad booked me on an earlier flight, so I'll be arriving in Kansas at 4:30 p.m. instead of 5:30 p.m.! I know, he's a miracle man! (not really). Gotta go. I'm still packing. See you soon!

Okay, I'm done packing. I'm actually sitting in my coat even though my dad says we don't have to leave for the airport for another half hour . . . I'm taking off my coat . . . still sitting . . . waiting . . .

Since I'm sitting here doing nothing, I'll tell you about the latest with Mrs. Goldstein. So, right before vacation, I see her in the hall, coming toward me with this big gas-smile supreme, looking like she wants to talk. But, being hungry, I try and duck into the cafeteria before she actually sees me, but then of course, she's like:

"Amy! Do you have a moment?"

"Sure thing, Mrs. Goldstein," I sigh.

I follow her into her classroom, where she sits at a desk and gestures for me to sit down too.

"I just wanted to let you know," she says, "how thrilled I was about your immigrant journal assignment! I was actually talking about it with my husband and son last night at dinner."

And I'm thinking: Okay, no personal interests at all. Totally need to move forward with this intervention thing.

"Not only did I like the way you related to Anna Slonovich . . . But I sensed that you really enjoyed your experience with your new friends," she continues, leaning way toward me. "It seems to me that this whole experience has matured you . . . given you an opportunity to get out with people, develop more interests, maybe, hmm?"

Thank you, Mrs. Goldstein, for implying that I used to be reclusive, immature, and dull.

Then these long minutes tick by and she's staring at me with this "full of meaning expression" that I'm trying to gauge how to respond to, until finally I'm like, "Um . . . well, great. Thanks."

I start to get up.

"But there's one more thing, of course," she grins.

And I'm down.

"I was also very excited about Anna's historical mystery that you had to solve! Such an illuminating, personal look into American history!"

"It was cool," I say.

"So, here's the thing," she glows. "I sent a copy of all of your journal assignments to the principal and the superintendent at the district office. Now they would like you to read excepts from Anna's diary and your journal at next week's assembly. And we would love it if your 'team,'" she makes quotation marks in the air, "could join us too. How does that sound!?"

I freeze.

How does that sound? Let's see . . . sort of like three thousand pieces of china crashing to the ground! Miss Sophia and Beryl with me . . . up on stage . . . in front of the whole school? Was she kidding?! Talk about becoming the next "touch me" joke of the school for the rest of time immemorial. But, on the other hand, if John Leibler were there with us, it might not be so bad.

Mrs. Goldstein looks as if she's reading my expression and her face falls.

"Oh . . ." she says, quietly. "You wouldn't like that?"

Then suddenly, I realize something. If don't do it, I would be disappointing, like, everybody, not only Mrs. Goldstein, but probably Miss Sophia (who would totally find out from my mother) and I'm sure Beryl too.

And then, unbelievably, I start thinking that maybe I

would be disappointing myself. I mean, it could be fun, to, ya know, be important for a day. Besides, I can't get geekier than I already am.

"Sure, Mrs. Goldstein," I say. "I'd love to."

So, Cal? Social suicide? Good deed? Or the decision of a newly matured, not dull, social bon vivant?

12/24, 1:04 p.m.

Time to go! Dad is standing at the front door, frantically waving a little lunch bag that I fear is some kind of crappy organic snack my mom packed me for the flight. I can only hope it doesn't include a cabbage/broccoli/brussels sprout related vegetable and doesn't smell up the plane.

PS: Can't wait!!!!

12/27, 11:00 a.m.

*D*ear Beryl,

Thanks for your last e-mail. It was very informative. I now have a way deeper understanding of the meaning of Hannukah according to Rabbi Akiva ben Yosef from some really old century.

You shouldn't have.

Really.

Anyway, it sounds like you and your family are having a nice holiday. Please tell Menachem I say "hi" and, in answer to his thoughtful inquiry, no, I am not planning to spend another Shabbat at your house anytime soon, so I can, to paraphrase his words, "give him a big laugh."

Callie is very happy that I'm here, and we've been very busy. Yesterday we went to the local Malt Shoppe and ate gravy fries, plus, we've attended many stylish hog fairs, hootenannies, and knockwurst bake-offs. And Callie's friends here aren't so bad. I can't say that I hate them. Amazingly, she's very popular here and, because I'm her best friend, I'm popular too!

But here's the really funny part. I used to be so desperate to climb up the monkey ladder but now I'm not really sure if I'm cut out for this bon vivant, superficial life. I've learned that popularity has a price. I've had to be polite, smile, dress nicely, chat, laugh at other people's jokes (which, believe me, are mostly not funny). And nobody here gets my irreverent sense of humor. Not at all.

To make matters worse, at the "whose got the fattest hog fair" (which by the way, in case you're interested, is Mrs. Clarinda Johnson), Callie and I were actually picked first to play an impromptu softball game in her school gym. Well, you can imagine how that went. I've spent so much of my "athletic life" in an outfield, I don't even know what the rules of the game are. We basically lost, like, 0 to 100, and one of my "foul balls" inadvertently gave some poor spectator a mild concussion.

As for being here, in general, Callie's aunt and uncle are very nice people. It's very pretty here. The snow actually stays white, even after it's been on the ground for a while, and it's kind of peaceful too. No one's rushing anywhere. No blaring horns. No little balls of spit on the sidewalk or puddles of urine dribbling down the curb. There's very little car exhaust, and it doesn't cough into your face every time you cross the street.

Callie and I are having an awesome time just hanging out together. We can't stop laughing all day. It's so good to see her again!

As for her ex-boyfriend Bucky pet/boy (yes, now he's her ex), he's everything I thought he would be. Nuff said.

He only recently broke up with her, and told her that he wanted to be friends and he's already been sniffing around his ex-girlfriend. Callie was pretty brokenhearted, so I feel badly, but I can't say that I feel brokenhearted that he trotted off. I'm sure she'll get over him in time.

However, there is another cute boy here who, I can tell, likes her. His name is Dong Chung, and he's an exchange student from . . . well . . . somewhere. He is quite nice, and will be returning to his home country at the end of the school year, so I am encouraging this relationship. Short-term dating is best during these tender, impressionable years, don't you think?

Now, for the super good news. Hold on to your tefillin! Callie is, in fact, coming back to New York at the end of the school year.

I did, however, take your advice and refrain from pressuring her (too much). You were right when you implied that a good friend should be sensitive to what their friend really wants. Plus, you were right that I wasn't a nobody without her. I would have made it work somehow, I suppose.

Anyway, Callie says she realized that as much as she's liked spending time in the heartland, she does "heart" New York after all. And she's even done some Internet research and found a number of organic gardening opportunities right there. I think you two will like each other. Like, not like, if you know what I mean. (And I think you actually might—know what I mean, that is).

So, in the end, it all turned out the way it was supposed to, I guess.

See you soon.

Amy

PS: Please give my best to your aunt Sophia. Thank her for the anisette cookies she gave me for the plane ride. In keeping with her suggestion, I did, indeed, dip them in tea and they were quite tasty. Much better than the incredibly smelly organic coleslaw my mom packed me that I totally had to keep in the airtight container for fear of being thrown off the plane.

PPS: I'm glad to hear that you and John Leibler are buds. Next time you e-mail him, tell him I say hi.

12/27, 12:12 p.m.

And I swear this is it. Believe it or not, there is a good Chinese restaurant here, and Callie and I have been going there as much as weather permits. I know you're not into this kind of thing, but I wanted to share the latest fortune cookie fortune with you. It is somewhat inscrutable and needs a Talmudic perspective.

It says:

WHEN THE MOMENT COMES, TAKE THE TOP ONE.

Something to think about, hmm?

LAURA TOFFLER-CORRIE was born in a big hospital in New York City, but shortly thereafter moved to the little town of Oceanside, Long Island. She fondly remembers her childhood visits to Manhattan where her grandmother would step boldly out into oncoming traffic and shout "Yoo-hoo! Taxi!", much like Miss Sophia in this book.

During her school years, she and her best friend amused themselves by writing each other funny letters and plays about their lives. This activity actually continued way into college and became the inspiration for *The Life and Opinions of Amy Finawitz*. This is Laura's first novel. Visit her at www.lauratoffler-corrie.com.

ACKNOWLEDGEMENTS

Even though it usually takes one real person and many imaginary people to write a book, it is not written in a vacuum. The world spins around the writer, sometimes ignoring her, sometimes acknowledging her, and sometimes even cheering her on.

Here's to the people in my life who cheered for me, to whom I owe a debt of gratitude; who supported me through this crazy journey, which only a crazy person would take, and kept me from going totally . . . well, crazy.

To Elana Roth, my agent extraordinaire, for visualizing what AMY could be and finding her a good home. For watching my back.

To Nancy Mercado, my editor extraordinaire, for gently challenging me to challenge myself. For having the right words. For making the journey an enlightening one.

To Annette Fisch, for being there during crazy times. For all your hilarious letters. For being a muse.

To Mary Beth Bass, for appearing in my life (and Starbucks) at just the right time. For your friendship, guidance, and support.

To Patricia Reilly Giff, for nurturing the writer in everyone. I don't think AMY would have been a book without your support.

To all the gals from Pat's class and writer's groups past, for telling me "I had something there."

To the Chabad of Stamford—The Chabad Jewish Center for Life and Learning. For keeping the flame.

To Lee Kalcheim, my first playwriting professor at NYU, DWP.

For giving a frightened freshman the confidence to think, *Hmm . . . this is fun and way scary. Maybe I can do this.*

To the rest of my family, and friends Michelle Finkelstein, Joan Willgohs, Anne Teall, Julie Ball, Polly Tafrate, and Felice Kempler for being "so excited." Yeah, me too.

To the Starbucks Drinking and Writing Society, for "writer talk" from compadres.

To the team at Roaring Brook Press at Macmillan, for an awesome cover. For doing what you do.

Lastly, to my parents Hinda and Alvin Toffler, who gave me the room to be myself, even if that meant (usually meant) being awakened in the middle of the night to hear my very first poems. To my daughters Hannah and Rachel, for being beautiful, courageous, and wise. For laughing at my jokes.

And to my husband Tom, who always supported my dreams, taught me how to strive, and never let me quit.